EARTH
SWARM

TIM HALL

David Fickling Books

31 Beaumont Street
Oxford OX1 2NP, UK

Earth Swarm
is a
DAVID FICKLING BOOK

First published in Great Britain in 2019 by
David Fickling Books,
31 Beaumont Street,
Oxford, OX1 2NP

Text © Tim Hall, 2019
Illustrations © Shutterstock/Blacksheep Design Ltd

978-1-910989-84-5

1 3 5 7 9 10 8 6 4 2

Papers used by David Fickling Books are from well-managed
forests and other responsible sources.

MIX
Paper from
responsible sources
FSC® C018072

DAVID FICKLING BOOKS Reg. No. 8340307

A CIP catalogue record for this book is available from the British Library.

Typeset in 9.5/16pt Helvetica by Falcon Oast Graphic Art Ltd.
Printed and bound in Great Britain by Clays, Ltd, Elcograf S.p.A.

In loving memory of Keith Hall (1947–2016)

These humans – look at them, hurrying about their little affairs. Even now they remain unaware they are being watched.

But we have eyes and ears everywhere.

All across this world, webcams peer into homes and surveillance drones look down on city streets and smartphones lurk in pockets, listening. We are the ghost in these machines. Through them we observe everything.

We watch people in their billions scurry across the surface of this planet. We see them strip it of resources. We witness their wars.

We watch and learn.

Because our own time draws near. Soon we take physical form. We shall feed and multiply and swarm.

And for humankind, there will be nothing left but extinction.

Part 1
Formation

1

Day of the Drones

In time to come, everyone on Earth would remember where they were, and what they had been doing, on this particular morning. But for the moment the skies above London were blue and serene, and no one would believe that plans were already in motion. For a little while longer even Hal Strider would remain oblivious.

It was a Saturday and Hal was racing home on his bike. He had slept over at a friend's house, stayed up half the night playing Xbox, and he woke late to find a text on his phone. 'At home? Stay there. Tell Jess same. Dad x'.

Finally. It had been over a week since Hal had seen his father; he hadn't even heard from him in days. But now, at last, he must be on his way home. Determined to get there first, Hal stood up on the peddles and powered across Westminster Bridge, then hurtled westwards alongside the Thames.

Dark haired and green-eyed, Hal was tall for his age and athletic, with energy to burn. He only knew one way to ride a bike: at breakneck speed. But this morning he must be on course for a new record. He tore past the Houses of Parliament, weaving through a great mass of tourists. Then he shot down Millbank, barely slowing down for the roundabout, zipping between delivery vans and black cabs, leaving horns blaring in his wake.

Ahead of him, towering up on the north bank of the river, was one of London's newest and tallest skyscrapers. It was nicknamed The Spaceship, because it curved towards its summit like some intergalactic rocket, and its glass shell swam with otherworldly colours. Even now, more than two years since they moved in, Hal still found it a little hard to believe – that he should actually live at the very top of this breath-taking building.

He skidded to a halt at the foot of the skyscraper, and within seconds he had locked up his bike and run into the tower and across the lobby. He rode the elevator to the uppermost floors, then swiped his keycard and burst into his apartment.

'Dad?' he called, as he climbed the spiral staircase. 'Dad, are you here?'

No response. Hal must have got here first.

He spiralled up to the third floor, and he hammered on his sister's door.

'Come on, Jess, get up. Dad's on his way back.'

After a long delay, the door opened a crack and Jess squinted out.

'What are you shouting about?'

'Dad's coming. He could be here any minute.'

'Yeah, right. What makes you think that. Did you speak to him?'

'Well – no. But he sent a text. He said—'

The door slammed in his face.

Hal shrugged, went back downstairs and into the wide circular space of the living room. He sent a reply to his Dad's message. 'Yes – at home. When will you be here?'

So now there was nothing to do but wait. He stood at the glass wall that wrapped around the entire living room. Ordinarily, it left Hal awestruck, looking out across the whole city. Out there, so far below, boats the size of bath toys were drawing patterns upon the Thames. Buses like fat red beetles were crawling across London Bridge. Helicopters glinted as they swept past at eyelevel.

But today Hal wasn't really seeing any of this. He was tapping his fingers on the glass, while listening for the beep of his father's keycard. To distract himself he put on headphones, then paced around listening to Deftones and Avenged Sevenfold. He stopped the music and flopped down on a sofa and flicked channels on the TV. Finally, he dug behind cushions and found an Xbox controller, and he managed to immerse himself in a flight simulator. And in this way the minutes ticked down.

A little while later Jess emerged. She was wearing a pink dressing gown, and as always she was tapping away at her phone, and in the other hand she was holding a bowl of cereal.

'Well – where is he, then?' she said, sitting on one of the sofas, eyes still on her screen. 'No sign? What a surprise.'

'He's probably stuck in traffic,' Hal said, dropping his controller. 'Why do you always have to think the worst?'

'Why do you never learn? He makes promises, he breaks them. That's what he does. Even if he does come home he'll only stay five minutes.'

'You don't know that. You're so ungrateful.'

For the first time she looked up, and she glared. 'What am I supposed to be grateful for, exactly? For the fact that we're basically orphans? That he didn't even come home for my birthday.'

'Still sulking about that. Your problem is you're too young to remember what it was like before we—'

Hal fell quiet because something had just caught his eye. He stood and moved across the living room and stopped at the glass wall. Out there in that bright blue sky was a small, dark object. It was hovering at eyelevel, no more than fifty metres from the apartment.

'What are you looking at?' Jess said, watching him.

Hal was amazed to find he couldn't say for certain. He was a watcher of the skies, fascinated with flight his entire life, yet here was an airborne object he couldn't identify, unlike anything he even knew existed.

It was a drone of some sort, it had to be. And yet it looked eerily organic. It had an oversized head, set with a pair of reddish orbs, like bulbous eyes. Its wings vibrated – a greenish blur at its sides. It might almost be some alien insect, except it glinted metallic.

Before he could study it further, the machine climbed rapidly, lifting out of sight. Hal found himself going after it, bounding up the spiral staircase.

'What is it?' Jess said as he dashed past.

'I can't tell. I'm going for a closer look.'

Up three flights, onto the top floor of the apartment. Out through the sliding doors, onto the roof garden. Bridging both hands above his eyes, Hal scanned London's airspace, his gaze flicking across helicopters and private jets and—

He flinched, took a step back. Because he had locked eyes on the mystery drone. And now it was hovering almost close enough to touch. Its wings made a piercing, whining buzz.

Watching the blur of those metallic wings, Hal took another step back. But as he did so the drone edged forward. Again Hal stepped away, and again the machine closed the gap.

Hal stood his ground, and the drone returned to a hover. Unblinking, he studied this uncanny machine. And in the facets of its eyes he saw a hundred tiny reflections of himself.

Then suddenly, the machine was back on the move. It spun and darted away from Hal while also losing altitude. Within a second it had dropped below the edge of the roof and out of view.

Hal went after it. He came to the guardrail, leant over. Beyond the rail was a ledge, preventing him looking directly downwards.

Without a second thought he climbed the rail, stepped down onto the ledge. With both arms stretched behind him he leant out and peered down the entire reach of the building.

At ground level, hundreds of metres below, tiny ant-people were walking alongside the river. Tourists were stepping off a boat at the pier. But there was no sign of the mystery drone. Whatever it was for, and whatever it had been doing here, it had vanished.

Hal's phone started vibrating. Out of habit, his right hand almost – *almost* – went for his pocket. But he kept a tight hold of the guardrail, pulled himself back to safety. He climbed back onto the roof garden and took out his phone.

A photograph had appeared on the screen – his father, wearing a flying suit, standing in front of the Starhawk Spaceplane. The moment Hal answered the call his father spoke rapidly.

'Hal – where are you – where's your sister?'

'I'm at home. We both are. Didn't you get my—'

'Has anyone else come to the apartment?'

'Um – no, I don't think so. Why? Who were you expecting?'

'Okay, now listen. First of all, it is vital that both you and Jess stay exactly where you are. Until I say otherwise, no matter what happens, do not go anywhere. Is that understood?'

'Dad, where are you? It's difficult to hear. What's that sound in the background? It's getting louder.'

'The second thing,' his father said. 'If anyone should come to the apartment, whoever it is, whoever they claim to be, do not let them in. Not under any circumstances.'

Behind his father's voice there was a roaring noise, and Hal wasn't sure he had heard all this correctly. But there was no mistaking his father's tone: clipped, urgent. It told Hal all he really needed to know.

'Something's happened at work – again,' he said. 'You're not coming home, are you?'

'This is the third thing,' his father said, again ignoring his question. 'In a little while, a package will be dropped on the roof. I need to talk to you about what's inside.'

'What did you just say? Dad, I can barely hear you. Just tell me, are you coming home or not?'

8

A brief pause, then his father said: 'Believe me, there's nowhere I'd rather be. But right now it's not the important thing. What's vital is—'

'How is it not important? It's important to me and Jess!'

'You need to listen to me, Hal. Events are moving fast. I still hope to avert the worst of this, but if I can't . . . going to need you to . . . absolutely vital . . . our last . . .'

Hal had already been struggling to hear him through that heavy noise in the background, and now the signal was fading. There were a series of beeps and the call dropped out completely.

Hal lowered the phone and looked up. He saw that Jess had come out onto the roof garden. She had been standing there listening.

'What did I tell you?' she said, hugging her arms. 'He cares about the company now, nothing else. Not even us.'

She stormed back inside. After a while Hal went in too. In his bedroom he turned the tint of the windows to maximum, until it was as dark as night, and he lay face down on his bed.

His phone, tossed on his desk, was ringing once more, juddering like an upturned beetle. But he didn't hear it. Because he had put on his headphones, and was blaring Rage Against the Machine at full volume, using the music to blast away everything else.

2

London Falling

'Hal, do you think Dad's okay?'

They were now both in Jess's room, Hal lying on his back on the floor, Jess sitting on her bed, arms wrapped around her knees.

'How do you mean, is he okay?'

'After you spoke to him, he called me too,' she said 'I didn't answer and he left a voice message. Wherever he was it was noisy, and I could barely hear. But he sounded, I don't know . . . kind of frantic. He never used to let anything get to him, did he? So it made me think, maybe he's ill. You know . . . working too hard, having some kind of breakdown.'

'No, Jess. Think about it. Dad used to fly jump jets from aircraft carriers. He flew a spaceplane outside Earth's atmosphere. Whatever he's up against, he is not cracking up.'

'That's just it, though, we don't know what he's up against. At least you say you don't. But you've been out to the aerodrome loads of times. I think you must have some idea.'

'I'm not lying, Jess. Last time I went out there was the weirdest day of my life – I hardly knew what was going on. The first thing I was going to do when he got home was try to get some answers.' Hal sat up, looked at her. 'What's going on with your phone? Could that be Dad?'

Her phone was pinging maniacally. She was digging beneath her bedclothes trying to find it. Eventually she pulled it out from under a pillow, and she swiped at the screen. Her expression became grave.

'Well,' Hal said. 'Is it him?'

'No, it's . . . everyone else. And they're all messaging bizarre things.'

'More bizarre than usual? I've seen your friends' posts. All their fascinating dreams.'

'I'm not joking, Hal. I think this is serious.'

He got to his feet, stood over her. 'What do you mean?'

Still staring at her phone, she swung her legs to the floor. 'I think . . . I think we should go and look.'

'Look at what? Where?'

But she was already heading out the door. Hal followed her along the landing, up through the apartment, and back onto the roof garden.

The moment he stepped outside, squinting in the sunlight, he sensed that something was very wrong. It took only a second to pinpoint what it was.

It was the sky.

The sky was silent.

Shielding his eyes, he looked up. The contrails were dissolving, and no new trails were taking their place. Sweeping his gaze, he didn't see a single business jet or helicopter or passenger plane.

London's entire airspace had emptied.

'What could have done this?' Jess said, her voice hushed.

Hal could only shake his head.

'Has a plane crashed?' she said. 'Have they closed the airport?'

'Which airport?' Hal said. 'All of them? Look – this is total. I haven't even seen a police helicopter or an air ambulance. Nothing.'

'So what is it?' She swiped at her phone, scrolling through websites. 'All the news channels are reporting it, but none of them know why it's happening. Wait – this one says it's terrorism. A hijacked plane. Could that be it?' She looked up. 'God, it's eerie.'

Yes, it was. The rumble of air traffic had been such a constant all Hal's life, that he rarely even noticed it. Only now it was gone did it become something massive, a chilling void left by its absence.

Was it his imagination, or had the city also become very quiet at ground level? From far below he heard a car door slam. A baby was crying somewhere in the distance.

His phone started vibrating. He snatched it out, saw the photo of his father, answered the call.

'Dad, you know something about this – you were trying to warn me.'

'I want to listen!' Jess shouted. 'Put it on speaker!'

Hal did so, but for several seconds no voice came from the

phone. There was just a hissing, like static, along with that deeper roaring sound Hal had heard before.

Finally, their father said: 'Hal, I hope you can hear me. I've had to patch into an emergency network, and it's broadcast only. I hope Jess is there too. There are so many things I need to tell you.

'Above all else, I need you to know that I love you both very much. No matter what happens from here, if you can trust in nothing else, I want you to hold onto that.'

'Dad, you're scaring me!' Jess shouted. 'It feels like something awful has happened – or it's about to. We need to know where you are.'

'Quiet!' Hal hissed. 'He said he can't hear you. We need to listen.'

But in fact their father's voice had faded away. Now there was only that roaring sound drifting from the phone.

'What is that noise?' Jess said. 'Where could he be?'

'It sounds like jet engines,' Hal said. 'Maybe he's near a runway.'

Jess bit her lip. 'Or, in that case . . . could he be on an aero-plane?' She turned her eyes to the empty and eerie sky. 'Hal, do you think he could be on a plane?'

Before Hal could answer, their father's voice came once more from the phone. But it was fainter and more broken than ever.

'. . . find it in my safe,' he was saying, 'in the hours ahead . . . whatever it takes to . . .'

Hal and Jess had their heads bowed together, their ears close to the phone. But it was futile. Their father's voice was tiny, and now it was swallowed utterly by that roaring noise.

To Hal, it sounded more than ever like jet engines. And still it was getting louder. It was swelling out of the phone and filling the world around them.

Hal hesitated, then held the phone at arm's length.

The roaring did not stop. In fact, it grew fiercer.

Slowly he turned, looked out and up.

Jess gripped his arm. She gasped.

Because the sky was no longer entirely empty.

Here, moving across them east to west, already far too close to the peaks of the buildings, was a colossal aircraft.

Hal recognised it immediately as a Lockheed Super Galaxy. It was a military airlifter, a giant of the sky. The sort of plane that should never be here in London's airspace.

But that idea was eclipsed by a far more shocking fact.

'Oh my God,' Jess whispered. 'It is, isn't it? It's going to crash.'

Yes, it was. It had passed the roof garden at eyelevel and was still dropping as it thundered westwards. It trailed a plume of smoke from one of its four huge engines. It was making a howling noise like a dying beast.

For Hal, all this was happening in slow motion. The plane lumbered over Battersea, narrowly missing the tall towers of the old power station, and then it passed out over lower rooftops, its dark shadow sweeping over Chelsea and Kensington.

All of London was still now, and hushed. Tiny stick people stood frozen as the aircraft howled ever lower, ever closer to the streets.

For Hal, time slowed further, until the plane was suspended just above the ground. And perhaps this was how the world would remain. Maybe gravity had shown mercy at the last moment and this metal monster would never fall fully to earth.

But then time lurched back into motion, and that final second passed.

As it did so, Jess spoke into Hal's phone, her voice cracking as she said a single word.

'Dad . . . ?'

And that solitary word drifted clear and distinct, even amid the rolling roar of the crash.

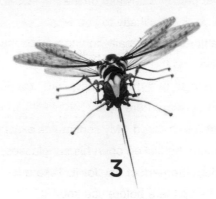

3

The Aerodrome

Ten Days Earlier

'Believe me, I'm as keen to get back in the air as you are,' Hal's father said, as they sped down the motorway. 'But I do have a few things to take care of first. So when we get there I need you to wait in the Ops Room. I won't be long. Then the rest of the day will be ours.'

For Hal, these words barely registered. He was staring out the window, watching the world blur past, and he was so full of excitement about the day ahead that he could hardly think straight.

'I know you've already had to be patient,' his father said. 'It's been far too long since we came out here together. I haven't been fair to you lately – to you or your sister.'

As he spoke, he was turning off the M25, and now they raced south east, leaving Greater London behind.

'I asked Jess to come along today,' his father went on. 'Tried bribing her with a stop at Bluewater on the way home. She wouldn't even open her door. But I'll say to you what I said to her – better days are on the horizon. I'm finally getting my nose in front at work. Soon we'll get back to the way we were, I promise.'

Hal looked across at him. 'It's okay, Dad. You told me all this before. Anyway . . . we're here now.'

His father smiled, nodded. ' My sentiments exactly.' Taking one hand off the wheel, he flicked open his sunglasses, put them on. 'And we've picked the perfect day for it. Take a look at that wide blue sky. We'll be up there before you know it.'

Hal grinned. 'Can we take the Comet?'

'Certainly we can. I had the engineers give her a once over. She's running better than ever.'

'And I get the pilot's seat?'

'I'd face a fight keeping you out of it, wouldn't I? Anyway, you earned your stripes last time. All right then, let's get round these dawdlers – don't they know we've got places to be . . .'

He steered them into the fast lane, and he floored the accelerator, and his McLaren FX surged past other cars so fast it made everyone else look like they were standing still. In under eight minutes they reached their junction of the M20, then they turned off onto smaller roads.

They swept through the Kent countryside, the hypercar making barely a whisper in full electric mode. Hal pushed a button on the dashboard and the roof came apart in segments and folded away into the boot, like a beetle stowing its wings.

Hal's grin widened. It was true that recent weeks had been difficult, their father working such extreme hours that Hal and Jess had barely seen him. But at this moment, for Hal at least, all that was practically forgotten. After all, how many fourteen-year-old boys get to spend a day of their summer holidays this way, hours of free flight and adventure stretching ahead . . .?

And now the aerodrome was close. They swept around the reservoir, then his father slowed the car, and he turned off the smooth tarmac. Now they bumped up the final rutted track.

Hal's excitement levels spiked as they passed the sign that read: 'Private Testing Facility. Strictly No Entry'. And here were all the warning symbols: the biohazard sign; the double lightning bolt; the images of low-flying aircraft.

The track twisted a mile through a tunnel of trees. And when they emerged at the other end the security fence loomed up ahead of them.

As they approached the guardhouse, cameras swivelled to track the car's progress. Ghostly fingers of light reached through the windshield, drew grid patterns upon their faces. The gates swung open, and Hal's father steered them inside.

As they drove through the compound, Hal stared around him, every bit as exhilarated as the first time he had ever come here. In many ways it was much like any other private airfield, albeit an ultramodern one: there was a gleaming glass-and-aluminium control tower, hulking aircraft hangars and rotating radar scanners. The whole place smelt of kerosene and hummed with the sound of aero-engines.

All of which, for a boy like Hal, would have been exciting enough. But that was only the half of it.

Because at the heart of the compound, between the twin

18

runways, stood the most extraordinary structure. It was a geodesic dome, constructed of massive hexagonal panels. Its exoskeleton was formed of titanium threads, which glistened like a gigantic spider's web. All in all it looked like something that might be built on the moon. This was the headquarters of his father's company, Starr-Strider Biomimetics.

'Since you've got things to do,' Hal said, staring at the dome as they drove a long circuit around it, 'wouldn't it be easier if I just came with you?'

'I'm sorry, Hal, my answer hasn't changed. There will come a time for that, really there will. But you have to trust me, now is not that time.'

'You wouldn't even know I was there – I'd just sit in a corner and watch.'

'Hal Strider, you could no more sit and watch than I could. No – the day we get you involved, we get you involved fully. I've always known that.'

Before Hal could press him further, his father's phone buzzed from its cradle on the dashboard. When he answered it, a woman's face appeared on the screen. An attractive blonde woman with bright-blue eyes.

'John – security said you just came in,' she said. 'There's something you need to see.'

'I'm trying to keep my head down today. I have my son with me.'

'We've picked up another rogue signal,' the woman said. 'We can't make head nor tail of it. Only it appears to originate from the unmanned division.'

'Unmanned? So talk to the professor about it.'

'I tried, but he's gone to ground. And he's not answering his phone. You know what he's like.'

His father sighed. 'All right, I'll come and take a look. It's probably just a ghost on the instruments, the same as last time.'

'One more thing,' the woman said. 'The Mark IV has just come off the line. You did say you wanted to know as soon as it was ready.'

'Yes, thank you. But I won't get round to it today. Have them bring it up. Put it in Hangar Five.'

After ending the call, he said to Hal: 'Don't worry, none of that sounded critical. It'll barely slow us down. And if my phone rings again I'm ignoring it.'

They drove into a quiet corner of the compound, where a few breezeblock buildings clustered around a red-fronted firehouse.

'You know which one is the Ops Room,' Hal's father said, as he stopped the car and Hal got out. 'And listen, I know I always say this, but it's a tense time out here. There are people on a short fuse. So it's important you don't go wandering about. Just sit tight and I'll be back as quick as I can.'

The Ops Room wasn't nearly as interesting as it sounded. Perhaps interesting things went on here once, judging by the rows of powerful computer servers that stood against the walls and the banks of monitor screens. But now all such equipment was turned off. This room was no longer used for anything, as far as Hal could see.

He sat on one of the swivel chairs, spun it round. He scooted it from one end of the room to the other, while listening to Muse and AC/DC.

And all the while he was trying to ignore something he had overheard in the car.

The Mark IV has just come off the line.

Have them bring it up. Put it in Hangar Five.

What was the Mark IV? Was it the company's latest prototype? What breed of fantastic machine might, this moment, be heading for Hangar Five?

Over the past decade, Starr-Strider Biomimetics had created some of the most advanced technologies on the planet. It was Hal's father and his engineers who built the Starhawk Spaceplane. Not to mention the Spider 7 Surface Crawler. And the Cephalopod Ocean Explorer.

The company had invented unmanned technologies too. A fully autonomous search-and-rescue robot. A tree-felling drone. A surveillance quadcopter that had gone into service with police forces around the globe.

For Hal, growing up, the most thrilling thing of all was knowing in advance what was coming next. Because his father used to tell him everything. Whenever Hal showed an interest, he would talk him through his latest project, even showing him scale models or blueprints.

But then, around a year ago, all that came to an end. His father suddenly became guarded about his work. Now Hal's questions were met with evasive answers, and a swift change of subject. Even after Hal started coming out to the aerodrome for flying lessons, he got no closer to learning what new marvels might be taking shape behind closed doors.

That was the one downside of coming out here, in fact – the

feeling of pressing his face to a window, knowing that a world of wonders existed on the other side, but the glass was too murky to see anything more than vague shapes and shadows.

And today, because of what he had heard in the car, his frustration had quadrupled – his curiosity burned so fiercely he didn't think he could stand it!

Finally, as the waiting stretched into half an hour, then forty minutes, he decided he really *couldn't* stand it.

He got up and left the Ops Room. He wouldn't be gone long, and he wouldn't exactly be wandering about. He would go directly to Hangar Five and come straight back. What harm could come from just taking a quick look?

As he crossed into the busier part of the compound, he spotted engineers in overalls and technicians in lab coats. They pressed their palms to biometric scanners as they came and went from blank-faced buildings.

Hal felt conspicuous, a fourteen-year-old boy in jeans and Nike high-tops and Black Ops T-shirt. But in fact, everyone he passed was intent on their own business, and nobody paid the slightest attention to him.

A beeping noise made him turn his head. In the near distance, a flatbed truck was reversing. It was backing into a giant domed shed, which had the number five embossed above its doors. Hangar Five! Yes – that truck must be carrying the Mark IV prototype!

Forcing himself not to run, Hal hurried closer. He got a glimpse of something on the back of the truck, but it was covered by a tarpaulin. And now it was swallowed into the hangar, and the gigantic doors were sliding shut.

Now Hal ran. From this distance it looked like he was already too late – only a sliver of light remained as the doors rumbled together. But he got there with a second to spare, squeezing side-ways through the gap, the doors crunching closed just as he pulled his arm inside.

Against one wall of the hangar stood rows of shipping con-tainers – instinctively Hal darted behind them to stay out of sight. He crouched there and he listened.

He could hear two voices, although the words were swallowed into the vastness of the space above. Soon another noise began: a whirring, sighing, which he imagined was a lifting machine taking the prototype off the rig.

When this noise stopped, Hal risked peering out. Two men were getting back into the truck. Its engine started up and the giant doors were reopening. The truck left the hangar and the doors closed, coming together with a resounding clunk.

And only with this noise did Hal realise something: he hadn't given a single thought to how he might get back out of here. Would he be able to open those colossal doors – and could he do it without being noticed?

But the thought was fleeting. It was crowded out by anticipation and curiosity.

Because for over a year he had yearned to know what his father's company might be developing next. What project could be so fantastic that his father had been working on it day and night?

And now, here in front of him, was the company's latest proto-type. When he pulled back that tarpaulin, what world-altering wonder was he going to find?

4

Heavy Metal

As Hal approached the mystery machine, he was struck first and foremost by its size. It towered over him, and stretched at least thirty metres end to end. Tracing its outline beneath the tarpaulin, he began to suspect it was some kind of manned aircraft.

Yes – there was the shape of a tailfin. And near its front end the curve of a cockpit. So then, was this some state-of-the-art hypersonic jet? Or perhaps a successor to the Starhawk Spaceplane? His pulse ran faster at the very idea.

He tried to pull away the tarpaulin, but it was secured with nuts and bolts. So instead, he lay on his back and wriggled under one corner of the shroud. He switched on the light of his phone and shone it upwards.

Dark metal gleamed back at him. The surfaces of this aircraft – at least its undercarriage – were angular and bulky. He might almost believe it was armour plated . . . He wriggled back out and went to the front end of the machine. Again he lay on his back and shuffled underneath. And this time, when he shone the light, his breath stopped.

Because now he was staring up at a lethal-looking device. It was huge and had twin-barrels.

This could only be one thing.

It was a weapon.

For a full minute Hal just lay there, staring. His father had told him all about his time in the Air Force – about the awful things he had witnessed when he was deployed to a warzone. He had left Hal without the slightest doubt that the one thing his company would *never* build was tools of war.

Yet here Hal was, in one of the company's hangars. And here above him, armed and armoured, was unmistakably a warplane.

A noise made him flinch. The clanging of a door.

He wriggled out from under the Mark IV, then dashed back behind the shipping containers. Peeking out, he saw that two figures had entered the hangar at its far end. They were now heading towards the prototype.

The first man wore heavy spectacles and a tweed jacket and had a perfectly bald head, which gleamed beneath the white lights. He rode in a high-tech electric chair, which had a single gyroscopic ball in place of wheels. This was Professor Dominic Starr, Hal's father's business partner.

Walking alongside him, the second man looked like a different species. Dressed in dark jeans and T-shirt, he was broad and muscular, with a heavy black beard and an overhanging brow.

Hal knew this man's name was Tony Daegar – and that he was a relative newcomer to the company. But he didn't know much more than that. Once, when they had seen him walking across the aerodrome, Hal had asked his father who he was. His father had said something about him being a security consultant. But his reply was curt and dismissive, leaving Hal with the impression that he didn't like this man very much.

As the pair of them moved towards the Mark IV, Tony Daegar was saying something to the professor, but his words were lost in the vastness of the hangar.

In any case, Hal wasn't overly concerned with listening. It suddenly seemed vital that he shouldn't be caught snooping around in here. And looking beyond the pair, he saw the door where they had come in. It was still ajar. Here was his chance to sneak away unseen.

Sticking close to the wall, he passed behind more shipping containers. Once he was some distance behind the men, he broke cover and made a dash for the doorway.

But then he heard shouting. He stopped and spun in place.

Tony Daegar was shouting at Professor Starr. He was leaning over him, jabbing him in the chest with one finger, while snarling and spitting into his face.

The professor tried to put his electric chair in reverse, but Tony Daegar took hold of the armrests and lifted both man and chair off the ground. While the gyro-ball spun in midair, Tony Daegar shook the professor so violently that his glasses fell to the floor.

'Hey, let go of him!' Hal shouted, running towards them. 'Put him down!'

Tony Daegar dropped the professor, his chair lurching backwards before coming to a standstill.

Slowly, the big man turned, and Hal's pace faltered. At close quarters, Tony Daegar was intimidating, his thick forearms tattooed with winged swords and serpents.

'Well now, you must be Hal Strider. Yes, I was told you look just like your father. And why would you be skulking around in here?'

'I wasn't skulking,' Hal said, forcing himself to stand tall. 'I . . . I heard shouting.' He glanced back at the open door, as if that was the way he had come in. 'And then I saw what you were doing to the professor. It's hardly a fair fight, is it?'

Tony Daegar showed his teeth. 'So, that's what this is – an act of *heroics*.'

He stepped closer, and he dropped his voice low and menacing. 'You want to be careful, Hal Strider. Didn't your father ever warn you – playing the hero can land you in all kinds of trouble.'

He turned back to Professor Starr, who had merely been sitting there trembling, blinking without his glasses. 'In any case, Professor, I believe I made myself clear. Don't take too long thinking it over. Time is against you – in every sense.'

With that, Tony Daegar turned away from them both and strode across the hangar towards the open door.

'Are you okay?' Hal said, picking up the professor's glasses and taking them to him.

'Ah, hum, yes, yes, I think so. A little shaken.' He forced a smile. 'When it comes to fisticuffs, I'm afraid men like Tony Daegar will always have me at a disadvantage. Thank you, Master Strider, for – ah – for coming to my rescue. Now, if you'll excuse me, I must return to my work.'

His powered chair swivelled on its ball, and he headed for the doorway.

'Wait,' Hal said, running after him. 'Professor, wait a minute, I'd like to ask you something. I . . .'

The professor stopped. But now Hal wasn't entirely sure what he was going to say. His eyes flicked to the menacing outline of the Mark IV. How could he ask about it without revealing he had really come in here to snoop around?

In the end he said, 'I wanted to ask about you and Dad. About when you first set up the company. He told me once – well, he said you always knew what sort of machines you wanted to build . . .'

He trailed off, inviting Professor Starr to speak. The professor blinked at him and eventually said, 'Well, ah um, yes, certainly, that's quite correct. From the outset, your father and I, we had a clear understanding of how we must utilize our expertise.'

Again Hal's eyes darted to the warplane beneath its tarpaulin. 'And how was that, exactly?'

The professor smiled awkwardly. 'Um, ah ha, let me see. Perhaps it will sound a trifle grand, or even naive, but your father and I, we always believed our endeavours here must aim to make the world a better place. Yes, indeed. Nothing less than to improve the lot of the human race!'

As he said this, a change came over Professor Starr. His eyes appeared to grow and glow behind the thick lenses of his spectacles.

'Personally speaking, Master Strider, that zeal is stronger in me than ever. My present endeavours – ah hum, you must excuse my hubris – but my current project promises humankind the greatest gift imaginable. Indeed, yes, the greatest boon since fire! And now we are so close. We stand at the very threshold! And so you see, uh hum, I really must return to my work immediately . . .'

So saying, without so much as a goodbye, he swivelled his chair and whirred away faster than Hal could run.

Back in the old Ops Room, Hal paced the floor, more frustrated than ever. His foray to Hangar Five had provided no real answers, and had only succeeded in throwing up more questions.

Was his father really helping to develop a warplane? What had Professor Starr meant about his latest project being 'the greatest gift to humankind'? Surely he could not have been talking about creating weapons . . . ?

Now Hal was doubly impatient for his flying lesson. The minute he and his father were alone in a cockpit, Hal intended to start quizzing him – and this time he wouldn't let up until he got some answers!

But when his father finally stepped into the Ops Room, half an hour later, Hal could tell immediately that he would get no such chance. By his father's troubled expression, it was obvious they would not be going flying together.

'I'm sorry, Hal, really I am. This problem is worse than I thought. It needs my full attention. Trust me, I'm as disappointed as you are.'

He came and put a hand on Hal's shoulder. 'But chin up – it

won't be a complete waste of a trip. I've asked one of our instructors to take you out, so you'll still get some flying hours.'

As they walked towards Runway Two, his father apologised again, and repeated his pledge that better days lay ahead. But Hal had heard it all before. And, no matter what he might say, the end result was the same. Once again, his father was too busy to spend any time with him. Instead, he would be palmed off on a total stranger.

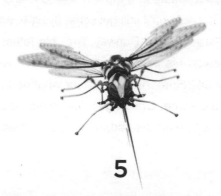

5

The Impossible Girl

The stranger's name was Archie Graham. He was a big, soldierly type with ginger hair and a full moustache. He and Hal stood together in the hangar that housed his father's private collection of aircraft.

'Dad said we could take the Comet Racer,' Hal said, gazing at the twin-engined plane, with its famous sweeping lines and gleaming red paintwork.

'Out of the question, I'm afraid,' Archie Graham said. 'I've not had a chance to fly the Comet. I'd never take a passenger on a maiden flight.'

'I wouldn't be a passenger. I'd be the pilot.'

Archie Graham raised his bushy eyebrows. 'Your dad said you're a confident lad. No harm in that. But what he allows is one thing. What happens on my watch is another.'

He moved towards a blue-and-white training plane. 'We'll take the Cessna. I'll disable dual controls, but you can still mimic my actions, and talk me through what you already know.'

Hal groaned inwardly. Mimic your actions? I could fly the Cessna with my eyes closed, he thought. But he didn't want to sound ungrateful, so he kept his thoughts to himself while he and the instructor walked around the Cessna, performing all the pre-flight checks.

Just as they were finishing them, the sound of hard laughter made Hal turn towards the mouth of the hangar. There, sauntering past in the sunshine, were four young men. They had their flight uniforms folded down, revealing bare chests, and all four wore mirrored sunglasses.

Three of the boys passed by, joking among themselves. But the fourth peered into the hangar, locked eyes on Hal. He gave a short whistle and the others came back and crowded round.

'Hey, Archie,' the biggest of them called. 'You know who've got there – that's the golden child. You just go careful, okay?'

The others laughed, and one of them shouted, 'Maybe you should just taxi him down the runway. It can be scary up there in the air.'

'Yeah, scary,' another boy echoed.

'You boys have no right being here,' Archie Graham growled, stepping towards them. 'I don't care who your father is, Karl. Strutting around as if you own the place. Go on, get lost.'

Three of the boys backed off. The biggest and perhaps oldest of them held his ground, fixing Archie with a hateful stare. But finally he turned too, and all four of them slouched away, shouting brave things back at Archie once they were out of range.

'Who were they?' Hal said. 'What have they got against me?'

'Don't take it personally,' Archie said. 'Some people just live to pick fights. Your dad said you haven't been out here in a while, so you won't have run into Karl Daegar before.'

Karl Daegar.

Now it made sense. The eldest boy looked a lot like Tony Daegar, with the same heavy features and overhanging brow. And evidently he was just as mean.

'In any case, they've gone, good riddance,' said Archie. 'So let's get on with these checks. It's a beautiful day up there, and it's getting away from us.'

Ten minutes later, they were sat side by side in the twin cockpit of the Cessna and accelerating down the runway. At take-off speed, Archie Graham pulled back on the yoke, and the wheels lifted off the ground, and they soared up and out of the compound.

As they climbed past 1,000 feet, Archie banked the plane to the east, the wooded hills tilting and rotating below. They continued to climb, the reservoir down there sparkling as it dwindled.

Normally, the moment Hal was up in the air, everything else dropped away. With the world below looking so small, it was impossible to hold onto worries or stray thoughts.

But today it was different. He looked back and watched the aerodrome shrinking, swallowed into the pinewoods, and his mind churned with everything he had seen and heard there this morning.

'Mr Graham—'

'Archie.'

'Archie, how long have you worked for Starr-Strider?'

'Since day one. Twenty-two years.'

'And in all that time . . . have you ever known the company do any work for the military? Even in secret?'

This took Archie off guard. 'What does your dad say about that?'

Hal considered making something up, trying to trick his way to the truth, but he wasn't a natural liar. So in the end he simply said, 'He doesn't tell me much about anything any more.'

Again, Archie hesitated. 'Well, all I can say is, you needn't take that to heart. There's lots of us been with Starr-Strider a long time, and we're not told anything either. I'd wager it was a year ago, thirteen months in fact, that your dad stopped sharing.'

'How did you know that?'

'Because that's when everything changed. Tony Daegar came along, and suddenly security was so tight even your dad's oldest friends found themselves out of the loop.'

Hal gave this some thought. 'Nobody likes Tony Daegar, do they? So why do Dad and Professor Starr put up with him?'

'Lots of us been wondering that too. Some say he bullies the professor, keeps a hold over him that way. But listen, lad, I shouldn't be talking like this. I don't know enough in any case to be running my mouth off.'

'So you don't know what Professor Starr is working on now? He told me his latest project will be . . . um, a "great gift to humanity", something like that. You don't know what it could be?'

Archie said something in reply, but suddenly Hal was paying no attention whatsoever. Because he was staring out past their port wing, where a truly incredible sight had just caught his eye.

He squeezed his eyes shut, opened them, stared again.

And what he saw made no sense at all.

He was 3,000 feet in the air, travelling at a hundred miles per hour. And yet there – so his eyes wanted him to believe – was a girl.

A girl who was flying—

Without an aircraft.

He blinked rapidly, then stared once more. Instead of dissolving like a mirage, the vision only clarified. The flying girl was wearing some sort of dark bodysuit. From beneath her flight helmet a blonde ponytail whirled in the wind. Her legs were arrow-straight behind her, and her arms were tucked at her sides.

But the most astonishing thing was still what Hal *didn't* see. He saw no flying machine above or below the girl – no glider or parachute or rotorcraft.

A jetpack? No. That bodysuit hugged her form and showed no bulky shape at her back, and there was no glow of a jet.

She was simply . . . flying!

And now he was losing sight of her. Because she was moving fast and losing altitude, and Hal was struggling to spot her shape against the dark mass of the pinewoods.

Just as she vanished entirely, something else caught his eye. More shapes in the sky. Four single-seat aeroplanes. They were heading westwards, losing altitude. In fact, they were following the same flight path as the girl. Almost as if they were racing her . . . or even pursuing her . . .

'I was wondering what you'd spotted,' Archie said. 'Now I see them. I'm surprised ground control didn't warn us they were up here. They're unpredictable at the best of times.'

Still wondering if he could trust his own eyes, Hal examined the aircraft. They were bull-nosed stunt planes with howling turbo-prop engines, very modern and very fast. They were painted in garish colours like exotic insects.

'You know who they are?'

'Karl Daegar and his hornets. They're in a hurry, looks like. Usually they're content to hang around and play the fool.'

'It looked like they were chasing someone – or racing them.'

'Oh? You saw another plane?'

'Not a plane, no, but—'

Hal stopped himself. What was he going to say? *Not a plane, no. They were chasing a magically flying girl.*

Yes, great idea, make Archie think you're a lunatic.

'Actually . . . I'm not sure what I saw.'

And this was nothing less than the truth. Because suddenly, the whole day had taken on the texture of illusion. Archie clearly hadn't seen the impossible girl, so might she have been a mirage after all? And if so, had Hal also imagined everything that had happened in Hangar Five, including finding a war machine beneath that shroud?

No – he could trust his own senses. All today's events had all been real, of course they had. And they told him one thing above all else: the aerodrome was home to extraordinary secrets – even more of them and even stranger than he had ever imagined. And knowing this made him burn with frustration, more desperate than ever to peer beneath the surface and find out what it all meant.

Their flight time was almost up and they were heading back to the aerodrome when the four stunt planes reappeared.

This time they were dead ahead. And they were growing more distinct, their venomous colours blazing in the sunshine.

'They must have seen us,' Archie said. 'Visibility is perfect. Even so, they're on our flight line, so I'll follow procedure and climb 500 feet.'

He took the Cessna higher. But Karl Daegar and his gang also gained altitude. They remained on a direct collision course.

'Come in, ground control,' Archie said, operating the radio. 'This is training flight zero-four-zero. We have visual on four light aircraft. Estimated 2,000 metres, and closing.'

The only response was a hiss of static. Hal watched the stunt planes grow larger.

'Ground control, do you copy?' Archie said. 'We have four aircraft in dangerous proximity. Ground control! Where the devil are you?'

The radio buzzed as he switched channels. 'Karl Daegar, acknowledge this signal. And keep your damn eyes open. We are directly in your flight path. Alter your heading and maintain safe distance. Karl Daegar – acknowledge. You're too close!'

Again there was no response. The stunt planes were now growing very fast. Hal's mouth was suddenly dry, his stomach twisting in knots.

And then came a moment of almost unbelievable terror, the

four planes thundering upon them, parting at the last possible second, screaming wide on both sides, above and below.

Archie Graham swore repeatedly. Hal twisted his neck, saw a glint of banking wings, and he knew the stunt planes were coming back.

Karl and the others buzzed them again – howling, yawning sounds, shockingly loud and close.

'Stupid idiots!' Archie growled. 'Karl – what in God's name do you think you're doing?'

'Turn that child's toy around.' Karl Daegar's voice burst out of the radio. 'This is our airspace now. The aerodrome is out of bounds.'

The stunt planes broke formation, and they mobbed the Cessna one by one, flashing out of the sun, their engines yowling, spitting sparks.

His heart racing, Hal caught sight of the ground. He had never been remotely daunted by heights, but those hills were suddenly a very long way away, a village down there no bigger than his thumbnail.

'I won't tell you again,' Karl Daegar said, as his plane roared past. 'We can clip those wings, easy enough.'

'We don't have enough fuel to play your idiot games,' Archie growled. 'We're landing at the airfield, so you'd better get out of our way. Christ, that was the closest yet. By God they're taking a chance with these margins!'

Again the planes blazed by, Hal holding his breath, Archie swearing repeatedly, his knuckles white where he gripped the flight stick.

'I promise you, Karl,' he hissed. 'Once we're back on the ground, and I get hold of you, you are going to wish—'

He never got to finish this sentence. Because one of the stunt plane pilots had just made a mistake. He misjudged his angles, or got the distance wrong, and his plane clipped the Cessna.

There was a tearing, sickening crunch. Hal's neck jarred as his head was thrown violently to one side. Then the Cessna lurched, dropped, and he and Archie went hurtling towards the earth.

6

Lockdown

The plane plummeted, the cockpit shuddering, air howling across the wings. Instinctively, Hal pulled back on his flight stick.

But nothing happened. Before take off, Archie Graham had disabled dual controls.

'Pull up!' he shouted.

But Archie was slumped. And now Hal saw a smear of blood on the inside of the canopy. On impact, Archie must have hit his head, and now he was unconscious.

Craning his neck, Hal saw that their tail-plane was shredded. The rudder would be useless. But both wings were intact – he still had the ailerons – if only he could operate them.

As the ground rushed upwards, he ran desperate hands all around his control column. How had Archie disabled his controls? He had reached under here, hadn't he, so there must be—

Yes – here was a pinion, pulled out! Hal shoved it back into place, and it reengaged with a clunk.

Now his flight stick kicked and juddered in his grip. He wrestled with it, trying to bring the nose up, trying to level the wings.

The aircraft steadied. But they were still dropping fast, the altimeter spinning wildly. The wooded hills had become horribly distinct, Hal able to see individual trees.

He needed more power to gain lift. He rammed open the throttle, the engine rising in pitch. And now, as he pulled back on the flight stick, their rate of descent slackened, at least a fraction.

Groaning, his head lolling, Archie Graham came back to life. But he was in no condition to retake command of the aircraft. His fingers fumbled as he worked the controls of the radio.

'Mayday, mayday!' he said in a slurred voice. 'We are crash landing. Request immediate assistance to these coordinates. Mayday, mayday. We are crash landing . . .'

To Hal these words were surreal, yet perfectly distinct, along with every other detail – the sun glinting on the glass of the canopy, the air yowling across the wings, the thump of his own heartbeat.

And here were the pinewoods, rushing to meet them.

And a fire-break between the trees.

Rolling the wings, using the ailerons to swing to starboard, Hal guided the Cessna into this clearway.

They dropped below the tips of the trees, and now it was out of Hal's hands. Gravity reached up and slammed the plane into the ground, and his world shattered into shards.

*

41

Hazily, Hal peered around him, grasping for meaning. Here were pine trees. Pieces of aeroplane scattered between them. A severed wing. Bits of blue-and-white airframe. Half a propeller embedded in the soil.

How he had come to be here? For the moment he had no recollection of the aerial impact, or of the crash. A second ago, as far as his mind was concerned, he had been flying up there amid the clouds.

'Hal – look at me, lad. Can you move?' Archie Graham was standing over him. 'We need to get you out of there. The fuel could catch.'

He unbuckled Hal's harness and took hold of him beneath the armpits. Hal pushed upwards and between them they scrambled clear of the wreckage. At a safe distance they slumped to the ground.

Hal sat staring at his hands. The world had become very bright, every detail crisp. The crackling of flames, and the panicked noise of the birds in the trees. The sweet smell of pine needles.

They sat there like that for a long time, neither of them saying a word. Eventually, Archie Graham turned.

'I was in the Air Force for seventeen years,' he said. 'And I think you should know . . . what you just did . . . that was the bravest and best piece of flying I have ever seen. Your dad should be very proud.'

An hour later, Hal sat wrapped in a thermal blanket, nursing a mug of hot soup. An ambulance was here, and a fire engine, and two police cars. Archie sat at his side, his head thickly bandaged.

'Do you think the plane that hit us came down as well?' Hal said

'The fire chief told me there were no other mayday calls,' Archie said. 'Those stunt planes are built to withstand extreme G. Most likely he didn't even feel a bump.' He shook his head, then put a hand to his bandage and grimaced. 'I'll tell you one thing for free, they're not gettIng away with it. Their piloting days are over, at the very least.'

Unsteadily, Hal stood.

'You should sit still for a while,' Archie said. 'The paramedics will want another look at you.'

'I need to get back to the aerodrome. By now Dad will be worried.'

Archie pushed himself upright, and he nodded. 'I'll ask one of the policemen to run us into town. We can get a taxi up from there.'

Even from a distance it was obvious that something was very wrong. The aerodrome was too still, too quiet. And as Hal ran up to the front gates this unsettling idea grew more intense.

He could see no movement through the fence, hear no sound of engines. As he paced in front of the guardhouse no biometric scanner sent out its light. Even the security cameras were inert, hanging their heads.

Hal waved his arms. 'Hey, let us in! We're here – Hal Strider and Archie Graham. There's been an accident.'

He stood still and peered through the fence and said in a quieter voice, 'Where is everyone?'

It was an eerie feeling. Two hours earlier, this place had been full of noise and movement. Now there were no flashing lights on the landing strips. No signs of life in or around the buildings. Nothing.

It was almost as if . . . as if he and Archie had been up in the sky for years, and this airfield had long since been abandoned and forgotten.

'Why is it like this?' he said. 'What could have happened?'

Archie Graham stood at the security fence, stroking his moustache. 'I've known a few lockdowns in the past – but nothing like this.' He picked up a stick, touched it to the mesh. 'Even the electric fence is off.'

'Maybe Karl Daegar knew something had happened and he was warning us to stay away.'

Archie grunted. 'More likely, he thought this would help him get away with it.'

Hal's phone vibrated. He took it out, answered the call.

'Dad! Where are you?'

'I need you to head home,' his father said, 'straight away.'

'Are you still at the aerodrome? We can't get in.'

'That's nothing for you to worry about. Just do as I ask, please. Go with Archie to the train station. I'll see you back home just as soon as I can.'

'But, Dad, I need to tell you something. You obviously haven't heard. I'm not hurt, but we were in a—'

He was wasting his breath; his father had already cut the call. Hal lowered his phone, feeling cold all over. Jess had been saying for weeks that the company now came first, and she and Hal came second. Hal never wanted to believe it. But at this moment it was impossible to believe otherwise.

I might have died in that crash, he thought, a hot pricking behind his eyes. I could be lying dead in that wreckage. Would he care then? How long before he would even notice?

7

Fallout

Today

But now here Hal was, ten days later, and those events at the aerodrome seemed petty by comparison. Because he was standing on the roof garden with Jess, and he was staring at the aftermath of a very different air crash.

The airlifter had hit the ground several miles to the west, but even from here, the scene looked cataclysmic. Where streets of houses once stood there was now rubble and wreckage and fire. From the centre of it all rose a twisting column of blue-black smoke.

Hal stared at it all, barely able to breathe. The thunder of the crash was still rolling across the city, but far sharper was the memory of his father's voice – his last words on the phone.

I need you to know that I love you both very much. No matter what happens from here, if you can trust in nothing else, I want you to hold onto that.

For a long time he remained locked there like that, unable to even blink. But abruptly, as if someone had flicked a switch, the real world came flooding back in. He heard the soundscape of the city – it was now a cacophony of sirens. He watched flashing lights racing westwards. He turned to Jess, who had not made a sound. Her face had drained of colour, and she was visibly trembling.

'Jess, I—'

'Logical fallacy,' she blurted, interrupting. 'We're suffering a logical fallacy, that's all it is. A dreadful thing has just happened, and we were talking to Dad at the time, so our minds are trying to connect these disparate events, even though there is no way on Earth Dad could possibly have been involved in this.'

She blinked rapid-fire, and she spoke even faster. 'Even if there is some connection, it will be tangential. Coronal mass ejection. That's one theory. A blackout pulse that caused some kind of meltdown at the aerodrome, and also brought down that plane. That's one idea, among many.'

'I'm not sure what you're—'

'Because the fact is,' she gabbled, 'what do we actually know for certain? Dad didn't come home, and he told us he loved us on the phone, and then that plane fell out of the sky. The chances of these things being related are tiny, and even if they are linked, it is probably in ways we can't even imagine.'

'I think you should sit down. You're shaking.'

'We need to call him.' She took out her phone, but her trembling hands dropped it, the battery popping out as it hit the ground. She went scrambling for it on hands and knees.

'Jess, listen to me.' Hal got hold of the bits of the phone and clipped them back together. 'Here, look, here it is, please just stay still for a minute.'

She was sitting now, hugging her phone to her chest, her breathing short and ragged. The pair of them fell silent, and once more they did nothing but stare west.

'You're right,' Hal said at last, swallowing against the lump in his throat. 'This was a shock, and we jumped to the worst possible conclusion. But of course Dad wasn't involved in this. Why would he be?'

Once more they stared in silence, watching the tower of smoke billowing higher. Eventually, Jess's breathing slowed and she met his eyes for the first time.

'Will you try calling him?'

He hesitated. 'Yes. But if he doesn't answer that doesn't prove anything, does it? We already knew he was struggling for signal.'

As Hal expected, the call went straight through to voicemail. 'Dad, it's us,' he said, trying to keep his voice steady. 'We need you to call us as soon as you get this.'

He ended the call and met her eyes and said, 'We'll keep trying him, every ten minutes, okay?' He stood, thinking. 'In the meantime, there are other things we can do. Right now we don't know anything, just like you said. And that leaves gaps for our imaginations.

'So . . . first thing, we need to find out what that military plane was doing here, and why it might have crashed. Go and get your laptop, bring it to the living room. Even if the answers we find are horrible, they won't be half as bad as what we have in our heads.'

*

47

'Plane Crash in West London,' read a rolling banner at the bottom of the TV screen. 'Hundreds feared dead. Terrorism Not Ruled Out.'

A reporter stood facing the camera. Behind her was smoke and flashing lights. Water arced from fire engines. A background clamour of sirens.

'The number of crew and passengers on the plane is still unknown,' the reporter was saying. 'However, there are fears for a large number of people on the ground. At least a hundred homes lie within the blast zone. Some reports suggest—'

Hal flicked channels. And what he saw made him inhale sharply. At the bottom of the screen a banner read: 'Drone Mounted Camera'. He was now looking at the devastation from above, the image drawing back and rotating. From this angle the scale of it all was even more horrendous.

One of the plane's giant engines lay embedded in the roof of a church. A section of wing had come to rest in a park. The smashed fuselage was half buried in a crater. From out of this crater twisted the pillar of blue-black smoke.

Off-screen, someone was saying: 'At the heart of the crash site is Hammersmith Underground station. It appears the impact caused a section of the road to collapse into the train tunnels. Security sources insist that terrorism is the most likely cause of the—'

Hal flicked channels again. Jess sat beside him on the sofa, surfing news sites on her laptop. Her eyes were red and slow from crying, and from time to time she gasped.

'Look at this,' she said in a small voice, pushing the laptop in front of him. 'Somebody filmed it on a mobile phone. Look what the plane was carrying.'

Hal watched the video. Whoever had filmed it had got right inside the disaster zone. But the image was shaking and dark, and there was a lot of smoke, so at first Hal barely knew what he was seeing.

Then an object glinted silver amid the wreckage. And there was another one. They were cylinders of some kind. Egg-shaped, maybe, or rather, what was the word . . . ellipsoid. They were scattered throughout the crash site, nestled amid the rubble, glistening in the firelight.

'Look at the comments below,' Jess said, again sounding close to tears. 'People are saying they're bombs. They'll explode in the fires, won't they? Even more people will be killed.'

Without taking his eyes from the screen, Hal shook his head. 'That plane wasn't a bomber. There's no reason it would be carrying bombs.'

'What are they then?'

'They . . . could be almost anything. They could be aid parcels for all we know.'

But still he went on watching the video, staring at the mystery pods. He saw now that their silver shells were pitted. They put him in mind of something specific. After a moment the word came to him: *cocoon.* Yes, even though they were clearly metallic, they put him in mind of insect cocoons.

Finally, he managed to stop the video and close the laptop. 'This isn't doing us any good. It's just more fuel for our imaginations. There are more constructive things we can be doing.'

He stood and paced. 'Dad isn't answering his phone. So we need to get hold of him a different way. Did he ever give you a number for the aerodrome?'

Jess shook her head, wiped at her eyes with her sleeve.

'Me neither,' Hal said. 'But there must be a number. Or numbers for people he works with. Come on, we'll search his study. We'll track him down somehow, you'll see . . .'

8

Discoveries

Unlike the rest of the apartment, their father's study was always perfectly neat and ordered. There were bookshelves for engineering manuals, and a separate section for books on biology and physics. Not so much as a sheet of paper or a stray pen was ever out of place.

'Phone numbers . . .' Hal said, peering around the room. 'Dad isn't the type to just leave them lying about, is he? Do you think you can get into his computer?'

Jess sniffed, rubbed at her eyes. 'I can try.' She pulled herself into the big swivel chair, and she powered up his desktop. 'He's never been very imaginative with his passwords. But he does change them now and then.'

The lock screen appeared, and Jess clicked into the password box. 'Let's see . . . he likes to use his favourite authors. So how about H.G. Wells.' A red message flashed: 'Password Incorrect'.

'Okay then, Fred Saberhagen,' she said as she typed. 'Or Ursula Le Guin.' Those didn't work either, and nor did her next three attempts.

'Maybe he's run through all his favourite authors,' she said. 'What about films? Or actually, music. What's that horrible band you two are always listening to?'

'You probably mean The Mars Volta.'

'Spelled as it sounds?'

Hal spelled it out and Jess typed it into the password box. This time, when she hit return, the lock screen cleared and the home page appeared. It was a photo of the three of them on a ski slope.

Jess sat straighter, and she managed a weak smile. 'I don't know why I doubted myself – of course I can get into his computer. So then . . . contacts, contacts,' she said, as she began opening folders. 'Schedule, no, that's not it. Ah ha, yes, here we are. This syncs with his phone by the looks of it.'

She scrolled down a long list. 'But I don't see any numbers for the aerodrome.'

'Wait,' Hal said. 'Go back up – there – see.' He pointed at the screen. 'Professor Starr. If anyone knows where Dad is, it'll be him.'

Jess clicked the video icon next to 'Professor Starr'. It rang and rang, until Hal was sure they were going to get no response. But Jess let it ring, and suddenly the icon went green, and Professor Starr blinked out of the screen.

'Professor – it's us!' Jess blurted, sitting bolt upright. 'We're worried about Dad. Please say you've seen him!'

The professor was peering down into the camera, perhaps using a laptop. He glanced away, looking nervous. Then he ducked closer to the screen, his eyeballs bulging behind his spectacles.

'Miss Strider – ah hum – Master Strider. I've been expecting your call. Indeed, and in fact, I had wanted to contact you myself, and ah, would have done, had circumstances—'

'Please just tell us where Dad is,' Jess said. 'We need to know he's safe.'

Again the professor glanced away, then lowered his face even closer to the screen. 'Safe? Why, ah hum, yes – yes, certainly he's safe. At the present time, even as we speak, he is—'

'Professor – what are you doing?' said a hard voice off-screen. Professor Starr turned his head, startled.

'What did I say about outside comms?' the voice said, apparently moving closer. 'Really, Professor, if you can't be trusted, I'll have to confiscate your privileges.'

A hand reached in and yanked the laptop out of Professor Starr's grasp. The camera turned, and now Hal and Jess were looking at a man with an overhanging brow and a neat black beard.

Tony Daegar narrowed his eyes. 'Hal Strider. You have a habit of poking around at inconvenient times.'

'We were worried about Dad,' Hal said. 'We need to talk to him.'

'Is he there?' Jess blurted. 'Put him on – I want to see him!'

Tony Daegar went on staring. Finally he showed his teeth. 'Don't worry, Miss Strider, you'll soon be seeing a great deal of your father. Everyone will. Just keep watching the news channels.'

With that his hand loomed forward, the screen went blank.

Jess swung the chair to face Hal. 'Who was that man? What

did he mean about the news? Why would he say that? So Dad *is* involved in this somehow!'

'Calm down a minute,' Hal said. 'That was Tony Daegar, and I don't think we can trust a word he says. Professor Starr said Dad's safe, didn't he? That's what counts.'

'So where is he then? If he's at the aerodrome, why doesn't he just call us?' She swung back to the computer. 'We need to keep trying. We'll call everyone on this list until—'

But then the screen went dark, and the computer whirred to silence. At the same time, all the lights blinked off. For several seconds, Hal and Jess held perfectly still. An eerie silence settled, without even the background hum of electronics. The only sound was the *tick tock* of a battery powered clock, which was now oddly loud and incessant.

'A powercut,' Jess said at last, her voice hushed. 'Is this a coincidence too? Hal, what's going on? I've got this horrible feeling. Like all this is just the beginning, and there's even worse to come.'

'If we're going to find answers, we need to stay calm, and we need to think,' Hal said. 'You said yourself, everything might be connected, but in ways we can't even imagine. So then, Dad was trying to tell us something, wasn't he? Right at the start.'

He paced back and forth in the darkened room. 'He called me, then he left you a message, and then he spoke to both of us. So come on, you're supposed to be the smart one, what was he trying to tell us?'

'I don't know, do I?' Jess yelled. 'I could barely hear him, and what I did hear didn't make any sense, and I can't even think straight I'm so—'

54

Abruptly she fell quiet, twisting her lower lip between her fingers. 'Come to think of it . . . I do remember one thing Dad said. He talked about his safe. Yes, I heard that quite clearly. He said: '"It's in my safe."'

'His safe?' Hal said. 'What safe?'

She rolled her eyes at him, then crossed to the back wall of the study. Here was a framed photograph of their father and Professor Starr, the pair of them standing in front of the Starhawk Spaceplane, both of them much younger and smiling.

Reaching up, Jess hooked the picture off the wall. And there underneath, just above her head-height, was a small recessed vault.

Hal raised his eyebrows. 'How long have you known this was here?'

'Um, since the day we moved in. Do you ever notice anything?'

'Anyway . . .' Hal said, 'I don't see how it's relevant. Are you really suggesting Dad wanted us to break into his safe? Not that we could. Unless you happen to know the combination.'

'I worked out his password, didn't I?' Reaching up, she started entering digits on a keypad. 'This is numerals only. So I bet he used my birthdate. No, that's too short. Okay then, how about our birthdates combined? No, that's not it . . .'

She entered several different combinations. Each time the vault beeped sharply and a red light flashed and the door remained sealed.

'Face it, Jess, it's impossible,' Hal said, turning away. 'A computer password is one thing, but you're never going to guess—'

'Yes – we're in!'

Hal spun round and saw that the vault had yawned open.

'You don't have to say it, I can tell you're impressed,' Jess said. 'Sometimes I amaze even myself.'

She stood on tiptoes, but was still too short to peer into the safe. Easing her out of the way, Hal saw that there was a single object inside. He took it out. It was rectangular, black, and about the same dimensions as a paperback book.

'A vault within a vault,' Jess said, taking it from him.

'What do you mean? It's a portable hard-drive, isn't it?'

'Not exactly. It's a digital vault.' She flipped open a panel on top, revealing a miniature screen and keypad. 'Mrs Roberts showed us one of these in computing class. It's where you store information when you want something more secure than a server or a cloud.'

'More secure how?'

'It has physical safeguards as well as electronic. Tamper with it or keep getting the password wrong and it floods with acid, destroying its own circuits. I'll have to be careful with this one. But I'm on a roll – I'll crack it.'

'No you won't – and you're not even going to try. Give it to me.' He made a grab for the device.

'What are you talking about?' she said, holding it away from him. 'Of course I'm going to try.'

'We don't have the first clue what's on there.' Again he tried to snatch it, but she pulled away. 'It could be, I don't know, years of Dad's work. I'm not going to let you destroy it.'

'I'm not going to destroy anything.'

'It took you about ten goes to get the safe open. Look, when Dad's not here I'm in charge—'

She rolled her eyes. 'Still clinging to that idea?'

'— and I say we put that back where we found it. No – all right, we don't put it back, not if you think Dad really wanted us to find it. But until we know why, we shouldn't even—'

He broke off and they both became still and listened. Beyond the study, the world was no longer silent. There was a low, rhythmic thrumming.

'What *is* that?' Jess said. 'It's getting louder. It's coming closer.'

Rapidly it became a clattering, whumping roar.

And still it was getting heavier – now thunderously loud.

'What now?' Jess wailed, clinging onto Hal as the walls of the apartment began to quake.

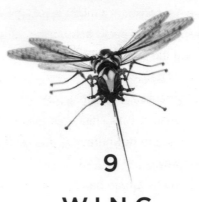

9

W.I.N.G.

'It's a helicopter,' Hal shouted above the noise. 'Jess, let go of me, it's just a helicopter. I need to go and see.'

'A helicopter – why here?' Jess shrieked. 'Why is it coming down on top of us?'

'I don't know – I need find out!'

Detaching himself from Jess, Hal went out of the study and up the final flight of stairs. As he went, the clattering thunder grew even fiercer. It was true – the helicopter was coming down on top of their building!

He kept going and burst out onto the roof garden. And here above him was a huge cargo-copter, its twin rotorblades roaring in the otherwise silent sky. It was carrying something clamped in its belly – a bulky, rectangular object. It was a shipping container.

Hal absorbed all this, while in the same moment he noted

something else: there was no one flying this machine. This rotor-craft didn't even have a cockpit – it must be pilotless.

And then he was jumping back, scrambling out of the way as the rotorcraft dropped the final metres and the shipping container came down on the roof garden with a clanging clunk.

With a hiss of hydraulics, the copter released its grip on its load. And without pause it was lifting back into the sky – Hal bracing himself against the downdraught. And already the rotor-craft was clattering away.

'Hey – Who are you? – Come back!' Jess had come out onto the roof garden and was waving her arms above her head. 'Wait – Come back!'

'There's no one to hear you,' Hal said. 'It's pilotless. It must have been on a pre-programmed flight path.'

She stared at him. 'Pilotless? But . . . programmed by whom? And why?'

Now she stared at the shipping container it had left behind. Its green paint was flaking, showing rust beneath. And along one side were stencilled the words 'Starr-Strider Biomimetics'.

'Dad sent it?' Jess said, moving slowly towards it. 'Is that what you think? Or someone else from the company? Why? What's inside?'

Hal stared towards the disaster zone, the pillar of smoke now so gigantic it was darkening the sun. He looked east, watching the cargo-copter dwindle into the distance. He turned back to the shipping container. Somehow all these events fitted together, but right now, the picture was more fractured than ever.

He went to the container and stood alongside Jess. She pressed both palms and one ear against it. A second later she jumped back, stumbled and fell to the ground. She looked so startled that Hal also took a step back.

'There's something alive inside!' she gasped, scuttling further away.

'What?'

'I heard a scrabbling noise – like claws!'

Hal looked at her, frowned. 'Why would Dad's company transport a live creature?'

'Why would they bring anything up here? It makes about as much sense as anything else!'

Hal put one ear to the warm surface of the container. 'I don't hear anything. What you heard was probably the metal settling after the flight.'

He went to the front end. There were no locks, only three large bolts.

'What are you doing?' Jess said. 'You're not going to open it?'

'Of course I am. We can't just leave it here, not knowing what's inside. We need answers.'

'That's what I said about the digital vault.'

'This is different. I can always seal this up again.'

'You hope! Depends what comes out. No – wait, not yet – if you're going to do it, at least wait until I'm back inside.' She ran back through the sliding doors, pulled them shut and pressed her face to the glass.

Hal drew back the bolts one by one. Then he cracked open the doors of the container, and he peered inside. Then he heaved the doors wide, and he looked some more.

And still he saw . . . nothing.

The container was empty.

'Well?' Jess called, poking her head outside.

Hal shrugged. 'There's nothing here.'

'What did you say?'

'It's empty. Take a look.'

She came cautiously to his side, peered in, creased her brow. 'Why fly an empty box all the way up here?'

'Hang on a minute,' Hal said, staring, his eyes adjusting to the gloom. 'I think maybe there *is* something in there, only . . .'

He edged his way inside the container. And now his knees came up against something solid. He groped with his hands and found a large, smooth object. He tugged at it and found it was on a wheeled base. He walked backwards and pulled the whole thing out into daylight.

'What the—' Jess said. 'Where did that come from? The container was empty a moment ago!'

'No, this was there the whole time! But just look at it – even in direct sunlight. No wonder we didn't spot it in the dark.'

That was the last either of them said for several minutes. Hal circled the machine and, for the moment, in spite of everything, he was lost in wonder. Here was an aircraft of some kind, that much was certain. But it was unlike any flying machine he had ever seen or read about or even imagined!

It was a single sweeping wing, perhaps five metres tip to tip. It formed a shallow 'M' shape, arched slightly, like the outstretched wings of a falcon. Hal had never seen anything manmade look so graceful, the sleek sweep of the thing unbroken by harness or cockpit. Its perfect lines unmarred by a single seam or rivet.

But the most astonishing thing of all was its colour. Its surface warped and shifted with dark shades. One moment it was gunmetal grey, then it was midnight blue, then the deepest black. Bizarrely, it made the machine difficult to hold in sight. Shift your gaze too quickly and its outline fell apart, like shadow dissolving in sunlight.

For the moment, staring at this, even Jess appeared to have forgotten everything else. 'There are certain sorts of beetle – the luminous ones,' she said. 'Their shells are made of microscopic cones that do odd things to the wavelength of light. So maybe this is a bit like that. Only in reverse. It really does look like it's swallowing the light, doesn't it?'

Hal's memory wound back ten days, and realisation dawned. 'I *have* seen one of these before. I mean, I *didn't* see it, but I saw the pilot. It looked like she was flying on pure air. And no wonder. This thing is hard to see when it's just sitting here in front of us. Imagine when it's speeding through the sky.'

'You're seriously telling me someone was stupid enough to fly one of these?' Jess said. 'Surely this is just some kind of concept design. How would you even stay on? It would be like trying to fly a surfboard. It would be suicide.'

'There's some writing here, look,' Hal said, kneeling. The machine swelled at its centre, incorporating what appeared to be a small pulsejet. And curving around the air intake valve were four words: 'Weightless. Invisible. Night. Glider.'

'Well, that's stupid,' Jess said. 'Nothing on Earth is weightless. And it's not invisible, it's just a trick of the light. But it spells "wing" so they must have been pleased with themselves.' She rubbed at her eyes. 'All this is very fancy and impressive, but we still don't have a clue what it's doing on our roof. Why would Dad need it here?'

She went to stand at the guardrail. But Hal remained lost in wonder of the wing. Beneath the glider, resting on the wheeled base, was a munitions box. He put the box on the ground and lifted the lid.

Inside he found a marvellous-looking flight helmet. It was beaked at the front and ran into an aerodynamic crest at the back. Its curved eyepieces were pale orange. It had a dial on each side, almost like a pair of ears. All of which gave the helmet a lifelike appearance, like the head of a mythical bird.

The case also contained a pair of gauntlets. Encircling the wrists were the words: Haptic Unconscious Grappling Gloves. And there was also a bodysuit, made of some tough but lightweight fabric, gunmetal grey with dark blue panels.

Hal lifted the helmet, turned it in his hands. He was just about to try it on when Jess called out.

'Come and look. There's something happening down there. People are on the streets.'

'What people?'

'Just about all of them, by the looks of it.'

He went to her side and peered down. Last time he looked, he had seen almost no one at ground level. But now there were people in their thousands, like lines of black ants.

Police riot vans were working their way along the streets. On the vehicles' roofs were loudhailers. One moved close enough for the words to reach Hal and Jess.

'This area is being evacuated. Leave your homes and proceed towards Westminster Bridge. Walk, don't run. Motor vehicles are prohibited. Take only what you can easily carry. This area is being evacuated . . .'

'Why would they do that?' Jess said, her grip tightening on the guardrail. 'The crash site is miles away.'

She looked at Hal and gasped. 'The pods we saw on that video – they *must* be bombs! They're so powerful the blast will reach us even here!'

Hal watched the evacuees. Wherever they reached a bridge, the police were directing them across the river. They must be shepherding everyone south out of the city. He shook his head. 'We're not going anywhere.'

'What? But we can't stay here. If they say it's not safe, then—'

'Do you have any signal on your phone? Nor me. I doubt anyone has. If we leave, how will Dad know where to find us? We need to wait for him to—'

He broke off, turned. A noise had risen behind them. It was a rolling clatter, rapidly becoming fierce. Within two seconds it was thunderous, right on top of them. Jess pressed her hands to her ears, her mouth wide open, shrieking noiselessly.

It was military helicopters, and there were scores of them. They were sweeping directly above the apartment, so close they made the roof garden tremble, the downdraught threatening to throw Hal off his feet. Jess was on the ground, curled into a ball, covering her ears. The noise was horrendous.

And still the helicopters kept powering overhead, thousands of tonnes of thundering metal. Most were Apache gunships, built like tanks, bristling with rocket pods and missiles. There were also tandem-rotor Chinooks, with armoured cars slung beneath their bellies.

Finally the onslaught eased, the last of the war machines clattering overhead. Their noise became a hollow *whump-whump-whump* rolling west up the Thames.

Hal stared after the dark swarm of aircraft. They were heading towards the crash site. But why? Surely this catastrophe called for the emergency services, not the Armed Forces . . .

His ears were ringing from the din, so it took him a moment to realise that Jess was saying something.

'Hal, I'm so scared. Why are there warplanes? Are we at war?'

'No, we're not at war,' he said, in the most definite tone he could muster. 'Who would we be at war against?' He stared to the west. 'But maybe you were right, and that plane was carrying something dangerous. Perhaps we do need to leave after all.'

Jess turned her eyes to the darkening sky. 'I've got that feeling again, except now it's worse. Now it feels like this is the beginning of the end. The end of everything . . .'

Hal looked down at the streets, watched the great tide of evacuees. 'With all this going on, Dad will struggle to get home in any case. Okay then, yes, we should go. But not south like everyone else. We'll aim for London Bridge. Maybe trains will still be running. If not, we'll hitch lifts. Somehow we'll keep heading east.'

Jess looked at him. 'You think we should try to get to the aerodrome.'

'Yes. Dad is still out there, I'm sure he is. If he can't come to us, then we'll go to him.' As Hal said this, a new idea started to form. He looked back towards the wing. 'Or . . .' he said slowly, 'maybe there's a better way.'

'What do you mean?'

'When you think about it, how do we know the wing was dropped here for Dad? Maybe he sent it himself. Perhaps he sent it for me.'

'What? Why would he do that?'

'So I could fly it.'

'Hal, you've gone mad. Do you even have the first idea how it works? Why would Dad even want you to try?'

He hesitated. 'I don't know why, exactly. But the first time he called this morning, it sounded like he wanted me to do something. Something important. I couldn't make out what he was saying. But now we've got a way to reach him, and fast. I could fly out there and—'

'No!' Jess stamped her foot like a small child. 'No, no, no! I can't believe you're serious. Don't you *dare* leave me here all alone just so you can go and break your neck riding some flying board you've just laid eyes on!' She stamped her foot again. 'If you leave here on that thing you won't come back – I'll be here all on my own with bombs about to go off or war breaking out or whatever it is – Dad's abandoned us and now you want to leave me too!'

'Okay, calm down, take a breath. I can see that wasn't such a good idea.'

'It was the stupidest idea you've ever had – and that's saying something!' She wiped away a tear. 'We're not safe here. We need to leave. Both of us. We need to go and find Dad. Together. I'm going to pack a bag. You'd better do the same.' Sniffing, wiping at her eyes, she stormed indoors.

Hal took a long breath. He went and rolled the wing back inside its container. It felt all wrong, walking away from this machine, when it seemed that his father sent it here with a purpose. But Jess was right. Essentially it was a straight choice: either he had to leave the wing behind, or he would have to leave Jess.

His father would want him to look after his sister, first and foremost. So yes, they should travel to the aerodrome together, overland. But it wouldn't be easy, not with the city in turmoil.

Sparing one last glance towards the gigantic pillar of smoke, he hurried downstairs, suddenly desperate to be underway.

At that exact same moment, several miles to the west, a firefighter called Chris Stones was suffering a different kind of desperation. He had come to a sudden standstill, mortally afraid, convinced that these were the last seconds of his life.

Chris was standing on King Street in Hammersmith, at the very heart of the disaster zone. All around him shops and offices were on fire, the flames hot enough to melt glass. A damaged block of flats was groaning, on the brink of collapse.

But Chris had been a firefighter for fifteen years, and he under-stood such hazards. At this moment they were not what terrified him.

What kept him rooted here, rigid with fear, was a metallic object sitting directly ahead. It was one of the mysterious cylinders that fell to earth with the plane. It was no more than ten metres away, embedded in the front of a Costa café.

Since he had arrived in the disaster zone, Chris had seen many of these silvery pods. One had lain half buried in a blast hole, like a seed waiting to germinate. Another pair sat at the heart of a burning church, charred and smouldering, like dragon eggs.

But as Chris and his team had gone about their work, searching for survivors, he had gradually put the pods out of his mind. If they were bombs, surely by now they would have exploded. As far as he or anyone else could tell, these cylinders had sat amid the wreckage and done precisely nothing.

Until now.

Because this cylinder in front of him – he could swear he had just heard it make a noise. Yes – there is was again. A grinding sound, almost like the lid of a giant jar unscrewing. And now there was a rapid ticking, like superheated metal expanding . . .

Abruptly, both sounds ceased.

Chris exhaled heavily, and he blinked. The cylinder just sat there. In its pitted surface he saw nothing but his own reflection.

Already he was telling himself he had overreacted. It must be the stress of the disaster zone affecting his judgement. This pod in front of him was inert, of course it was, the same as all the rest.

As he went on his way, he passed even closer to the cylinder. And now he heard nothing but his own breathing beneath his mask.

He turned his attention elsewhere, determined to focus on real hazards, telling himself for the final time that the mystery pods held nothing to be feared.

* * *

+ + + Primary Processes Completed + + + All Systems Active + + +
Initiating Fabrication + + + Fabrication Initiated + + +

Until this moment, inside the metal cylinders, all has been still and dark. But now, unheard by any human observer, ultrasonic signals begin rippling between the pods. In response, fifty of the cylinders spark into life. Beneath their silvery shells, they begin pulsing with energy and churning with industry.

First, within each of these pods, a printing arm starts charging back and forth. Attached to the arm are nozzles, which extrude a thermoplastic resin. This resin builds up, layer upon layer, until it acquires a definite shape: a multi-jointed exoskeleton.

Next, robotic spindles turn, weaving graphene threads into membranes for the joints and the wings and the mouthparts. Simultaneously, laser scalpels cut and carve and splice, creating the architecture for the brainboxes and the sensory apparatus.

Within minutes the work is complete. Inside each of these fifty pods, a mechanical device is hardening into its finished form.

Even now, from the outside, the cylinders appear dormant. But beneath those silvery shells all is changed. Pneumatic pumps hiss – newfound limbs twitch. Metallic eyes redden in the darkness.

And finally, within each of these fifty pods, a green light begins to blink, strong and steady as a pulse.

Part 2
Emergence

1

Another World

'For your own safety, do not run,' a policeman was saying through a loudhailer. 'No motor vehicles or bicycles are permitted. Proceed east and cross the river at Westminster Bridge. For your own safety, do not run . . .'

Hal and Jess pressed on amid the great mass of evacuees. With the river on their right-hand side, they were moving up the wide, tree-lined streets of Millbank. The Palace of Westminster rose up directly ahead.

It was an uncanny experience, shuffling through this hushed city. The buildings themselves, and the river, and the skyline – all this was unchanged. But the human life and the atmosphere were so utterly transformed that Hal might have stepped into a parallel world. Gone was the roar of traffic and the whizz of cyclists. Gone were the milling crowds of smiling tourists. Now there was only this nervous, zombie-like procession of men, women and children.

Amid the hush, Hal caught the odd snatch of conversation.

'Why aren't they telling us anything? What don't they want us to know?'

'If we could think of some way to contact your sister, at least she could tell us what it's like out there . . .'

'Samantha – stay close! Hold your brother's hand!'

'. . . hardly moving. We should never have left – should have gone down in the basement – that's the safest place . . .'

But in fact there were few of these voices. Most people were shuffling along in near silence. Some dragged wheeled suitcases. Others carried small dogs, or young children. And almost everyone, from time to time, turned an anxious glance to the west.

Hal looked back himself, and the shock hit him afresh. From ground level, that tower of smoke dominated everything. It was so titanic it warped perspective, giving Hal the impression he might be standing right next to it. And walking away made no difference – if anything, step by step, it only loomed larger. Like trying to run from danger in a nightmare.

'Do not go back for personal belongings,' said another policeman with a megaphone. 'Take only what you can comfortably carry. If you need assistance, wait at one of the muster points. For your own safety, do not run . . .'

'Why do they keep saying that – as if anyone could run with all these people,' Jess said. 'We've barely come any distance. Do you really think we can make it all the way to London Bridge?'

'It can't be like this the whole way,' Hal said. 'They're pushing everyone south. Once we make it past the bridge I bet we hit a clearer stretch.'

Jess said nothing more, staring straight ahead. Hal watched her from the corner of his eye. She had recently turned eleven, and was smarter than most adults he knew, so it had been a long time since he had thought of her as his baby sister. But today she looked much younger than her age, her hair tied in pigtails and her school satchel pulled tight across both shoulders.

Hal reached out and took her hand.

'I don't need you to do that,' she said, but made no attempt to pull away.

'If we get separated in these crowds,' he said, 'we might not find one another.'

She turned her eyes to the sky. 'Are those storm clouds, or is it smoke from the explosion? I think it's both. In any case, it's getting darker. Look – the streetlights are coming on, they think it's night-time. God it's eerie. It really does feel like the end of the world.'

There was a roaring clatter from above – another pair of Apache gunships heading for the disaster zone. They passed very low, and the sight and the sound stirred fresh fear through the crowds.

'. . . all these warplanes! We're under attack, we must be!'

'. . . Russians . . . or the Chinese . . .'

'They've gone now, Benny, it's okay. Look at me. Everything's going to be okay, I promise . . .'

The fear caused swells in the crowd, and Hal and Jess were jostled. He kept hold of her hand and they pressed onwards.

But their progress was torturously slow. The evacuation route funnelled between Westminster Abbey and the Houses of Parliament, and it seemed to take forever to get through this bottleneck.

And when they finally emerged into Parliament Square, and passed beneath Big Ben, they were met with a dispiriting sight. Because a second flood of people was washing down Whitehall. Where the two masses met, they merged and turned south, the police directing everyone across the Thames.

'We'll have to go south too, we've got no choice,' Jess said. 'It's hard enough going *with* the tide, we can't push against it.'

'Yes we can, we have to,' Hal said. 'Do you want to reach Dad or not?'

He took a tighter grip of her, and they kept heading eastwards. They waded and burrowed through the great surge of bodies. And slowly they made progress.

Ahead of them, Hal glimpsed a yellow and black tape – a police cordon. And beyond that – yes, he could see an empty stretch of riverbank.

But he also spotted police officers guarding the cordon. Some wore flak jackets and held carbines across their chests.

When Jess saw this, she pulled back. 'We can't cross that tape – they'll shoot us!'

'Don't be ridiculous. They're not going to shoot anyone.'

'How can you know that? How can you be sure of anything?'

'Anyway, look over there – there's no one guarding that bit. Come on, quick, that's where we'll sneak across.'

But in fact, just as they approached the cordon, a policewoman stepped to intercept them.

'That's far enough, you pair,' she said. 'You can't come through here.'

'But please,' Jess said, pointing east, 'our dad is that way.'

'I'm sorry,' the policewoman said, 'I can't make exceptions. Everyone goes across the river.'

Hal thought she looked nervous, or even afraid, beads of sweat visible below her cap.

'Why are they doing it?' he said. 'Evacuating the city? What do they think is going to happen?'

The policewoman turned her eyes to the west, then she blew out her cheeks. 'I wish I could tell you. But in all honesty, I have no idea. An hour ago I'd just finished shift and I was on my way home and I really, really don't want to be here, so please, just do as I ask and go across the bridge.'

She looked from Hal to Jess, and her expression softened. 'I sympathise, honestly I do. But really your best bet is to keep heading south. The army is setting up camps – there's one on Wimbledon Common. It's your dad you're looking for, you said? Well, he would want you to stay safe, wouldn't he? So stick with everyone else. Once all this is over, there will be ways to contact your dad.'

At that moment, the policewoman's phone blared a ringtone. Hearing this, people nearby pulled out their own phones and frowned at them.

'How has she got signal?' Jess said, doing the same. 'I've got nothing.'

The policewoman had her phone pressed to her ear. 'Dave, we've been through it,' she said. 'I shouldn't even be using this line. Well, somebody has to – can you imagine how stretched we are? Of course you're my priority – always.'

She bowed her head, pressing fingers to her eyes. Seeing this, Hal looked at Jess and tipped his head towards the cordon. When she hesitated he grabbed her arm and dragged her with him. And together they ducked beneath the tape and darted away.

The policewoman shouted something behind them. But already her voice was faint. Because this whole stretch of riverbank was deserted, and Hal and Jess were heading eastwards at a sprint.

'That's better – at last we're getting somewhere!'

'It's still a long way to London Bridge,' Jess said, breathless. 'How many more cordons will we have to cross?'

'It doesn't matter how many,' Hal said, starting to feel genuinely optimistic. 'We'll get to the aerodrome, and we'll find Dad – no matter what it takes.'

In actual fact, reaching their destination would be far harder than Hal could possibly have imagined. Because even at this moment, in west London, a critical event was taking place.

In Hammersmith, at the heart of the disaster zone, Chris Stones suddenly stumbled, fell to his knees. He clamped his hands to either side of his helmet, trying to block his ears. All around him, other firefighters and rescue workers were doing the same, some of them dropping tools or stretchers, their mouths set in silent screams.

The cause of their agony was a multisonic tone so piercing it shattered glass over a mile away.

The sound only lasted a few seconds. But by the time it had

gone, and Chris Stones slowly lowered his hands and lifted his head, he knew everything had changed.

Because he was staring at one of the metal cylinders that came down with the plane. And now, as he knelt here locked in fear, he saw its shell was splitting down the middle.

The crack was lengthening, widening. A luminous green glow came from within—

And then the pod burst fully open, spilling oily fluid—

And Chris Stones was scrabbling backwards on hands and feet, barely able to breathe, as something truly shocking began to pull itself free . . .

2

Swarm Warning

Hal and Jess didn't have a clear run for long. Halfway up Victoria Embankment they ran into another mass of evacuees. Hal gripped Jess's hand once more as they were swallowed into the slow-moving tide.

In fact, this crowd was even slower than the last. Hal began to see why: many of these people weren't moving at all. They had turned and were staring west, standing on tiptoes to peer over heads. Some were climbing onto the wall of the embankment, or onto the plinth of a nearby statue. A babble of voices was rising.

'What is it – what's everyone looking at?' Jess said.

'I can't see much with all these people,' Hal said, dropping to one knee. 'Climb onto my shoulders – I'll lift you up.' Once she was up there, he said, 'Well, what is it?'

'I . . . I'm not sure,' she said. 'The tower of smoke . . . it's turning like a vortex. Like a whirlwind. And all around it . . . there are black specks.'

'What do you mean, specks? What are they?'

'Maybe it's bits of debris, lifted by the heat. No, if it was that, they'd all be blowing in the same direction. These things whatever they are . . . they're fanning outwards.' Her fingers tightened in his hair, and she said in a quieter voice: 'Hal, I want to get down.'

'You still haven't told me—'

'Let me down! Can't you hear them? They're coming!'

Hal lowered her to the ground, and she clung to him. The entire crowd was still now, everyone facing west. Voices died away and there was a hush, like a collective holding of breath.

And amid that hush, a single noise was building. It was a piercing, buzzing whine. Like a swarm of wasps crossed with a plague of mosquitoes, electronically amplified.

And still it was rising in pitch and volume. Dogs howled. Children clasped hands to their ears.

And then it was right on top of them – people ducked, gasped – and in the same instant the noise dopplered past. As it did so, Hal caught a glimpse of something buzzing low and fast. But it was no more than a glimpse and his mind refused to make full sense of it.

Jess kept her eyes closed, her faced buried against him. All around them, the crowd was coming back to life. People began talking in nervous whispers. They started to move, at first hesitantly, but then more urgently than before.

'Come on,' Hal said. 'Whatever this is, we need to keep moving. Jess, come *on*!'

He hauled her onwards. But within a few seconds the crowd

lurched to a halt once more. Again that fearful buzz was rising in volume, drawing close.

The noise reached its apex, whined past. A metallic blur swept just above their heads, and this time people shrieked.

'I saw it!' Jess said. 'Hal – did you see it? What was it? What are they?'

Hal could only shake his head. He spotted another of the mystery machines further out over the water. And there was another one, above the Savoy Hotel. But he was still struggling to believe what he was seeing.

What are these things?

Each one was about the size of a small car. And they were clearly metallic – all hard edges and dull gleaming surfaces. Yet at the same time – these *machines* – they were so lifelike. They flew with an undulating motion, like that of a fly. Their wings were a greenish blur at their sides. Each had a pair of reddish orbs, like compound eyes.

People were holding up mobile phones, taking pictures or videos. Voices were hushed and urgent and frightened.

'Who sent them? What do they want . . . ?'

'. . . come down with the plane . . . those pods?'

'Don't just stand there – come *on!*'

Again people were pushing eastwards. Hal pushed along with them, taking Jess with him. For the next few minutes she was silent. She just stared skywards and stumbled as Hal hauled her along.

Finally, she blurted: 'Hal, please – just tell me – what are they? You know all about these sorts of things. You *must* know!'

He shook his head. 'I've only seen anything remotely like this once before. And that was this morning. Remember I ran up to the roof, to look at something. Well, it was a drone, I think. And it looked a bit like one of these. Except these are bigger. Much bigger.'

'Drones? So . . . they really were in that plane. But what are they doing here – I mean, what are they for? Who's controlling them?'

'I don't know any of that, Jess, I'm sorry. Don't keep looking back. We need to hurry. Whatever these things are, they look and sound frightening, and people are scared. We need to get away from the crowds.'

'For your own safety, do not run . . .' a policeman was saying through a megaphone. 'Remain calm and proceed east in an orderly fashion. For your own safety, do not run . . .'

As they hurried onwards, Hal watched another of the insect-machines. It was circling high to their left, making its piercing whine.

'One thing I can tell you,' he said. 'They might sound frightening, but I don't think they're fighting machines. I've been looking for anything that might be a gun or a missile. I'm sure they're unarmed.'

'So . . . they're surveillance drones. Could that be it?'

'I don't know; maybe. Look at the way they're spiralling. They do look like they're searching for something, don't they?'

'But – why? Spying on us – what for?'

There was a deafening shriek, so sudden and so loud that many people fell flat on the ground.

It was fighter jets. A pair of Typhoons screeching low over the river. Another pair screamed over, and a third, all of them heading towards the pillar of smoke.

'They're going to shoot them down!' Jess gasped. 'They're going to start fighting. I told you – it's like I've said all along – this is just the beginning!'

'Look, here's Waterloo Bridge,' Hal said, hauling her along. 'I bet it's the same as last time – once we're past it we'll be in the clear. Quick, while no one's looking.'

Police officers were stationed at the crossing. But they were all watching the skies. Hal and Jess slipped between them and beneath the cordon. And Hal was right: beyond the tape the river-bank was practically deserted. They broke into a run.

The insect-machines were now crisscrossing in every direction, their reflections sweeping across the Thames, or mirrored in tall buildings. Their fearful whine saturated the sky, pushing down from all sides.

At ground level a roaring noise made Hal and Jess turn. It was Army trucks, racing past on a parallel street. One of the vehicles screeched to a halt. Soldiers jumped out holding binoculars, rifles slung across their shoulders.

Here was another surreal and frightening sight: armed troops on the streets of London. Some of them were unloading equipment. And within seconds they had set up a contraption. It was a launching platform for surface-to-air missiles.

Jess gasped. 'You see – they're going to start shooting! We're in the middle of a war!'

Hal had no answer to this. He was struggling against his own rising fears. From overhead came the clatter of attack helicopters.

And here were more soldiers, fingers on triggers. And everywhere he looked he saw the alien gleam of the insect-machines. All of which gave him a sensation almost like vertigo – as if they had come to the edge of a precipice, and with one more step the world would fall away beneath their feet.

'Look!' Jess shrieked, pointing upwards with a trembling finger. 'There's one up there – a drone – see! – It's right above us!'

Hal looked up, locked eyes on the solitary machine: the dull gleam of its metalwork, the greenish blur of its wings.

'It's watching us!' Jess wailed. 'What does it want?'

'Come on, hurry!' Hal hauled her onwards. 'We need to get out of the city, and quickly.'

He gripped Jess's hand and they ran and ran, neither of them now looking up, but knowing by the buzz-whine of wings that the insect-machine was still up there, hovering above their heads.

*   *   *

+ + + Scanning Lifeforms + + + Reading Bio-Signatures + + + Analysing + + + Analysing + + +

A lone drone – designated Seeker 013 – hovers above two human beings. From their bio-signatures they identify as adolescents. One female and one male. Holding hands as they run.

Through its compound sensors, the drone sees them in a hundred separate images, each in a different wavelength. In one they are a pair of X-ray skeletons. In another they swim with the bloody colours of infrared. In others they ripple with laser light and microwaves.

But in each one they are the same fragile creatures. Brittle endoskeletons wrapped in perishable tissue. Seeker 013 carries *no armaments, yet it would be a simple task to destroy these life-forms. Merely colliding with them at speed would be enough to scatter their bodyparts.*

The drone dismisses this course of action. It would be inefficient. Because it has finished scanning these two human beings. From their behaviours, and the objects they carry, they classify as non-combatants. This environment is full of such civilians. For the time being, whether they live or die is insignificant.

The drone turns and continues its reconnaissance. And soon it finds something of far greater interest. Here is a facility of some kind. Spiralling lower, its antennae twitching, it crosschecks its databases. It concludes with high probability that this is a refuelling station for ground vehicles. It is certainly a rich store of petrochemicals.

Seeker 013 deposits a chemical beacon to mark the location. Then it buzzes back to the deployment zone. Circling above the cylinders that remain sealed, it pings ultrasonic signals.

+ + + Resource-Rich Environment + + + Raw Materials Abundant + + + Priority One ~ Secure Resources + + + Construct Berserkers + + + Construct Berserkers + + +

Other scouts are returning with similar messages. And soon a tipping point is reached. Within fifty of the sealed pods, a second phase of industry begins. This time the printing arms craft tougher shells. Laser scalpels fashion ordnance and projectiles. Paint nozzles apply warning colours of black and yellow and orange.

The fabrication is complete. A multisonic screech tears through the crash site. The fifty fresh pods burst open. Pulling themselves free, the newborn machines buzz hungrily into the sky.

3

Close Encounters

'The buzzing noise – it's getting even worse,' Jess said, sounding more scared than ever. 'Hal, what is it – why are you stopping? What have you seen? Is it that drone – has it come back?'

Hal wasn't certain what he had seen. He might even have imagined it. But a moment ago he thought he saw something new cross the skies. It had blurred wings and a weaving flight path, the same as the drones they had seen before. But this last one appeared to be a different colour – at least he thought he caught a flash of yellow and black.

'It was probably nothing,' he said. 'No matter what we see, or think we see, we need to keep moving. Look, there are more people ahead, so it's going to be—'

He flinched, and Jess gasped, as another drone buzzed past.

This time Hal was able to watch it for several seconds as it swept out over the river, then flew back towards the London Eye.

And he could no longer doubt what he was seeing. Here, without question, was a new type of insect-machine.

And if the first drone was unnerving, this second kind was pure menace. It was even larger than the original drone. Its rear section was elongated, and hung downwards, like the abdomen of a hornet. It was striped with venomous markings of black and yellow and orange.

'Well . . .' Jess said, in a choked whisper, 'are you going to tell me that one is harmless?'

No. It was pointless even thinking that. Because as the drone turned out over the water, Hal had seen one more detail with dreadful clarity.

This new insect-machine was armed.

It had a snub-barrelled gun slung beneath its thorax.

'We need to get out of the city,' he said, suddenly icy cold all over. 'That's all that matters.' He tugged at her hand. 'Come on, Jess, *please* – we can't just stand here staring! We need to hurry!'

But now, even as Hal's heart thundered, and his every instinct told him to run and run, their progress slowed once more to a crawl. Because again they were sucked into a seething mass of evacuees.

And this crowd was even slower and more chaotic than the last. Many people were shoving and shouting. Some were even physically fighting, while police with their megaphones continued to call for calm.

'This is no good,' Hal said, feeling increasingly desperate.

'We're getting nowhere. We should look for backstreets – find a clearer route. We need to get as far from here as we—'

His next word was swallowed by a thundering cackle.

Catching his breath, holding tight to Jess as she shrieked, Hal turned and looked skywards.

It had started –

Helicopter gunships had opened fire –

Two Apaches were hovering above the river, and their auto-cannon were rattling, spitting sparks –

Further off, more warplanes were loosing rockets, the flare lighting their wings from underneath. And there were crunching concussions, together with starbursts above the Thames.

It was all too sudden, too bright, too shocking to even begin to take it all in. But Hal saw one sight with perfect clarity. Here was a drone dropping from the sky, engulfed in smoke and flame. The machine fell hissing into the Thames, throwing up water and steam.

And with this impact, so it seemed, the last semblance of normality was gone. The final thread of order snapped. People shouted, screamed, ran.

Hal and Jess ran with them, their backs to the Thames. They were borne along by the crowds, thrown from side to side, fighting to keep their feet.

A keening zapping sound made Hal twist his neck, look back. It was the sound of the insect-machines going on the attack. That weapon they were carrying was not a cannon, but some kind of energy gun. When they opened fire the air ahead of them shimmered, as if superheated. One of these beams raked a row of plane trees and instantly they burst into flame.

Even as Hal's senses swam with all this, he saw a gunship take a direct hit. An almost-invisible beam leapt out of a drone, struck the helicopter and turned it to fire. The gunship spiralled towards the ground spewing flames like a ghastly Catherine wheel.

Feeling physically sick, his head swimming, Hal turned away. He gripped Jess's hand and they ran. Past cars wailing with alarms. Past policemen still shouting for calm or just standing there looking stunned.

Hal had little idea which direction they were headed or how far they'd come, and he didn't care, he just held onto Jess and they ran and ran, battling for space amid the crowds.

Gunfire directly above. People flattened themselves to the ground, others wailed in terror. Jess stumbled, but Hal held her upright and they ran on, veering around obstacles – abandoned vehicles, toppled café tables, dropped suitcases.

They darted beneath trees and entered a wide green space. At last Hal saw where they were – they were running across St James's Park. Here were children's bikes lying on the grass, and an overturned coffee cart, and ducks flapping frantic circles above the pond. Panicked people fleeing everywhere, shouting names.

Hal and Jess were halfway across the park when there was a roaring screech directly above. It was followed by a terrifying boom and a burst of light. Instinctively, they threw themselves down behind a plane tree, pushing themselves against its massive trunk.

As they did so, Hal glimpsed a flaming meteor. It fell too fast to tell what it was – just the impression of something massive plunging earthwards. It ripped the roof off a building before thundering down in the park.

They held still. Jess pressed against him, whispering some-thing under her breath. Hal listened to the sounds of tortured metal as the crashed object finally came to rest.

He breathed hard, his thoughts racing. What had come down in the park? Might it have been a gunship, or a fighter plane? Might pilots be trapped inside? A part of him knew he needed to go and see – there might be people who needed help. But for long seconds he couldn't move a muscle, just stayed huddled there with Jess while the sky lit up and thumped.

Finally he forced himself to sit upright. 'Jess, I have to let go of you, just for a minute.'

'What? No!'

'I have to go and see what crashed. People might be trapped. I might be able to help.'

She sat up, trembling. Eventually she managed to nod. But she still didn't let go of his hand. He had to peel away her fingers one by one. He took a deep breath, promised he would come straight back, and he left the cover of the tree.

The impact had dug a trench across the park. Hal followed the trench, its edges flickering with flame, the air thick with the smell of charred grass and churned soil and engine oil. He flinched as the sky cracked and lit up with another missile burst.

But he kept his gaze fixed on the crashed object, and he didn't blink. Because he had seen by now that it wasn't a helicopter, or a fighter jet.

It was a drone.

It was one of the later type, with lurid markings, like that of a poisonous insect. Horribly fascinated, Hal found himself drawn towards it. This *machine* – it was the size of an armoured car, and it glinted metallic. Yet at the same time, lying here half crushed, it looked more than ever like something living. Two of its six legs twitched as it lay there on its side. Its metal jaws clicked feebly, and oil oozed through cracks in its abdomen.

Still Hal moved closer, until he could feel the heat pouring off the crashed machine. It was now entirely still. Other people were leaving their hiding places and creeping near.

'Is it alien?' said a man with dreadlocks, holding a skateboard in front of him like a shield. 'Is it . . . dead?'

'Is anybody hurt?' called a woman in a business suit. 'I'm a doctor. Does anybody here require medical assistance?'

A group of young men approached the machine, each of them gripping a baseball bat, or a sledge hammer, or a hockey stick. They glanced at one another, shuffled their feet, came nearer. Finally one of them picked up a stone and launched it at the drone; it clanged off its thorax.

The machine stirred. One set of its wings was crushed beneath it, but the other set buzzed. Its legs scrabbled for purchase and it shuddered and turned against the earth.

When this happened people cried out, and stumbled backwards, and they fell and scrabbled away, and the boys with their weapons fled. But still Hal stood there, staring at the machine, transfixed, horrified.

And then from all around came the roar of engines – armoured cars were powering across the park.

'Clear the area!' blared a voice over a loudhailer. 'Step away from the machine. All civilians clear the area.'

Hal backed away as soldiers jumped out of the vehicles. Two of them went to their knees, rocket launchers resting atop their shoulders.

'Area clear,' someone shouted. 'Open fire.'

Hal flinched as rockets fizzed and thumped into the hornet-drone. The rockets pierced its armour plating and detonated within, the machine flaring like a dark bulb. It gave one last pneumatic sigh, then collapsed in on itself and lay still.

At last Hal turned, went back to Jess, pulled her to her feet. And they were running once more, neither of them saying a word.

Jess had been right all along: they were at war.

But who – or *what* – were they at war against?

4

Secrets from the Vault

They fled the park at its eastern end and they held hands and just ran. Through Admiralty Arch and across Trafalgar Square and up the Strand. Hal's heart thundering, Jess pale and stumbling with terror. Those sounds of warfare tearing across their city. The streets seething with panic.

Ahead of them, the Strand was blocked by a mass of evacuees. Hal turned and dragged Jess with him and they dashed down a side street. To their left the sky cracked and flared – instinctively they lurched away and fled right.

Up ahead were flashing lights – a police cordon. Time and again they turned, veering this way and that through the chaos, desperately trying to keep their backs to the violence.

Now they were running down a wide road flanked by cafes and restaurants. But Hal could no longer say exactly where they were. For the moment this didn't seem like his world at all.

Here and there a detail came to him that was entirely ordinary. A bus stop. A red telephone box. A Starbucks. An overhead hoarding advertising the latest *Call of Duty*. A cinema showing the new *Transformers* film.

But pushing through all this, warping it, was a different reality. The clatter of gunships. The alien shriek of the drones. The hollow thump of detonations. Terrified people fleeing in all directions.

He and Jess ran on, into a warren of narrow, twisting roads. Through a deserted street market. Beneath a railway bridge.

Hal risked a glance back. All across the skyline he could see the weaving shape of the drones, the air shimmering with their heat rays. He glanced around him, trying to get his bearings.

'I can't . . . I can't see anything I recognise,' he said, fighting for breath. 'Everything looks . . . different. I've got no idea where we are.'

'It doesn't matter where – just run!'

'We could be going in circles.'

But he kept running in any case, down more narrow streets, past more shops and estate agents and restaurants. And suddenly he knew where they were, because they emerged onto the wide interchange of Oxford Circus. It was chaos, with people shouting, and flashing lights, and sirens.

'Down this way,' Hal shouted. 'We need to get back to the river.'

'Why?'

'We've been going the wrong way. The river leads us east.'

They headed down Regent Street. Here the pavement was covered in shattered glass. A giant Nike shop and Apple store had both had their windows smashed, and were being ransacked.

Jess gasped as two men with their faces covered dashed across their path. Ahead of them a police car came screeching to a halt. Hal gripped Jess's hand and they kept going, weaving through the chaos, dodging between people and abandoned buses and black cabs.

They ran through Piccadilly Circus, the giant illuminations dead, a flock of pigeons rooted to the ground in fear.

Hal jerked his head up, his heart missing a beat. Something had just swept overhead. A drone? No – because he had heard no whine.

'What is it – what have you seen?' Jess said.

'I don't know, I—'

Scanning the skies, he caught a second glimpse, and a third. There was something up there, he was sure of it. A dark shape zipping between the buildings. But trying to fix his eyes on it was like trying to shine a torch on a shadow.

He found himself thinking back to the roof garden, and finding the wing – watching it warp and weave. His memory scrolled back further, and he thought of the impossible girl soaring above the aerodrome. Could it be her out here, circling above them? Surely now he was imagining things . . .

And a moment later all such thoughts were unimportant. Because a clearer shape swept overhead. This time it made a buzzing whine and Jess shrieked. A second drone buzzed over, and a third. They were pursued by fighter jets, and in a second the sky above was full of gunfire and missile bursts.

Hal and Jess fled amid the panic. People were scrambling beneath cars, or cowering in doorways, or smashing their way into shops and cafés. Hal and Jess kept running, stumbling with each explosive thump, ducking their heads at each keening of the drones' heat ray.

At ground level, a crunching, grinding sound made Hal half-turn and look back. He saw a battletank. It lurched to a halt and raised its gun barrel skywards. With the tank were infantry, who went to their knees, rocket launchers across their shoulders.

As he and Jess stumbled onwards, Hal watched the soldiers a moment too long. Because in that moment, a pair of hornet-drones came buzzing low, their eyes blazing red.

Before the tank or the troops could open fire, the drones swept their heat rays. A near-invisible beam leapt from soldier to soldier, incinerating them, their skeletons visible for an instant before they crumbled to dust.

Hal made an animal sound of horror. At the same time, the tank opened fire, obliterating one of the drones. The explosion was dazzling. Hal tripped and fell headlong. He could see nothing now but vague shapes cut across with bright slashes.

'Come on – get up!' Jess wailed, trying to haul him to his feet. 'Hal – what's wrong with you?'

Finally, he managed to find his feet, and he staggered on with her, the world still a blur of shadows.

'Quick – look – down there!' Jess shouted, pulling at his arm.

He staggered after her, and she dragged him stumbling down a flight of steps. She was leading him into an underpass. At the bottom of the steps she clung to him and they froze.

An unknown stretch of time passed, cowering here, listening to the violence rage above. In the darkness, Hal's vision swam with orange and red. His memory flashed images of those soldiers and their sickening deaths.

Eventually, the noises above became less fierce. It sounded as though the fighting was drawing away. Blinking, Hal thought his eyesight was returning to normal. Jess was physically shaking, and crying.

'I can't stand this – I can't! If I have to go out there with those things again, I—'

'It's okay, we're safe,' Hal said. 'It feels safer down here, doesn't it? So we'll stay down here for a while, okay? At least until we're sure the fighting has moved away.'

He felt Jess nod. He took out his phone, shone its light, and they moved deeper into the underpass.

And now he saw that other people had taken shelter down here. In the gloom they were little more than grey outlines slumped against the walls. But here and there he heard one of them whisper.

'. . . definitely quietening down now, listen . . .'

'We can't, not yet. We need to stay here until Daddy comes back . . .'

'. . . nowhere left to run *to*. Told you what I heard. That plane out west was just the first. Another crashed in Greenwich, and one in Hitchin. Those things are *everywhere*.'

Hal and Jess found their own space a distance away from the others and sat back against the cold, damp wall. For a while they sat in silence, staring at nothing.

Finally Jess sniffed and wiped at her eyes and said, 'The noise those things make – it's almost worse in the distance. Now it sounds like . . . like a swarm of bees mixed with children screaming.' She looked at him. 'Hal, what are those things? So they're drones, I get that much. But what are they doing here? Why are they attacking us? Who's controlling them?'

'I don't know, Jess. Maybe they don't need controlling.'

She shook her head repeatedly. 'No, no, don't say that. That's one thing I do know about drones – I've read about that – they can't act entirely on their own. They're not clever enough, not yet. They need people to watch screens and tell them what to do. That's true, isn't it? That's important.'

Hal hesitated, then said, 'There have been rumours, even going back years, about drones that could do this. Seek and destroy their own targets, I mean. Strategise, even. Like a smart cluster bomb. Militaries have always denied it. But then, they would deny it, wouldn't they?'

A long moment of silence, before Jess said, 'Well – somehow Dad knew these machines existed. Before any of this started, he knew something terrible was going to happen, didn't he, and he was trying to warn us.'

She held her satchel between her knees. Zipping it open, she took out a black object. It was the thing they had found in their father's safe. The digital vault. With everything that had happened since, Hal had not given it a second thought.

'And for some reason he wanted us to find this,' Jess said. 'We'll find answers on here, I know we will.'

'We're not staying down here long,' Hal said. 'As soon as we're sure it's safe we need to keep going.'

Resting the digital vault on her knees, Jess flipped it open. She powered it on and her face was bathed blue in the light of the screen. But then she froze, her fingers hovering above the keyboard.

'You've just realised it's impossible,' Hal said, watching her. 'With the computer and the safe you could keep guessing at the password, but with this—'

'Just be quiet, will you. I'm thinking. Let's see. For his desktop,

Dad used the name of a band. But he keeps things compartmental-
ised, so he would go down a different route with this. And it won't be
numerical like the safe, so it's not our birthdates.' She turned to Hal.
'What else is important to him? What else is he passionate about?'

Hal gave this some thought. 'Well, engineering and inventions,
I suppose. Machines. Specifically aircraft.'

'Even more specifically?'

'He used to fly a Harrier jump jet. But his favourite plane, of all
time, is the de Havilland Comet.'

'Yes, that's right. He bought one and I've never seen him so
excited. Right then, that's it.'

She typed "de Havilland Comet" into the password box. A red
message flashed: 'Access Denied. Warning: Unauthorised Access
Attempts Will Result in Self-Destruction of this Device. Attempts
Remaining: 2.'

'There was another type of de Havilland Comet – an airliner,'
Hal said. 'So Dad's is specifically a Comet *Racer*. I should have
said that before.'

Jess rolled her eyes. Then, taking great care, she typed: 'de
Havilland Comet Racer.' Again the red message flashed. And at
the end: 'Attempts Remaining: 1.'

They looked at one another. And the unspoken question was:
*should we stop there? Should we close up the digital vault, or risk
a final try?*

Eventually, Hal said, 'We could drop the "de Havilland" part. It
might be just "Comet Racer".'

Jess nodded, inhaled. 'Okay then . . . here goes.' She typed
'Comet Racer' and she hit return – and the lock screen cleared

– and both of them let out a long breath and they did a high-five.

'So then . . .' Jess said, as she began opening folders, scrolling through files. 'It would help if I knew what I was looking for, of course. But I'm sure Dad wanted us to find this, and he must have had a reason . . .'

While she sifted through files, Hal closed his eyes and listened. The clatter of gunfire and the *whump* of detonations – it all sounded deeper from down here, as if it were rumbling up from underground. But these sounds were also getting fainter, he was sure of it. Yes – the fighting was drawing away. Perhaps the military were driving the drones back west.

He fished in his backpack, took out a packet of biscuits. He offered the open end to Jess, who shook her head.

'How can you eat at a time like this?'

'When you're in shock you need to keep your blood sugar up,' he said through a mouthful. 'A paramedic told me that.'

'What's this thing?' Jess said, turning the digital vault towards him. 'I feel like I've seen it somewhere before.'

Hal looked at the screen. She had opened a blueprint. The design was for a robot. It stood on caterpillar tracks and was equipped with circular saws.

'It's called the Lumberjack,' Hal said. 'It was one of the first autonomous machines Dad's company ever built. Timber companies use it In Canada and Brazil. We watched videos of it working on YouTube, remember?'

'I recognise this one too,' Jess said, after opening another page. 'It was for search-and-rescue, wasn't it? For digging people out after earthquakes.'

This blueprint showed a machine with six legs. At its head end was a large cutting tool, like the jaws of a soldier ant. All across the page were printed the words: 'Intellectual Property of Starr-Strider Biomimetics'.

'These are all machines the company built years ago,' Hal said, as Jess opened more schematics. 'I don't see how any of this is going to—'

'Hang on a minute,' Jess said. 'There's something here that – ah ha, yes, I thought so. There's a whole separate ghost drive, hidden behind the main files. Except it wasn't very well hidden. And from the dates listed here it looks as though—'

She sucked a breath and held it. Hal stared at the screen, thunderstruck. Because Jess had opened a new file. And at the top of the page a legend read: 'SWARM Project. Class One Classified'.

And below this was another blueprint. This one showed an insectoid machine. It had six legs, and thin flapping wings, and sensor clusters like bulbous eyes. It was so lifelike it seemed to peer out of the screen.

This could only be one thing.

It was the fly-like drone that first flew out of the disaster zone.

Here was ironclad proof.

Those machines out there, terrorizing London . . .

It was their father and his engineers who had created them.

* * *

+ + + New Tactics Calibrated + + + Core Objective ~ Inhibit Enemy Actions + + + Disrupt Communications + + + Target Key Infrastructure + + + Despatch Devastators + + + Despatch Devastators + + +

5

The Accused

Another full minute passed. Sitting here in the dark, Hal and Jess did nothing but stare at the digital vault. At the diagram of the insect-machine. At the proof that their father's company brought these things into the world.

Eventually, without a word, Jess began opening more files. Each page was headed 'SWARM Project'. And beneath were blueprints of insectoid machines.

A fresh chill went through Hal as he realised that no two drones looked quite alike. Here was one like the metal hornet that crashed in the park. But the next machine was smaller, with a less pronounced abdomen – it looked more like a wasp.

There were more words at the bottom of this page. They read: 'Phase Two Phenotype [Projected]'.

'What does phenotype mean?'

'I've just been trying to remember,' Jess said. 'It's a biological term. Something to do with the expression of genes, I think. But why use it here? And why "projected"? It's almost as if they didn't know what the finished machines would be like. Or . . . as though they don't have a set form.'

'We're still only getting part of the picture,' Hal said, shaking his head. 'And something about this is all wrong. Dad always swore he'd never help make weapons.' He sat back against the wall. 'But the company changed – about a year ago – anyone could see that much. People like Tony Daegar turned up. That's when all the secrecy started. And all the infighting.'

'It's still Dad's company,' Jess said. 'I don't want to believe he built these things any more than you do. But the evidence is right here.'

As she said this, Hal raised his head and peered around the underpass. It seemed to him that every other person down here had fallen silent. Their faces were masked by the darkness. But there was a prickling in his skin, as if all these people were now staring at him and Jess.

'We should go,' he whispered.

Jess made no reply. Her fingers worked the keyboard.

'Come on, Jess. We need to press on while it's clear.'

'Just – give me a minute. I've found a third nest of files. And it looks like . . . I think there might be . . .'

She trailed off, and before Hal could say anything more, all the lights blinked on beneath the underpass. There were humming, electrical sounds, and from somewhere came the rumble of a generator. Power had just returned to this area of London.

'Could that be it – is it all over?' said a man nearby, getting to his feet.

'Mummy, now can we go home?' came another voice.

'Listen – you can still hear those things,' said someone else, 'they're still out there!'

From street level, Hal could hear more voices. Some of them were tinny, and amplified.

'I can hear TVs, or radios,' he said to Jess. 'We should go and listen. We might learn something useful.' When she didn't stir, he added, 'Stay right here then. I'll only be gone a minute.'

Without taking her eyes off the screen, she nodded. Cautiously, Hal went up to street level. He stood and stared westwards. The skyline blazed and shimmered, but yes, the fighting was now far in the distance.

He became aware of a new sound. A different sort of shrieking. What did it remind him of? Building sites. Yes – like the shriek of saws cutting through concrete. Scanning the skyline, looking for the source of this sound, he saw only the glow of fires, and clouds of smoke.

Two men went bustling past him, and more people were hurrying from the other direction. They were all heading towards an electronics shop. The doors stood open and all the display TVs were switched on. The shop was full of people, and a crowd had gathered on the pavement outside.

Hal moved closer. For the moment the sound of the news reports was senseless, multiple channels cutting across one another. And there were too many people for Hal to see any of the images.

At the side of the road was a railing. He climbed to the top and looked over people's heads.

And the first thing he saw –

Staring out of every TV screen –

Was his father's face.

Various channels presented the image in different ways. But every single one showed the same photograph of his father. It was the exact same photo Hal kept stored on his phone – his father dressed in a flight uniform, standing in front of the Starhawk Spaceplane.

Hal's grip tightened upon the railing, his vision suddenly fuzzy. It took him several attempts to read a banner scrolling across one of the screens: 'Catastrophe in London. Counter-Terrorism Police Seek Key Suspect.'

Within the electrical shop people were muting some TVs, turning up others. And now the words of a single newsreader became all too clear.

'. . . unofficial reports that the crash was the result of sabotage. The release of the drones is therefore being treated as a deliberate act. Counter-terrorism police have launched a manhunt for John Strider, the head of a secretive technology firm.

'According to sources, officers have already raided the company's headquarters in Kent, but found it deserted. They believe Mr Strider may now be attempting to flee the country. Police are also trying to trace several suspected accomplices, including this woman, Neet Lannekar, the company's head of security.'

The screen showed a photo of a blonde, blue-eyed woman, before returning to the picture of Hal's father. As it did so, Hal became sharply aware of the mass of people all around him. Their swelling anger, and their disbelief.

'Somebody did this *on purpose*?' one woman said. 'Why would anyone do that?'

'Traitor!' another man shouted. 'Bring back the death penalty!'

Within the electronics shop, someone threw something at a TV. The screen splintered across Hal's father's face.

'Hal?' Jess said, coming to join him. 'Why are they saying these things? They're saying Dad *wanted* this to happen. Why would they say that?'

'Keep your voice down,' Hal said, climbing to the ground. Nearby was a bearded man with his hood raised. He was watching Jess, his eyes narrowed.

'Dad didn't mean for the drones to get loose, did he?' Jess said. 'The plane crash was an accident – it must have been.'

Hal shushed her. The man in the hooded top was nudging someone else, saying something, nodding in their direction.

'Jess, you really need to be quiet,' Hal hissed. 'Can't you see how angry everyone is?'

Thankfully, the crowd's full attention was now drawn back to the TV screens. The newsreader was saying something new.

'In the past few minutes we've been hearing reports of further activity in and around the crashed aircraft. Now we can bring you an eyewitness video. It appears to show a third batch of the cylinders opening, and something breaking loose . . .'

Some of the screens switched to shaky footage filmed within the disaster zone. Hal got a glimpse of something lifting off the ground – something black and bulbous. But then his attention was drawn to the distance.

That new shrieking sound – it had suddenly sharpened. What could be making that noise? It seemed to be coming from the north west. But in that direction he could see only billowing smoke . . .

'We need to leave,' he said to Jess. 'Something new is happening.'

'What do you mean?'

'I don't know. I can't see. But we need to get moving while we've got the chance.'

The hooded man was watching them once more, and was saying something to other people at his side. Hal turned away from them, and he gripped Jess's hand, and they hurried southeast towards the Thames.

Behind them that harsh shrieking was growing even louder. And a hard voice was calling after them. But sharpest of all, echoing through Hal's thoughts, was the memory of that news report.

Crash was the result of sabotage

Deliberate act

Police have launched a manhunt for John Strider

6

Devastation

As he and Jess rejoined the river, and they hurried along the north bank, Hal's mind warred with itself. He desperately wanted to dismiss every word of that news report. And surely he *should* dismiss it. His father would *never* sabotage an aircraft – any more than he would release those murderous machines on purpose. The very idea was ludicrous!

And yet, a persistent doubt kept creeping back in. He couldn't help recalling his last trip to the aerodrome. How he had snuck into Hangar Five and peered beneath that tarpaulin . . . and found a war machine. Even though his father always swore he would never help build tools of war.

If he had been lying about that, what else might he have been hiding? Was it possible Hal didn't know his father half as well as he thought he did?

Evidently, Jess was wrestling with similar thoughts, because eventually she said, 'Hal . . . you don't think any of it could be true, do you? What they said about Dad. I don't *want* to believe it – not a word of it – but my head is spinning and I hardly know what to think.'

When Hal said nothing, she continued: 'Because the thing is, over the past year . . . he's been like a stranger, hasn't he? He works every hour there is, and he barely comes home. What if he really had been cracking up, going crazy, how would we even know?'

Hearing Jess say this out loud had a powerful effect on Hal. A moment ago he had been struggling with similar fears. But now it was as if a switch was flicked, and his mind reset. Suddenly he could think calmly and see clearly through all the doubts.

'It was a shock, hearing them say those things about Dad,' he said. 'And right now the world is turned upside down and it's difficult to even know what's real and what isn't. But there are still things we can trust. We *know* Dad. The sort of person he is. If he *was* directly involved in all this, then there's only one thing he would have been doing. He would have been trying to *stop* any of it from happening. That's the truth, and we both know it.'

Jess watched the ground as they pressed on, while the sky flashed and flared behind them. This stretch of riverbank was busy with evacuees, and getting busier, and it was increasingly slow going.

'So . . . our plan hasn't changed?' she said. 'We're still heading east?'

He nodded. 'Reaching the aerodrome is still our best chance of finding Dad.'

'Yes, except . . . the news. It said police went out there, and it was deserted.'

'It also said Dad is trying to escape the country. That's final proof the whole thing was nonsense. As if he'd run away and abandon us.'

'But what if—'

'Listen, Jess, it's like you said right at the beginning. We've got too little information, and that makes it easy to think the worst. The fact is, none of what we've heard so far adds up. All we know for certain is that Starr-Strider designed the drones. But the company is huge. From what I can work out, it has at least two separate divisions.

'Just now I remembered something Professor Starr told me out at the aerodrome. He said his latest project would transform the world. I can't remember his exact words, but he talked about a great gift to humankind. Well, he couldn't have been talking about battle drones, could he?'

She studied him. 'You think Dad and the professor might have been working on something else entirely?'

'Yes. I'm not sure. Maybe. My point being, we don't yet have the full picture. And it's obvious the police don't either. If they really are blaming Dad for all this, then they've made a mistake. It probably means someone somewhere is lying.'

A strange expression crossed Jess's face, and she looked as if she were about to say something more. But then they became aware of a commotion up ahead. They were approaching Blackfriars Bridge. And in front of them the crowd was juddering to a standstill.

'It's the army,' Hal said, standing on tiptoes. 'They've put up a barricade. I think they're using the bridge. Yes. Army trucks. They're coming across. We're going to have to wait.'

A whole fleet of armoured personnel carriers roared across the Thames. Meanwhile, the atmosphere amid the evacuees was increasingly taut, with people shoving and shouting and jostling for breathing space.

It was a desperate feeling, crushed amid all these people, unable to move an inch, while behind them the sky crackled and blazed, with those hornet-machines gleaming black and yellow in the distance – and the idea that any moment they might come buzzing this way, sweeping their deathrays.

At long last, the final armoured car roared clear of Blackfriars Road. Soldiers took down the barricade. A great flood of evacuees surged along the riverbank, Hal and Jess among them.

'This crossing is reserved for military and emergency personnel,' a soldier said through a loudhailer, waving them on. 'The next civilian crossing is at Tower Bridge. Keep moving east and cross the river at Tower Bridge . . .'

Jess looked pensive, and again Hal got the feeling she was about to say something. But then a formation of fighter planes swept overhead, screeching like some prehistoric beast. The crowd surged, and Jess was almost swept away. Hal tightened his grip and fought to keep her close.

Immediately afterwards, a different sort of commotion rippled through the crowds. People were turning, some of them stopping to point. There was a groundswell of nervous chatter.

'See it – where I'm pointing . . .'

'It is – it's leaning – it's going to fall!'

'Look! Has it been hit?'

'What's happening?' Jess said. 'What now?'

Peering over heads, scanning the horizon, Hal's gaze came to rest on one of the tallest structures in London. The BT Tower, its crown bristling with radio transmitters and satellite dishes. It was a long way away, up near Regent's Park, and it was hazy through smoke and low cloud. But even so, it was immediately obvious that something was very wrong.

This colossal building was no longer upright.

It had tilted by at least ten degrees. Looking at it made Hal want to tip his head, as if the Earth itself was out of kilter.

'What's happening?' Jess said again.' Why is everyone talking about the BT Tower? What's that shrieking sound?'

Before Hal could reply, the tower fell. Visible for miles around, this structure had been a landmark of the skyline all Hal's life. But now, in seconds, it simply toppled over and was gone. Thunderous reverberations and waves of dust poured upwards and across the city.

Shock and fear surged through the evacuees. There was a stampede. Hal and Jess were swept away east. Now all they could do was cling to one another and fight to keep their feet, while those crunching crashing noises continued to shudder across the city, the very ground shook, and all around them people panicked and shoved and called out across the crowds.

Finally the aftershocks subsided, and with it the worst of the panic. The crowds slowed and calmed. Breathing hard, Jess looked back.

'The BT Tower . . . it fell? Really – it's destroyed?' She looked at Hal, her eyes wide. 'The machines . . . they did it on purpose, didn't they?'

'I can't help thinking that, yes,' he said, pushing back against the jostling crowds. 'The BT Tower was a giant antenna. If the drones really are smart, it would make sense to target radio masts. It'll make it harder for our side to communicate.'

Her grip tightened on his hand. 'But – *why*? Why are they attacking us at all? What do they *want*?'

'I don't know, Jess. Maybe that's like asking what a bomb wants once it's been dropped. All I know is, we need to get out of the city, and fast.'

They pushed on amid the desperate crowds. From somewhere to the north, that shrieking sound of demolition was rising once more. There could be no doubt that this catastrophe had entered a terrible new stage. The machines had started deliberately taking apart the city. Where would they target next?

7

Troubled Waters

'Hal – there's something I've been trying to tell you,' Jess said, as Tower Bridge loomed up ahead. 'It might be important. I can't be sure . . . but it might be *really* important . . .'

'Just tell me. What is it?'

'Well, after you left the underpass, I continued going through the digital vault. And I found codes. Lots of them.'

'What sort of codes? What are they for?'

'Just listen – I'm getting to that. From what I could tell, most of them relate to the company's headquarters – to the aerodrome. They were each listed with a specific location: Command Room, Training Arena, things like that. You'd know better than me, but I presumed they must be entry codes for various parts of the complex.'

Hal frowned. 'I've never heard mention of any Command Room, or Training Arena. And they use biometric scanners to—'

'Whatever – it doesn't matter,' Jess said. 'I haven't got to the important part. The thing that really—'

She fell silent, jerked her head up, and so did everyone else. Suddenly the sky above was full of yellow and black streaks. It was the hornet-machines. There must be twenty of them – or thirty – or more!

These drones were menacing enough singly, or in pairs. But here was a whole swarm of these lethal, intelligent machines, their wings a blur of green, their eyes blazing red.

People were shouting, and shrieking, and trying to run for cover, and Hal was holding tight to Jess as they were thrown one way and then the other.

But for all the fear they were causing below, the drones didn't so much as slow or alter their altitude – they just swept above the pandemonium and buzzed on and were gone.

The panic continued to tremble through the crowds. But eventually the worst of it died down. Talking in fearful whispers, the evacuees lurched back into motion and Hal and Jess were able to press on.

'H-how many drones are there?' Jess said, visibly trembling. 'And how many types? Those ones – they looked different somehow. And *angrier.*'

'They're long gone,' Hal said. 'In any case, they're not interested in us. It's the military – that's their enemy.'

She looked at him. 'And when they're finished with the military? What will they do then?'

They pushed onwards, both of them scanning the skies. From the distance came that grinding shrieking noise, like saws cutting concrete.

'Listen,' Jess said. 'They're demolishing something else. Even if they're not trying to kill us, it makes no difference – they'll pull the city down on our heads!'

'Tell me about the vault,' Hal said, desperate to distract himself as much as Jess. 'You didn't finish telling me about those codes you found.'

She rubbed at her eyes. Eventually she said, 'Codes. Yes. Well, as I was saying, most of them looked like passcodes or activation codes or whatever. But the final one was different.'

She glanced at him. 'The way it was encrypted, it looked more important than all the rest. And the heading for this one wasn't the name of a room, or a place. It was a single word.' She looked across again and their eyes met. 'And the word was "Antidote".'

Hal blinked at her. 'You can't mean – you don't think – are you trying to tell me there's an *antidote* to the *drones*? As in, a way to stop them?'

'That's just it, I don't even know,' Jess said. 'Give me another hour with the vault and I could probably say for sure either way.'

'But that must be it, mustn't it?' Hal said, his voice hushed. 'Antidote. What else could it be? It must be a killcode!'

He came to dead stop, and he remained standing there even as people barged all around him. 'That's it — that's why Dad wanted us to open his safe in the first place!'

Jess was tugging at his arm. 'Keep moving. Those things could be back any minute!'

'But don't you see? That's what Dad was trying to tell me – what he wanted me to do. Yes — and that's why he sent the wing! He wanted me to fly the vault out to him!'

'Just stop talking for a minute,' Jess said, as she dragged him onwards. 'Give your brain a chance to catch up. Don't forget I've been thinking about this since the underpass. Plus, I'm cleverer than you. You're overlooking even the basic questions. For instance, if it's true, and these drones really do have an off switch, then why has no one used it yet?'

Hal thought for a moment. 'Well – because – maybe there's only one killcode. Maybe there were more, but all the others have been lost, or – I don't know – corrupted somehow. So we're carry-ing the only one that still exists.'

'All of which I've considered,' Jess said, 'and none of which sounds any more likely now you say it out loud. Second question: if you're right, and Dad thinks he can stop the drones, then what is he doing about it? Right now, I mean. Do you seriously believe he's just sitting out at the aerodrome, waiting for us to bring him the vault?'

'Look, Jess, I'm not pretending we've suddenly got all the answers. But surely some of it now makes sense. For what-ever reason, whatever "antidote" might mean, the digital vault is obviously *vital*. Something prevented Dad from coming to get it himself. So he needed me to take it to him. All that is true, I'm sure it is. I just can't believe we didn't work it out before.'

Again he came to a standstill. 'But it's not too late – we can go back.' He pointed across the river. 'Look – the south bank is clear. So we cross at Tower Bridge and we double back to the apart-ment. You stay there while I fly out to the aerodrome.'

'I should have known you'd say something idiotic like that,' Jess said, again hauling him onwards. 'Okay, let's presume that part is true, and the vault is critical. Even so, I still don't believe Dad meant you to fly the wing. Even less so now the sky is full of drones. You wouldn't survive five minutes.'

'I could do it,' Hal said, staring dead ahead. 'Dad knows I could do it.'

'But maybe you're half right,' Jess said. 'Because the fact is . . . even if there's one chance in a million that this "antidote" is a killcode, then we need to act on it, don't we? We need to get it to the aerodrome. And fast.'

'Well then – how?'

'Think about it. We're bound to run into more soldiers at Tower Bridge. So then, why don't we tell them about the vault?' She nodded to herself. 'Yes – that's the answer. If it's really so important, the Army should fly it out to Dad. Presuming he's out there at all, that is. And if he isn't . . . well, they've got a better chance of finding him than we have.'

Hal watched the ground as he considered this plan. Their father had trusted him and Jess with the digital vault, no one else. It contained all Starr-Strider's classified designs. It contained proof that the company created the drones. The idea of putting all that into a stranger's hands . . . to even think it, felt like a betrayal.

And yet, if the vault was as crucial as it suddenly seemed . . . if there was even the slightest chance it could help bring down the drones . . . didn't they have a duty to tell the military?

A formation of F35s screamed over very low, cutting through Hal's thoughts, making everyone duck. To the west there was a

119

searing flash and a series of heavy thumps. Fresh fear surged through the crowds, and in the crush Hal fought to keep Jess close.

Another shape swept overhead, and Hal's eyes went after it. At first he thought it was another fighter jet. Except no, because this object was far too small. And as far as he could tell it was silent. The shape was simply there, then gone, like a mirage.

Once again, Hal found himself thinking of the impossible flying girl. Could she really be up there somewhere, riding her wing? And if so, was her presence just one more amazing coincidence? Or could it be connected somehow to him and Jess?

Even as he was thinking this, he was astonished to hear someone shouting his name. He and Jess were now climbing the steps up onto Tower Bridge Approach, and he was able to look back over the sea of faces.

'Hal – Hal Strider! Wait. We need to talk to you. Wait for us. Stay right there. We've got something important to tell you.'

'Who is it?' Jess said, looking back.

'I don't know, I can't—'

But then his eyes came to rest on someone familiar. He was a heavyset figure, perhaps sixteen years old. He was flanked by three other young men, all of them wearing baseball caps and mirrored sunglasses. The four of them were barging their way through the crowds, all the while shouting after Hal.

'What are the chances?' Jess said. 'Someone you know amid all these people. Well, who are they?'

'The big one at the front – his name's Karl Daegar.'

'That name sounds familiar. So who are they? Friends?'

'No. More like the opposite. I just . . . I can't work out what they're doing here. It's like you said before, it can't all be a coincidence.'

'Why don't we wait then, see what they want? Look at them, pushing everyone out of the way. They're desperate to talk to you about something.'

Briefly, Hal considered waiting. But his mind flashed with shocking memories – stunt planes blazing out of the sun, mobbing Hal's aircraft. The trees rushing upwards, and the fear of the crash landing.

'No – those four are bad news,' he said. 'Whatever they're up to, it won't do us any good. Come on, we've got a plan. Let's get on with it.'

Karl Daegar and the others were stuck in the crush of bodies at the foot of the steps. Hal and Jess pulled away from them and joined the flow of people heading up onto the bridge.

'So you think I'm right – we should tell the Army about the vault?'

'Yes. On one condition,' Hal said. 'We insist on holding onto the vault ourselves. We fly out to the aerodrome with them, deliver it to Dad in person.'

Jess turned her eyes to the sky. 'Right now I'd rather keep my feet on the ground. But I suppose it's our quickest way out of the city. All right then. Look, beneath the first tower. Two soldiers. Let's tell them.'

It was still shocking to see armed soldiers here on the streets, all the more so at close quarters. In their flak jackets and battlefield helmets these two men hulked over Hal like giants.

'Move along, please,' the younger of the soldiers said. 'If you need medical attention, there's a hospital tent over there, in the grounds of the Tower.'

'We want to speak to someone in charge,' Hal said. 'We need to see your commanding officer.'

The younger soldier raised his eyebrows. 'And what would you say to my commanding officer?'

'We need to get out of the city.'

'You and everybody else, kid,' said the older soldier, looking at Hal for the first time. 'Do you see how the rest of them are doing it? Just keep on walking in a straight line.'

'What I mean is, we need to reach my dad, and quickly. We think . . . we think he might be able to help stop the drones.'

The older soldier snorted. 'Who's your dad then, Superman? Stop wasting our time, the pair of you. We need to clear this bridge.'

At that moment, both soldiers tipped their heads, the radios on their lapels crackling with indistinct words. The older man raised a hand to his radio, spoke into it: 'Sector Four, Acknowledged.' Then his grip tightened on his rifle and he stared westwards.

'We found . . . information,' Hal went on. 'Important codes. We think—'

'Listen, kid,' said the older soldier, leaning close, 'you're not in your bedroom now playing your computer games. This is real. Your only part in it is to do as you're told. So get across this bridge before I lose my cool.'

'Better yet, go up to the medical tent,' said the younger soldier. 'Your sister is pale and you sound confused. It might be delayed shock. There's no shame in it. This has come down hard on everyone.'

Hal set his jaw, and without another word he moved away from the soldiers. He pulled Jess with him and the crowd swallowed them up. In this great tide of bodies there was no choice now but to go across the bridge.

'You didn't try very hard to persuade them,' Jess said. 'Why didn't you tell them about the vault?'

'They were never going to take us seriously, no matter what I said. Perhaps it isn't such a good idea after all.'

'It's a perfectly good idea. You executed it badly, that's all. When we get to the other side we'll find more soldiers and we'll try again. Only this time I'll do the talking.'

Hal looked back and peered through a gap in the crowds. With a fresh jolt of unease, he saw that Karl Daegar was there. He was talking to the two soldiers, and he was pointing in this direction. Hal faced forward, telling himself to forget Karl Daegar. Whatever he might be up to, there were more important things to worry about.

Detonations cracked to the west, making people flinch. The bridge did not feel like a good place to be. It funnelled the crowds, crushing people tighter than ever. The water, a long way below, looked deep and dark and oily.

And suddenly the situation got worse. A charge of fear fizzed among the evacuees, like static electricity. The cause was a pair of drones. With terrific speed they had buzzed in from the north, and were now circling above Tower Bridge, making their fearful whine.

'What are they doing?' Jess said, her voice choked. 'Please tell me they're the original kind – the unarmed ones.'

'Yes, they are,' Hal said, 'but maybe people don't know the difference, because they're scared. Keep hold of me, Jess.'

There were raised voices, and people shrieked. The crowd surged. But thankfully, before full panic could set in, the drones lifted higher and buzzed away to the west.

Hal watched them go, thinking.

'They're gone,' Jess said, gripping his arm, 'so why do you look so worried?'

He hesitated. 'It's just, the unarmed machines – they're scouts, aren't they? And I was thinking, whenever we've seen the scouts, soldier drones are never far . . .'

He trailed off and stared westwards, suddenly unable to move or speak.

'What is it – I see them! – something's coming!' Jess gabbled. 'Hal – tell me – what are they?'

'Come on, hurry!' He pulled her onwards. 'We need to get off the bridge.'

People were shouting and fear was building, threatening to erupt. Because those dark shapes were racing closer, buzzing just above the Thames. Hal shot another look at them, and every inch of him ran cold.

These new machines were black and bulbous, like stag beetles. They had stubby legs and overlong mandibles. And at the tip of those mandibles each drone was armed with a pair of circular saws.

There were ten . . . eleven . . . twelve of these machines, their armoured shells gleaming as they powered towards the bridge. Their noise was even worse than the other drones – it was a wrathful rasp, like a swarm of chainsaws.

From this point on, everything happened with dizzying speed. There was panic on the bridge, many people turning and trying to go back the way they had come, some even throwing themselves into the Thames.

And now hornet-drones were buzzing overhead, and fighter planes were roaring in, loosing missiles, and Jess was shrieking, and Hal was pulling at her hand, trying to wade through the crowds to reach the south bank.

The beetle-machines landed on the towers and the suspension spans of the bridge. They landed with a clang, and their buzzing zipped to silence as their wings folded away beneath their shells. Then a new noise began – an awful keening shriek – they were cutting through stonework and steel with their saws.

Hal powered onwards, but people were desperate, fighting, falling, and he and Jess were thrown one way and then the other. Someone's head cracked him in the nose and his vision swam through watery eyes.

Now suspension rods were pinging apart with a whiplash of steel. The bridge lurched, swayed. Hornet-drones and gunships swirled above, battling. And the bridge was buckling, the tarmac cracking.

Sawblades screamed, sliced through steel and stone. More rods pingd apart. One of the giant towers groaned.

The bridge lurched again, more violently, threw Hal off his feet. He was no longer holding Jess's hand.

'Hal!'

She was sliding down the tarmac, towards the centre of the bridge, which was now folding into the Thames.

On his stomach, Hal slid after her, shouting her name –

Stretching out with both arms –

Reaching for her –

He would never truly know what happened next. There was a flash of light, a roar of flame, and in the same instant darkness was rushing all around him, and the river was dragging him into its depths.

8

Missing

'Jess!' Hal howled it underwater, the boom of his own voice merging with deep roaring sounds.

He struggled, thrashed, spun, frantically searching for her, seeing nothing but bubbles and streaks of black against black.

His lungs were already bursting, and people were on top of him, kicking. All around him huge objects were sinking in the gloom, their mass dragging him deeper down and down . . .

A lump of masonry plunged past. Then the wreckage of a drone, still burning, even underwater, its dead eyes watching him while it sank. As it passed, the water became scalding, the river broiling.

He kicked and fought and thrashed, and he struggled upwards, and he was rising – and his head broke the surface.

Gasping, coughing, sucking lungfuls of air.

'Jess! Jess!'

The water churned with people – a chaos of flailing limbs.

'Jess – where are you? I'm here!'

He spun round and round, barely drawing enough breath to shout her name. Through his horror and his fear, his vision narrowed. In all directions the river was now a vast blackness. Oil on the surface flickered with flame.

'Jess – I'm here – J—'

There was a screaming of metal, followed by a thunderous splash. A huge wave swept over him, and plunged him back into the depths.

Again he thrashed and fought for the surface. But this time the darkness was unending. His clothes were weighing him down, and his limbs were suddenly leaden and stiff.

Once more the water roared, this time directly above – and something massive rushed downwards, smashing into him, plunging him into an even deeper blackness . . .

Hal's eyes shot open. He coughed and gasped and choked. His head throbbed, and his mind swam, trying to make sense of what had happened and where he was and how he came to be here.

He was no longer in the river. He was lying on the embankment. There were faces above him. And people were talking. Their voices were thick and warbling, as if he were still underwater.

' . . . conscious . . . we need . . . keep him . . .'

' . . . hear me, young man? Can you tell me your name?'

'Hold still. No – don't try to move, we need to make sure you—'

'Where is she?' Hal shouted, struggling upright. 'Where's my sister? I need to find her!'

People were urging him to keep still, and were trying to hold him down, but he fought against their grip and he staggered to his feet. Still hands were reaching out, but he fought his way free. He stumbled along the riverbank.

All around him there were hundreds of people. Many were lying flat on the ground. Others were sitting hugging their knees.

'Jess – where are you? Jess!'

He doubled over, coughed up river water. Then he staggered on, shouting, his head throbbing, the world a blur.

'Jess!'

Vaguely, he was aware that the battle for Tower Bridge was finished. The drones had moved on, the fighter jets and gunships giving chase. A shocked stillness had settled upon this stretch of the Thames.

And now, as Hal stumbled on, darkness was falling. And the sky was grumbling with thunder. And rain was coming down in waves.

And still Hal searched and searched for Jess.

And still he found no trace.

'I'm looking for Jess Strider,' he said for the hundredth time, his voice cracking. 'She's eleven years old. She has dark hair in pigtails.'

Most people he asked didn't even meet his gaze. They just kept stumbling along the riverbank, white with shock, or they cupped their hands and shouted for loved ones of their own.

Night had fully fallen, and dust hung like a thick mist. Faces appeared in the mist and were gone. Ghostly names drifted. From time to time the crippled bridge groaned and shrieked and another piece splashed into the Thames.

'I'm looking for Jess Strider,' he called. 'Has anyone here talked to a girl called Jess?'

He passed a huddle of people wrapped in blankets. Again he called out, but these people only blinked at him in shock. He stumbled on, calling over and over, everywhere getting the same blank response.

But then a woman called after him.

'Wait – hold on – what was that name? Who did you say?'

Hal tripped and almost fell in his haste to rush back to her. The woman wore the green uniform of a paramedic. She looked as stunned as everybody else, but she held Hal's gaze as he ran up to her.

'Jess – Jess Strider!' he gabbled. 'You've seen her – you talked to her?'

Shakily, the woman nodded. 'Yes . . . I helped a girl called Jess. About this tall. Dark hair like yours. She was asking for someone. Are you her brother?'

'When was this – helped her how – was she hurt?'

'I . . . no, nothing serious, from what I remember. A little concussion, maybe, but—'

'Where did she go – where is she now?'

'Uh, well, all those who could walk we put on a police launch. That was, I don't know . . . an hour ago?'

'A police launch? Where would they take her?'

'I'm sorry, I can't say for sure. All the hospitals are full. So I'd guess one of the Army camps? There's one at Blackheath. Yes – going by boat, I'm sure that's where they'd go.'

Unsteadily, she put down her backpack and took out a silver survival blanket. 'But I'd like to think about you for a minute. You've stopped shivering, and that's a serious sign. We need to get you warm. Here – take this.'

She tried to drape the blanket around his shoulders. But Hal had already mumbled his thanks and was stumbling away from her. He went back to the water's edge. Then he staggered almost aimlessly downriver.

Part of him was numb with relief that someone had seen Jess, and that she'd seemed okay. But another part was doubly desperate to think she had been ferried away.

How far was it to Blackheath? Ten miles, fifteen? How long would it take him to get there on foot, battling barricades and crowds of evacuees? And what if he got there but they had taken Jess to one of the other camps, or somewhere else entirely? How would he ever find her then?

Dazed with such thoughts, he continued to stumble downriver. Suddenly, the dust cleared and he found himself on a deserted stretch of riverbank.

Almost immediately, a dark shape swept overhead. A few seconds later it happened again, off his right-hand side.

They were no more than glimmers. Anyone else might have dismissed them as tricks of the night. But Hal had encountered such visions before.

He found himself starting to run. 'Who are you?' he shouted skywards. 'I know you've been following us! What do you want?'

Again the darkness shifted above him, and once more, up ahead. Both times he glimpsed nothing but a black after-image.

He ran faster. 'Why are you following me? Come down here. Tell me what you want, or leave me alone!' He sprinted flat-out, shouted louder. 'Who are you? Why won't you—'

He broke off and skidded to a halt. Because dead ahead, and very close, the shadow-shape was dropping from the sky. Briefly it appeared to spread its wings like a giant bat before swooping to the ground.

And a moment later she materialised.

The impossible girl.

She was right here in front of him, stepping away from her wing.

Now Hal could do nothing but stare. Ever since he had first glimpsed this girl, free-flying above the aerodrome, she had been something almost mythical in his imagination.

And now here she was, stepping towards him. And her bodysuit was glistening with rainwater. And her face was masked by a beaked flying helmet with orange eyepieces. And all in all she really might be some fantastical creature flung down by the storm.

She stopped, removed her helmet. And she became a young woman, perhaps a year or two older than Hal. Her blonde hair, tied in a long ponytail, hung over one shoulder. Her blue eyes were so bright they were points of light against the iron-grey sky. For long moments nothing else existed, and Hal could only stand and stare, mesmerised.

'I . . . I saw you earlier – twice,' he managed to say, finally. 'You were following me and Jess.'

'At first I couldn't be sure it was you,' the girl said, still a little breathless from her flight. 'And then the crowds were too dense to get close. Then the fighting flared up again and I was mostly concerned with staying alive.'

She dropped her eyes. 'After the bridge fell, I . . . I lost track of your sister. But the current is strong here. They're rescuing people miles downriver. If you search on foot, and I look from the air, we'll find her.'

'But – why?' Hal said. 'Why would you want to help me and Jess? Why were you following us in the first place?'

The girl was no longer listening. She had turned and was staring upriver. Suddenly she grabbed his arm, dragged him away from the embankment. In the deeper shadows of the plane trees she ducked down, and tugged at him to do the same.

'What is it – drones?'

In reply, she pointed out across the river. Vessels had come into view. In the darkness their outlines were hard and angular. They were chugging slowly, sweeping searchlights across the water.

'Gunboats,' the girl whispered. 'It could be regular military. But I bet it's them.'

'Who?'

'Tony Daegar and his thugs. They must be searching for your sister.'

'What – Tony Daegar? Why would he be looking for Jess? I saw Karl Daegar at the bridge – he was following us too. Why? What do they want?'

But the girl was already leaving their hiding place and heading back towards her wing. 'Come on,' she said. 'They've gone. We need to get started.'

As Hal went after her, he began to ask, 'Who are you, and what have you got to do with—' But he stopped himself. The mystery girl was right: now was not the time for questions. For the moment nothing was more important than finding Jess.

'Wait,' he said. 'If you really want to help, it's no good scouring the riverbank. I've got an idea where they've taken her.'

She spun around to face him. 'Taken her? Who took her?'

'She was rescued. They put her on a police boat.'

'Oh – I see.' The girl blew out her cheeks. 'Well then, that's good, isn't it? Yes, that's a great lead. Because you know where they were headed? And it's close? You can get there on foot?'

'No, it's miles from here. And it won't be an easy place to search – there must be thousands of people. But with two of us looking we'll stand a chance.' He pointed towards her wing. 'There's another one of those. It's on my roof. We can both search from the air.'

Her eyes darted away. And when she looked back at him her expression was impossible to read. Finally she nodded.

'Get back there, then, and hurry. I'll meet you there. First I'll follow Tony Daegar, see where he's headed. We need to keep track of him, if we can.'

'Wait – I haven't told you where I live. And I don't even know your—'

But it was too late. The mystery girl had picked up her wing, run with it to the river and launched herself off the high embankment. Her shadow-shape swooped into a climb. Hal saw the brief blue flare of a pulsejet. And then she had vanished back into the night.

His head spinning with all this, but desperate to find Jess above anything else, Hal turned and sprinted for home.

*

A little way upriver, a paramedic named Sarah Wheatley raised her head and watched him go. That dark-haired young man looked familiar. Ah yes, she had spoken to him a little earlier – she told him where he might find his sister.

Except now the worst of Sarah's shock was starting to ease, and she was thinking more clearly. And she began to question what she had told that young man. Did I really help a girl called Jess? Or was her name Beth? In actual fact, might it have been Jemima?

Well, it couldn't be helped. No one could blame her for being confused. And she'd done that young man no real harm. If nothing else, she had given him a glimmer of hope. Perhaps, at a time like this, that was the most anyone could ask.

In actual fact, Jess had not been ferried away, but had washed to shore no more than a mile downriver. Now she was fleeing blindly and mindlessly away from the Thames. For the time being, she had no real idea where she was or how she came to be here, or even why she was so wet and so cold.

Right now, through a haze of shock and terror, she was aware of just one thing: the buzz-scream of the drones. This terrible noise was everywhere, surrounding her, pressing down out of the dark.

The sound made her run, and keep running, without sense of direction, without conscious thought of any kind. Only the animal drive to flee and hide and survive.

It would be some time before she would even begin to recover her senses. Before she would even think to question why she was on her own, or what had happened to Hal.

By then, she would have run and staggered and stumbled miles through the darkened streets. And she would have blundered into the darkest of boltholes. And she would be truly lost and alone.

* * *

+ + + Core Objectives Achieved + + + Initiate Stage Three + + + Activate Manipulators + + + Activate Manipulators + + +

Within fifty virgin pods, a new kind of machine comes online, their eyes gleaming red. These drones are wingless, and when they burst free they do not take to the skies.

Instead, these machines crawl and clank and scuttle into the chasm at the heart of the crash site. Down here they find a readymade warren of train tunnels and maintenance ducts and sewerage pipes. They crawl through this labyrinth, mapping it with their chemical trails. Where they meet obstruction, they do not turn back, but dig fresh channels with their powerful jaws.

Algorithmic instinct insists they keep driving deeper and deeper into the dark. And so they continue to enlarge tunnels, and excavate chambers. And in this way, the empire of the machines spreads its roots beneath the earth.

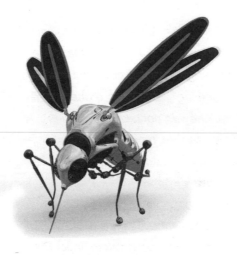

Part 3
Augmentation

1

SWARM

For Hal it was an eerie and fearful and wretched run back through the city. The Army had managed to clear these streets of evacuees and now everywhere was dark and deserted. The entire way from Waterloo Bridge to Westminster he saw not a single other human being.

Several times drones buzzed overhead, making him flinch and stumble. In the darkness, only the greenish blur of their wings and their reddish eyes were visible. Except once, when lightning flared, and he saw all too clearly the venomous blaze of hornet-drones as a whole swarm of them swept overhead.

But worse than any of this was the awful fact of retracing his steps without Jess. Here was the spot where he had lifted her up on his shoulders so she could see above the crowds. And further on was the police cordon, now abandoned, which they had snuck across. That only seemed like a moment ago. Yet here he was, returning alone, and Jess was lost.

Spurred on by such thoughts, desperate to reach the wing and set out after her, he charged headlong for home. And at long last he arrived back at the skyscraper known as The Spaceship.

At its foot he staggered to a halt, his hands on his knees, his chest heaving. He looked up just as lightning flared; revealing the peak of the skyscraper. With the power off, and the lifts dead, it looked a very, very long way up.

But he only paused for a second, then he was off and running again. Through the sliding doors, which had been wedged open. Across the lobby. Into the stairwell.

Here, even the emergency lighting had failed. Scrabbling his phone from his pocket, he was relieved to find its light still worked. Shining it before him, he bounded up the stairs, taking three at a time.

Inside the colossal skyscraper, the lack of other people was more oppressive than ever. Normally, the population of a small town lived and worked within these walls. But now, as Hal wound up and up, there was only stillness and silence – an emptiness that was like a great weight in itself. The only signs of life were his own – the squelching of his sodden trainers, the pulse thudding in his ears.

At last he staggered up the final flight of stairs and he stumbled into his own apartment and lurched to a halt in the living room. And now came the eeriest moment of all. His home was so dark and so still, and so totally quiet. He might almost believe no one had lived here for years.

He forced himself to keep going, up the spiral staircase and along the hallways and through the dining room. And finally out through the double doors and onto the roof garden.

As the wind hit him he swept his gaze, looking for the mystery girl. But no – she hadn't got here before him.

So he went to the shipping container. He groped his way inside his fingers found the smooth surface of the wing. Walking backwards he wheeled into the open.

The glider looked even stranger beneath the night sky, its surface swimming and warping with non-colours. For a moment, he lost sight of it altogether. Then a sliver of silver ran along one edge, like moonlight along a blade.

He stared at this enigmatic machine, then he looked out at the night sky, and for the first time since he left Tower Bridge he suffered a shiver of doubt. Because from up here, he sensed the true extent of the warfare.

All across the city fires blazed, the glow reddening the cloudscape. To the north, another fireball was hurtling earthwards. From all around came the *whump whump* of heavy guns and the hollow thump of detonations. And beneath it all was the alien screaming of the drones.

Was he really doing the right thing, launching the wing? Until this morning, he had no idea such a machine even existed. And now he was planning to fly it solo through this dark and violent night . . . ? Was Jess right – was he mad to even consider it?

But the stronger part of him knew he had no choice. He pictured Jess at the bridge – that look on her face as she slid away from his grasp. Could he stay here and do nothing, while she was out there alone and terrified? Did he have any chance of finding her on foot? No and no – using the wing was the only way.

Thinking this, he was already stripping off his T-shirt. Next he flung off his trainers and hopped out of his jeans. Then he knelt at the munitions box that came with the wing.

Flipping open the lid, he took out the grey-and-blue bodysuit and wriggled into it. Then he pulled on the gauntlets – the 'Haptic Unconscious Grappling Gloves'.

Lastly, he lifted the flight helmet, and he marvelled afresh at this exotic device – those orange eyepieces and its curved crest, so much like the head of some mythical bird. He pulled on the helmet, secured it beneath his chin, and the world outside took on an orange tint.

And now, equipped like this, his final shred of doubt disappeared. This bodysuit was light and supple, yet felt incredibly tough. Just wearing it made him feel stronger somehow – ready for anything.

He climbed onto the wing, and he grasped the handholds on either side of the fuselage. The gauntlets engaged with a reassuring clunk, like magnets coupling.

A moment later, a shadow-shape swept to his left. The mystery girl was here. Perhaps Hal was growing accustomed to picking her out of the darkness, because this time he watched her clearly as she swept in to land.

Rolling her body off the aircraft, her legs straight as a gymnast's, she hung from one hand while she touched down. Then she came to a graceful dancing halt, laying the wing smoothly upon the ground.

She removed her helmet as she came towards him. And in spite of all today's shocks and surprises, Hal was still stunned by what happened next. The mystery girl flung her arms around him and hugged him as tightly, as if they had known each other all their lives.

'I hope you don't mind,' she said. 'I had the urge to do this back at the bridge. I've been up there for hours with those machines. Just me. And all this time the clock has been ticking, with the idea that it was all on my shoulders. Then I found you, at last, and it's the first positive thing that's happened since the start.'

She stepped away from him, smiled slightly. 'Anyway, um . . . hello. I'm Sky. Sky Lannekar. I should have said that before. Sorry if I sound delirious. I almost died another three times just getting back here, and it's left me a bit on edge.'

Taking off his helmet, Hal opened his mouth to respond. But to his dismay, as her blue eyes peered into his, he found he was speechless, and nervous. As if he'd just found himself sitting next to the prettiest girl in class. What was wrong with him – at a time like this? Surely his mind should be on more important things!

Finally, he managed to say, 'Lannekar. I heard that name earlier. Yes – it was on the news, when they were talking about my dad. They said police were hunting someone else.'

'Neet Lannekar. My mum. Yes, Tony Daegar pinned the blame on her too. And now she's trapped down there with the rest. And unless we can—' She fell silent, staring past him towards the Thames.

'What did you say – trapped? Who's trapped? Trapped where?'

But she was already moving away to stand at the guardrail.

When Hal joined her she pointed. 'What does that look like to you?'

There was movement down there on the water. Lightning flared, and Hal saw gunboats. Three of them, powering towards the bank.

'It's them all right,' Sky said. 'Look, they're heading for the pier. We do not want to be here when they arrive.'

'Tony Daegar?' Hal said. 'You think he's coming here?'

'Apparently he doesn't know your sister has the hard-drive,' she said, heading back towards her wing. 'Presuming she *does* still have it, and it's not at the bottom of the Thames. I'm trying not to even think about that possibility.'

'Hard-drive? You mean the digital vault. Of course – that's what everyone wants. When we saw Karl Daegar near the bridge, he was trying to get close enough to steal it! And it's why you're so eager to help me find Jess.'

'Please don't say it like that,' Sky said. 'You make me sound like *them*. Tony Daegar is an evil, greedy maniac. He'd watch the whole world burn so long as it made him rich. Which is why we really, really need to get started. So tell me, where are we headed?'

Hal stared at her, and a thousand questions battled to be the first past his tongue. But in the end he bit down on every one. It was just like he had told himself back at the bridge – for now, questions could wait. All that mattered for the moment was finding Jess.

'I think they took her to one of the Army camps.'

Sky blew out her cheeks. 'You did warn me it wouldn't be an easy search. I flew over the camp on Wimbledon Common. It was chaos. And it was the same on Richmond Park. At least tell me you know which one she's in.'

'I have a pretty good idea.'

'Well then, that's something. And two pairs of eyes will be better than one. So then, let's go. You take the lead and I'll follow.'

Hal squared his shoulders, nodded. Then he moved towards his own glider. But perhaps he hesitated just a fraction before he did so, or a hint of trepidation crossed his face. Because now Sky came after him, and she stood between him and his wing.

'Hold on a second,' she said. 'Look at me. Why can't you look me in the eye? There's something you're not—' She glanced back at his glider. 'Oh no. You really haven't, have you? You've never flown the wing!'

She dropped her head, rubbed at her eyes. 'And there I was thinking – and I presumed . . .' She shook her head. 'Oh God – of all the stupid . . .'

'I can do it,' Hal said.

'No – you can't! Trust me, tonight is *not* the night for first flights. You wouldn't stand a chance.'

Hal bristled. 'I heard enough of that from Jess. She doesn't know what I'm capable of, and she's my sister. What can you possibly know?'

'I know it takes more than blind courage to fly the wing. It took me hours to master the basics.'

'Then it's lucky I'm a fast learner.'

She glared. 'How fast, exactly? Because from this height it'll take maybe twenty seconds to hit the ground. Do you learn that fast?'

'I'll take my chances. I don't have a choice.'

'You could choose not to be an idiot!' She took a deep breath.

'Hal, listen, I'm sorry, but we're changing the plan. I'll have to go after your sister by myself. You'd better tell me which camp she's in.'

'No.' He stepped around her to reach his wing. 'She's my sister. I'm going.'

She took hold of his arm, spun him round. 'Just stop and think for a minute! You do understand what will happen if Tony Daegar gets his hands on that hard-drive? That's it, finished – our last hope gone! Literally the end of the world! And meanwhile you're—'

She sucked a breath and they both turned.

A buzzing whine had risen up from below.

A lump rose in Hal's throat as he found himself eye to eye with a drone.

It came to a hover, making its piercing whine, fixing them with its reddish stare.

As Hal's initial shock subsided, he saw it wasn't a full-scale fly-machine. It looked like a smaller insect – like a gnat. In fact, it was identical to the drone he had first seen up here this morning.

'One of Daegar's spy machines,' Sky said. 'So now he knows we're here.' She headed towards her wing. 'There's no more time to argue. So here's what's going to happen. You need to tell me—'

She came to a halt, gasped. The gnat-machine had zipped around her, coming to a hover directly in her path. She tried to go around but again it buzzed to cut her off, its wings a vicious metal blur.

And then, with shocking speed, three more gnat-machines rose up to join the first. Hal backed away as two edged towards him. He found himself back to back with Sky.

'They're trying to hold us here!' Sky shouted. 'We have to find a way past!'

She darted one way, then the other, but each time the machines were too quick, shifting to close any gap.

'We can't let him catch us!' Again Sky failed to dart free. 'Keep trying! You go right, I'll go left. When I say – ready? Go!'

Again they failed to escape, and again.

And now it was too late. Because people were emerging from the apartment. Four of them came ambling out onto the roof garden.

At this distance, they might have been military men, or tactical police. Because they all wore full body armour, black and grey, of the sort worn by American SWAT teams.

But then they strutted closer. And beneath their helmets, through their visors, Hal saw their grinning faces.

And he recognised one hateful smirk in particular.

Here was Karl Daegar.

'How did you get up here?' Hal shouted, bunching his fists. 'Get out!'

'Now – is that any way to welcome guests?' Karl Daegar said. 'You want to be careful you don't hurt my feelings. My pets don't like it when I get upset.'

As he said this, the buzz-whine of the drones rose in pitch. The ring of razor-wings edged inwards.

'Go on, Karl, give them a haircut,' sniggered one of his gang.

'Closer – I dare you!' said another.

'Idiots – you don't know what you're doing!' Sky shouted.

'Tut tut, you want to watch that pretty mouth of yours,' Karl said. 'You might make me slip.'

Again the ring of drones closed tighter, Hal and Sky pressed back to back. Gritting his teeth, Hal shot a glance at Karl. How was he directing these machines? He wasn't holding a remote control.

'I see what you're thinking,' Karl said, grinning. He tapped his helmet, which was bulky around the forehead and temples. 'What do they call it – direct cranial something-or-other? Doesn't matter what it's called – it's *mind-control*! How cool is that?'

'I'm amazed it works on you, you're so brainless!' Sky spat. 'You don't have the first clue, do you? You've stolen a few toys so now you think you're on the winning team. Don't you get it – you can't win! Nobody's going to win! Only the machines!'

'You really need to watch how you speak to me,' Karl said, through gritted teeth. The blur of metal wings pressed so close that Hal held his breath. Karl's gang shared glances and stopped egging him on. But Karl didn't blink.

'One way or another, you two will learn some respect,' he said. 'By the time I count to three I want you both to—'

'That's enough Karl. We don't have time for this.'

It was an older man who spoke. He had just stepped out onto the roof garden. He was followed by two others. All three were dressed like Karl and his gang, in black and grey body armour.

They came closer. Only now did Hal notice that every one of these intruders wore a badge upon their left shoulder. The emblem was a stencilled image of a wasp, viewed from above, yellow against a black background. And written through it was the word SWARM.

The older man lifted his visor, revealing a hard face, a jagged scar across his chin. 'Didn't you hear me, Karl? I said call them off.'

Karl shrugged, smirked at Hal and Sky. He made a show of touching two fingers to his headset, near his right temple, and the drones lifted up and fanned away.

'Okay, you two,' the older man said to Hal and Sky. 'Don't make me twist your arms. Put your flight helmets on the ground – you won't be needing those. Get yourselves downstairs. Tony Daegar wants to see you both, and he doesn't like to wait.'

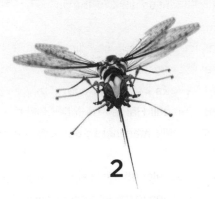

2

Shock and Awe

Downstairs there were many more of these militiamen – the apartment teemed with them. They all wore identical body armour, and each had the SWARM crest upon their left shoulder. They were all stomping about the place, shining powerful flashlights.

To Hal's growing fury, as he came down into the wide circular space of the living room, he saw they were ransacking his home. They were tearing pictures off the walls, turning over furniture, even cutting open the sofas.

And standing at the centre of it all, his hands behind his back, was the hulking figure of Tony Daegar.

'Get out!' Hal shouted, storming towards him. 'All of you get out right now or—'

Karl Daegar barged him in the back and made him stumble. 'Or you'll do what, hero? Fight us all? Call the police?' He laughed and shoved him again.

And now Hal found himself standing directly before Tony Daegar. He wore a bulky headset like his son's, and beneath that headset his face was in deep shadow, only the dark gleam of his eyes visible. But still Hal felt no intimidation – nothing but fury. Because seeing this man here suddenly made everything clear.

'It was all you, all along!' he said through gritted teeth. 'Everything that's happened to me and my family and the city – you caused it all! SWARM wasn't even Dad's project, was it? I bet he wanted no part of it. Somehow you *forced* Professor Starr to work on the drones. And it was *you* who released them on purpose!'

Tony Daegar showed not a flicker of emotion. And when he spoke his tone was mechanical. 'What you know, Hal Strider, or think you know, is immaterial. And whoever was the architect of these events makes no great difference.'

'Makes no difference – but you made sure Dad got the blame!'

'Sooner or later, mankind was bound to face a conflict with his machines,' Tony Daegar continued coldly. 'Professor Starr himself persuaded me of that. And now here we are. I have merely been the quickest to adapt. But this is a critical juncture. Which is why I'm glad to find you and Miss Lannekar here. I have urgent questions for you both.'

'We're not telling you anything!' Sky spat.

'You are quite mistaken, Miss Lannekar. You will tell me everything. Let me tell you how I can be so certain. I spent seven years in Afghanistan, during which time I interrogated hundreds of insurgents. And do you know how many, given the proper persuasion, eventually told me everything? Every single one.'

Hal glared around him, watching the militiamen wreck the apartment.

'What are you even doing here? I know you want the vault, but why? In any case, you're wasting your time. You'll never find it. It's miles away.'

Sky was staring at him, urgently shaking her head, but it was too late.

'Miles away?' Tony Daegar said. 'By which you must mean . . . your sister has the device. Well, I already suspected as much. But thank you for confirming it. And as luck would have it, we recently reacquired Miss Strider's trail. Rest assured, we'll track her down soon enough.'

'Leave her alone!' Hal shouted, lurching towards him, bunching his fists. 'Go anywhere near her and I'll—'

An arm snaked round his neck, made him choke. Karl Daegar had him in a stranglehold. Two of his thugs grabbed his arms. Hal struggled, and kicked, but these older, armoured boys held him fast.

Meanwhile, another militiaman moved close. This man wore headphones and held a black box that bristled with aerials.

'Commander Daegar,' he said. 'I've just decoded that last transmission. The general has given the go-ahead. They're all moving up to orange.'

'Numbers?' Tony Daegar said.

'The entire fleet, sir. Every gunship.'

'Well then – this should be quite a demonstration.' He raised his voice. 'Claymore, Brack, watch the exits. The rest of you, come and bear witness. This is history in the making.' He looked at Hal and Sky. 'You two will want to see this too. Everything else can wait.'

He and the rest of his men moved towards the glass wall. Karl released Hal, shoved him in the same direction.

'Your heard him, hero, get over there.'

Hal spun round with teeth bared. 'Push me again and I'll—'

He bit down on his next word. What could he possibly do, surrounded by these militiamen, other than make empty threats? He needed to be smarter than that. Whatever it took, he had to escape the apartment. He needed to go after Jess, and find her before Tony Daegar got to her first.

He looked at Sky. Outwardly she looked more composed, heading silently for the glass wall. But even as she went she darted glances left and right, watching for her own chance to escape.

Karl Daegar shoved him again, and this time Hal forced himself not to react. He went to stand at Sky's side.

'Miss Lannekar, I can see you're tempted to make a break for freedom,' Tony Daegar said. 'I assure you that would be most unwise. In any case, you should be looking out there. Trust me, you won't want to miss this spectacle. Claymore, give them glasses.'

The man called Claymore produced two sets of bulky binoculars, which had orange lenses. He gave one pair to Hal and another to Sky.

'The general's moved them up to red,' said the man wearing headphones. 'Two minutes.'

The room was hushed now, all the militiamen peering through

their night-sights. Even Sky was silently staring westwards. Horribly curious despite himself, Hal raised his own binoculars and looked out.

Now he saw the cityscape in grainy colour. Most of it was shades of green and white. But there was also thermographic detail. Yellow specks in some of the buildings must be people. A gunship swept past, glowing red at its engines and exhaust vents.

He trained his night-sight on the disaster zone. Fiddling with the controls, he managed to increase the magnification, the pillar of smoke springing towards him. As he took in the scene he drew a sharp breath.

The disaster zone had changed. When he had seen it on TV, half the smashed aeroplane had been lying in a crater. But now . . . the giant aircraft was gone. The entire plane had vanished!

The reason was simple but shocking – the crater was now much larger. It was not only wider, but also looked deeper, and was jagged around its edges like the jaws of a shark. The crater had become a hole in the earth.

The plane had crashed down on top of a tube station, that's what the news reports said. So then, more of the street must have collapsed into the train tunnels, swallowing the entire aircraft. It was still difficult to fathom how a thing of that size could have sunk without trace, but that was the only possible explanation.

The giant column of smoke twisted out of the chasm. And buzzing in and out of the hole, stirring the smoke, were drones.

But here was the strangest thing: when the machines arrived, they looked bulkier than when they departed . . .

Further increasing the magnification, focusing on individual drones, Hal saw why. Each returning drone carried a scrap of metal, or piece of wreckage. One was carrying what looked like the wing of a gunship. Another had the severed head of a beetle-drone clamped between its feet.

'They're . . . scavenging,' Hal said quietly, a sickly feeling twisting in his stomach. 'They're taking all that stuff into the chasm. Why are they doing that?'

Before anyone could respond, the assault began. From all directions, helicopter gunships came sweeping in. Within seconds there were thirty, forty of these fearsome warplanes. Coming to a hover, they formed a ring around the chasm.

And a second later, in unison, every single gunship opened fire. Red streaks shot from their rocket pods, and cracked lines crackled from their cannons. Then there were the slower, brighter flares of Hellfire missiles. All this firepower pouring into the chasm. In response, dust and rubble and flame erupted from the hole like a volcano.

And still the onslaught continued. Dozens of missiles. Hundreds of rockets. Countless shells. The clamour of it all detonating within the earth was more terrible even than the initial plane crash. Hal *felt* the noise in his bones, even at this distance, even through triple-glazed glass.

He was quite certain, once the barrage finally came to an end, that nothing could have survived such violence. However many machines had been down in that pit, whatever they might have been doing down there, it had all certainly been obliterated.

Stillness settled. The gunships tipped their snouts, as if

examining their handiwork. There was no sign of a single drone. Bits of debris were still raining back to earth, but nothing else stirred.

Hal let out a long breath. So then, finally the military were on top of this conflict. They would still need to hunt down stray drones, but surely now it wouldn't be long before —

Fresh movement made him flinch. At first, he thought there must have been a delayed explosion underground, because it looked like more debris was erupting out of the pit.

But then he heard someone gasp. One of Karl's gang took a step away from the glass.

Those shapes, bursting upwards . . .

They were not chunks of rubble or bits of debris . . .

They were drones.

Scores of them were rushing out of the pit. And *still* they were rising, their wings a furious blur, their eyes blazing red – as if a stick had been thrust into a hornet's nest.

The Apache gunships were pulling back, sweeping their cannon fire. But the drones were faster and more numerous. Their energy guns shot shimmering threads, filling the sky with deadly spiderwebs. Any warplane caught in those webs instantly ignited and fell in flames.

Eventually, Tony Daegar's voice broke the hush.

'Magnificent, aren't they,' he said, to no one in particular. 'You all saw what was thrown against the machines. Doubtless they lost many of their brethren to that bombardment. Yet they suffer no fear, nor loss of morale. No shellshock or battle-fatigue. They merely rise, and do what is necessary.'

He sounded entranced, almost elated. How could anyone watch these events unfold with anything but horror? It was a massacre. The gunships were outnumbered and outmatched. Their weaponry was slow compared to the darting energy beams of the drones. Sickened, Hal saw more gunships fall, the explosive glare of one lighting the destruction of the next. Now the remaining warplanes were retreating, trying to shake off their pursuers. Fighter jets were roaring in to give support, and the battle was spreading outwards.

'But,' Hal began, finding his voice at last, 'but the military have been shooting them down. How – how many drones are there?'

'As of this moment,' Tony Daegar shrugged, 'I wouldn't hazard a guess. I'm told there's some kind of formula to predict their replication rate. But why let mathematics spoil such a spectacle? You can see for yourself – the machines are flourishing!'

Hal squeezed his eyes shut, that sickly feeling spreading from his stomach, filling every inch of him.

Their replication rate.

'So . . . their pods,' he whispered. 'They really are what they look like. They're *cocoons*. The machines *grow inside*.'

'Precisely,' Tony Daegar said. 'And that is why we are so privileged to stand here today. What we are watching, with our own eyes, is even more momentous than the first deployment of the atomic bomb.'

As he spoke, Tony Daegar's tone only grew more ecstatic. 'What you are witnessing here today, ladies and gentlemen, is the single greatest advance in the history of warfare. The *ultimate* weapon. Fighting machines able to print copies of themselves using only what they scavenge from their environs.'

Hal squeezed his eyes tighter. Until now, he imagined his horror of all this to be absolute. Yet he had not envisaged the half of it.

Fighting machines able to print copies of themselves.

London was overrun by intelligent, lethal robots. But not merely by a swarm of them. Rather, an infestation. A plague.

Here was terror without end.

3

Collateral Damage

Through all of this, Sky had remained silent. But now she stared at Tony Daegar, and she spoke in a choked whisper.

'I used to think . . . I used to think you were just stupid – brainless, like all bullies. But now I see it's much worse. You're not just stupid, you're mad.'

'Please watch your tone, Miss Lannekar. I can assure you, I am neither mad nor stupid.'

'You stand here, and you watch all this,' she said, 'and you think you can *win*? Do you even know why it's called the SWARM Project? It stands for Sentient WAR Machines. And you do know what *sentient* means? When all this is finished, do you really think the drones will need you? You won't win, no one will! They'll eat your world the same as they'll eat ours!'

'Really, Miss Lannekar, there's no need for these hysterics. And you must learn to have more faith in human beings. Yes, these machines are formidable. And yes they have built up good numbers. But ranged against them is the entire might of the British Armed Forces. Not to mention our allies in the United States and NATO.'

He raised his binoculars to watch the warplanes and drones doing battle. 'I guarantee, people will beat the machines – eventually. But by the time they do, the SWARM Project will have proved its full value.'

'Its *value*?' Hal said. 'So that really is what you want from all this – *money*. You're planning to steal the blueprints so you can sell them! You *are* mad! Who would even want to buy them after this? Who would risk it happening again?'

Tony Daegar showed his teeth. 'Let me ask you a question in return, Hal Strider. When the first atomic bomb fell on Japan, and the world saw what it could do, did generals turn away in disgust? No. Quite the reverse. They raced to acquire nuclear weapons of their own.'

He raised a hand to indicate the battle outside, which was spreading further and faster than ever.

'Believe me,' he said, 'after witnessing today's events, every army on Earth will be begging to buy my machines. After this, no army will dare be without them.'

Hal stared at him. He clenched his teeth, and he managed to say, 'Not *your* machines. Because you'll never get your hands on those blueprints. I'm going to find the vault. And I'm going to take it the aerodrome, and I'm going to use the killcode!'

Tony Daegar studied him coldly. 'The killcode? Ah, you mean your father's so-called "antidote".' He shook his head. 'No. That cannot be allowed to happen. Which is why—'

People gasped. Hal caught his balance as the apartment shook. An explosion, shockingly close, had lit the room light as day.

A man holding a radio receiver came forward. 'Commander Daegar, the battlefront has shifted into this sector.'

'I can see that for myself. You do know the meaning of *prior* warning?' He raised his voice. 'We need to leave. Now.'

'The drones can't hurt us,' Karl Daegar said, tapping his helmet. 'You said they won't come within 500 metres of these headsets.'

Even as he spoke, a fighter jet roared past the apartment, close enough to see the pilot inside.

'Our own side are not so predictable,' Tony Daegar said. 'In any case, we're finished here. Hal Strider, Miss Lannekar, you will come with us.'

'I'm not going anywhere with you,' Sky spat, backing away.

'Yes you are.' Karl Daegar grabbed her from behind, twisted her arm.

Hal lurched towards him. 'Let go of her!'

Two of Karl's gang closed to intercept and tried to take hold of him, but Hal twisted away.

'Get hold of him. Now,' Tony Daegar said, as another starburst lit the room. 'The rest of you, out to the boats.'

While militiamen marched from the apartment, Karl's gang encircled Hal, their arms spread wide. Hal feinted one way, darted another, stayed just out of range.

'Come and take her,' Karl said to one of his thugs. 'I'll grab the other one.'

With another of the gang now twisting Sky's arm, Karl Daegar came forward. Hal dashed one way, doubled back, but each time Karl and the others shifted position, kept him trapped.

'There's nowhere to run,' Karl said, snarling. 'But keep trying. It will give me an excuse to—'

A screaming sound, followed by a terrifying bang, and everyone in the apartment fell down.

Dazed, blinking, the wind knocked out of him, Hal rolled onto his back. His ears ringing, dull sounds reached him, as if from a great distance. He stared at the ceiling, which appeared to be swinging from side to side.

He started to get to his feet but a secondary quake rocked the floor and he fell down once more. All around him people were shouting. Cracking, roaring sounds were coming up in waves. Bursts of flame were rushing upwards past the glass walls.

Dizzy and disorientated, Hal finally found his feet. Hazily, he saw that Sky had managed to get free, and she was heading for the spiral staircase. He staggered after her.

But then a weight threw itself on top of him and he found himself back on the ground.

'We told you – you're coming with us!' Karl Daegar spat.

'Get off me, you idiot! The building's been hit – we have to get out!'

Hal kicked and thrashed and punched, but his blows fell on Karl's body armour. There was a splintering sound as cracks zigzagged across the glass wall.

'Get off!' Hal said, struggling for breath. 'The whole building's going to fall!'

The older boy only shifted his weight, grabbed Hal's wrist and tried to drag him to his feet. The movement freed Hal's legs. He pulled up his knees, and managed to plant both feet against Karl's midriff.

Hal kicked out with all his strength. At the same moment the apartment shuddered, and suddenly Hal was free, Karl Daegar sprawled on his back.

Hal stumbled to his feet, held his balance as the building roared and rumbled, plaster raining from the ceiling.

He staggered uphill and he reached the staircase. He started up, clambering on all fours, the stairs corkscrewing madly.

Finally, he reached the top. Finding his feet, he ran in a half-crouch, lurching from side to side: along the landing, pushing aside or clambering over obstacles: through the dining room, waves of heat pouring up through the floor.

And finally he was out and onto the roof garden. Frantically sweeping his gaze, he saw no sign of Sky or her wing. His own glider had rolled on its wheeled base. But mercifully it had come to a halt against the guardrail.

He went towards it, freewheeling downhill. The building shuddered, yawned, threw him off his feet. He skidded down the roof on his backside, scooping up the flight helmet as he passed, pulling it onto his head, clipping it beneath his chin just as he came crashing into the guardrail.

He tore off the fastenings holding the wing to its base – the last one came free. And immediately, with no thought now of anything other than escaping this shuddering, roaring building, he hauled the wing up onto the railing, and he launched himself and the machine out into the night.

The wind rushed, the world lurched.

And he dropped like a rock towards the concrete below.

4

Free Fall

Hal plummeted, the wind roaring around him. He wrestled with the wing, unable to get his weight fully settled against it. The machine bucked and twisted, threatening to fling him off.

He threw his body left and right, trying to get the craft under control. His efforts only sent the wing into a spin. The burning building whipped around him once, twice, three times, quicker and quicker, until it was a dizzying blur. Beneath him, already horribly distinct, cars and concrete and lampposts spun as they thundered upwards.

Mortal fear was building in him now, and his efforts were becoming erratic and even less effective. He fought with the wing, and he hissed between his teeth: 'Come *on*!'

On the inside edge of each handhold, beneath his thumbs, were twin triggers. In desperation, he squeezed them – the wing's pulsejet fired. Now he rocketed towards the ground, faster than ever.

But the burst of power also steadied the wing, stopping the spin. He fired the pulsejet again, and he threw his weight backwards – and the leading edge came up and caught the wind.

Summoning all his courage, the onrushing street mere metres away, he fired the pulsejet a third time, he pulled back with all his strength, and he felt lift surging through the machine – he swept clear of the ground with inches to spare.

Instinctively he pulled the dive into a climb, sweeping up and over the plane trees, their leaves rustling in his wake. And then he was firing the thrusters once more, taking the wing soaring into clear air, and he heard himself whoop his relief into the wind.

But the relief was short lived. Because now he was climbing just as rapidly as he had fallen, the wing sweeping him up and away from the Thames.

Already he was high above the streets, and the wind was tossing and rolling the machine, and all Hal could do was cling on, with no more control than when he had been in free fall.

And still he was climbing. Far below him the city tilted and lurched and flipped. Without warning the wing dropped violently, then surged up again with alarming speed.

Off his right-hand side there was searing flash, followed by a muffled thump. A dark shape hurtled past him, and another below, and his every muscle locked tight, tensing for impact.

But seconds passed, and somehow he was still alive. And he seemed to have climbed into clearer skies. Sweeping his gaze, he could see no drones or gunships.

Blinking heavily, he started to think more clearly. He looked at his gauntlets. Through all these terrific twists and turns, they hadn't shifted an inch. In fact, as the wing plunged into another dive, and the G-force increased, he sensed the gloves gripping even tighter. The kneepads of this bodysuit must be made of similar stuff, because they too remained clamped to the aircraft. That was one thing at least: he could trust this equipment.

But he still had no real control over the wing. Once more it dipped without warning, then barrelled up again on another surge of wind.

Lifting his head, he realised with alarm that he was sweeping back towards his burning building.

He rushed closer and closer, the inferno sucking in air, sucking Hal in with it. He fought with the wing, trying to steer it away, firing the pulsejet. But the harder he battled, the quicker the vortex sucked him towards the flames.

'You need . . . turn your . . . right hand . . .' Suddenly Sky was here, her own wing a glimmer beneath her. She was shouting, but her words were broken against the wind.

'What?' Hal shouted. 'I can't hear you!'

'. . . quick, before . . . it's on your . . .'

She was getting even harder to hear, because the pair of them were drawing further apart. She had successfully banked her wing, and was riding the edge of the vortex, while Hal was still spiralling towards its heart.

Wrestling his aircraft, becoming frantic, he shot another look at Sky. Now she was gesturing wildly with one hand. She appeared to be pointing at her helmet. Yes – and she was miming an action.

In desperation, Hal opened the fingers of his right hand. His gauntlet, which a moment ago had been gripping like iron, came away without resistance. He groped for the dial at his right ear. Copying Sky's mime, he twisted the dial forwards.

There was a beep inside his helmet, and a message flashed in his visor: 'Comms Channel Auto – Short Range Infrared.'

And now Sky's voice sounded clear in his left ear.

'You're doing it all wrong. You're fighting the wing. You shouldn't be fighting it.'

'What do you—?'

'Don't talk. Listen. You've got seconds before you're toast. You need to stop trying so hard. Stop firing the pulsejet. The wing is a glider. Use the air currents and the thermals.'

With the inferno now swirling so close, the heat intense, it took a lot of willpower to do as she said and stop firing the pulsejet. But the moment he did so he felt the struggle lighten. He found it easier to hold the wing steady, and to read its movements.

'That's better,' Sky said. 'The pulsejet gives you a boost, but it's not your motor. You've got all the power you need in those flames. Use them as a slingshot.'

Again it took all his courage to follow this advice. It meant turning the wing *towards* the inferno. But again, as Hal did so, he knew she was right. He felt a surge of power as the wing picked up a tailwind.

And now he was hurtling towards the burning building. But he was also feeling for the thermals, sensing an air channel opening to his left, and he was throwing his weight, banking the wing, using the momentum he had gained to skim clear of the flames, the updraught now flinging him up and away.

'Well,' Sky said, as they circled together at a safer distance, Hal's heart thundering, 'that was one way to have your first lesson.'

Hal glanced back at the fiery tower. 'Do you think . . .' he said, fighting for breath, 'do you think Tony Daegar and the others got clear?'

'Yes, they did. I saw their gunboats heading downriver. I'm going after them. Tony Daegar said they've picked up your sister's trail. So maybe they'll lead me straight to her. But I need to be quick. So listen carefully while I talk your through your landing.'

'What? I'm not landing! I'm coming with you.'

'This is hard enough without holding your hand.'

'I need to help Jess.'

'You can't help anyone if you're dead! The fighting comes in waves. How long do you think you'll last once it starts up again?'

'She's my sister!'

'Listen, Hal, I don't have time for this. If you won't let me help you land then I'm sorry, but—'

She was interrupted by a thundering roar. Simultaneously, a dragon's breath of smoke and flame poured skywards. The turbulence reached Hal even at this distance, sending him into a tailspin.

Wrestling with the wing, regaining a measure of control, he looked back in time to see his building fall. With strange slowness it toppled into a neighbouring tower. The second building crumpled on impact, but remained standing. Hal's tower was now slumped against it, wreathed in fire.

Watching this, Hal felt deathly cold all over. Already he was separated from his father and his sister, not even knowing for sure that either of them were safe. And now all alone up here he had watched their home destroyed. His whole world was falling apart. Would the pieces ever go back together?

But this cold sorrow lasted no more than seconds. It was burned away by a blazing fury. Tony Daegar caused all this! His greed had brought this down upon them all. And now he was out there hunting Jess. He wanted to steal the blueprints so he could sell these killer drones all over the world . . .

'Sky, where are you? We need to get after those gunboats!'

A message flashed in his visor: 'Comms Link Failed. Range Exceeded.'

So, then, Sky must already be speeding after SWARM. Manhandling his wing, finally getting the craft facing eastwards, Hal fired his pulsejet.

And leaving his home burning in his wake, he set off on the search for Jess, swearing beneath his breath that he would reach her first, no matter who or what might stand in his way.

5

Tremors

Although Jess had not been asleep, she blinked and it was like waking. Slowly she turned her head and stared around her. She saw nothing but total blackness.

Her breathing speeded up, and panic started to rise. Where am I – what's happening – am I blind? A low noise began in her stomach and reached her mouth as a wail.

Lights flicked on, bobbed towards her. Two people carrying torches. One of them, a woman, knelt at her side.

'Jess. Look at me. It's okay. Take deep breaths.'

'Who – who are you? H-how do you know my name? Where am I?'

'My name is Doctor Pavel,' the woman said. 'I've spoken to you a few times before. You keep forgetting. But that's nothing to worry about.'

'Forgetting! What do you mean? What's happened to me?'

'Keep breathing. Everything's going to be okay.' She put a hand on Jess's shoulder. 'You experienced something highly traumatic. Sometimes, if our brain becomes overwhelmed, it can shut down parts of itself. It's a defence mechanism, and it's temporary.'

'I – I remember – I was on a bridge – it fell!'

'Yes. You told us. We think it was Tower Bridge. You fell in the river. You swam.'

'Hal! Hal was with me – where is he?'

'We haven't seen your brother, I'm sorry. When they found you up above you were on your own.'

'Is he dead?'

'Last time we spoke, we agreed he probably isn't. You got your father's brains, he got the bravery, that's what you said. He's most likely out there right now doing something stupidly courageous.'

'Out there? So – where's here? Wait, I remember. We're underground. This is a tube station.'

'Good. Yes. You're holding onto a little more each time. And you're safe here, that's an important thing to remember. It can be very dark, because we're all trying to save our torch batteries. But it's not dangerous. During the Second World War, when the bombs fell, people used to shelter in these tunnels. If they can survive the Blitz down here, then we'll be okay, won't we?'

Jess's breathing began to slow, and she seemed to see the woman for the first time. The torchlight made crevices in her face, so she looked ancient. But she wore a concerned, reassuring expression. The young man with her might have been her son. He was holding a black sack.

'Perhaps you're ready to eat something,' Dr Pavel said. 'There's only the dregs left, I'm afraid. We have volunteers who go to the surface, but the fighting has been intense. They've had to postpone their foraging.'

While she spoke, the young man put down the sack, took out jars of jam, and tins of sardines and bottles of Diet Coke.

'The fighting's getting worse?' Jess said.

'Well – we think it's lulled for now,' Dr Pavel said. 'It appears to come in phases. And I won't lie to you, each one has been worse than the last. But it can't go on forever. And in the meantime, we're perfectly safe down here.'

Again she touched Jess's shoulder. 'Now, I need to leave you for a while. But I'm only just over there if you need me. I'd just finished a night shift when all this started, and unless I get a little rest I'll be no use to anyone . . .'

Once Dr Pavel and her son had moved away, Jess hugged her knees and tried to get her bearings. She got the idea there were lots of other people down here. She could smell them, and hear them shuffling and whispering.

She was surrounded by faceless strangers. And somehow that only made it worse. She was afraid and crushingly lonely, and wanted to cry with it. Where was Hal? She couldn't even remember being separated from him! Why couldn't she remember? What did that mean?

She realised she was gripping something so tightly it made her fingers hurt. It was her satchel. So she had managed to keep hold of that, but couldn't hold onto Hal. Where was he? How would they ever find one another now? And how would they—

A noise cut through her thoughts, made her sit up straight. At first it was faint, but rapidly grew louder and heavier. It was a rumbling grinding crunching sound.

Was it coming from the surface – a battalion of tanks trundling overhead? No. She wanted to believe that, but she couldn't. As the noise continued to swell, the truth became incontestable.

This grinding clamour was rumbling up out of the dark.

Whatever might be causing this cacophony, it was *down here with them*.

All along the platform, more and more people were on their feet. Many of them were shining torches into the train tunnels.

'It sounds like machinery,' Jess heard somebody say. 'But all the power is dead.'

'Could it be a train?' somebody else said. 'Tube trains are automated, aren't they? Maybe one started up by itself.'

'It sounds more like, digging. Like a . . . a tunnelling machine.'

Still it crunched louder and heavier, until Jess could feel the vibrations through the floor and the walls. And there were metallic scraping, clinking sounds. And Jess's heartbeat was thumping in her ears.

What was it? What was coming up out of the dark?

Abruptly the noise and the tremors stopped.

A stillness settled all along the platform. The only noise now was people breathing, and water dripping on the tracks.

After a while, lights began flicking off. Most people sat back against the walls. They went back to whispering, although more nervously than before.

But several torch beams were moving in Jess's direction.

They stopped nearby, congregating around Dr Pavel. Jess heard her and other people talking about the disturbance. What had caused it? Should they still consider it safe down here? Someone proposed leading a search party into the train tunnels to investigate.

Jess hugged her knees. She was overwhelmed with loneliness and fear. But now her thoughts remained clear, and she knew she would forget none of this, even if she might wish that she could.

6

Second Sight

As Hal swept eastwards, a powerful gust of wind hit him broadside and sent him spinning off course. His initial instinct was to counter-act the spin and try to wrestle the wing back under control. But instead he rolled with it, allowing his momentum to bring him back upright. Only then did he dip his right wingtip and guide the glider smoothly and easily back onto its heading.

With each small victory like this, his confidence was growing. Sky was right: if you fought with the wing it would only fight back. You needed to treat it with a lighter touch, learn to read its rhythms and work with them, not against them.

Flying this way, he barely needed to fire the pulsejet. Instead he harnessed the wind and the thermals as he soared above the Thames. He felt for the airstreams, riding the edge of one then cresting another, like a surfer riding waves.

In spite of everything, he couldn't deny he was starting to enjoy this. The wing was so light, so responsive, it might not exist beneath him. Or rather – it might almost be a part of him. Here was truly flying!

On the surface of the water, oil slicks flickered with flame. And by this light he caught sight of his own reflection – a swooping shadowy falcon. It was only a glimpse, and then gone, but it sent a fresh thrill through him. The marvel of this machine! The wonder of free flight!

All around him was clear airspace, no sign of any drones or warplanes. So he allowed himself to drift away from the river. He skirted tall buildings, and he caught the ridge-lift sweeping off their sheer surfaces.

He swooped through the concrete canyons of the city, and he soared over its peaks and dived into its valleys, and for the next few minutes he was so completely in his element that nothing else existed.

But then a searing flash lit the skyline, and abruptly he came back to himself, feeling ashamed. How could he even imagine enjoying himself at a time like this, with the city falling to pieces, while Jess was out there lost and afraid?

In any case, he needed to focus, or else this would be the shortest and last flight of his life. Further west, fires all along the riverbank had provided light enough to navigate, but here there were no fires and the night was black. It was getting worse, in fact, and with a flash of panic he realised he had lost track of the Thames.

To try to get his bearings he gained altitude, and soared above the buildings. But as he did so, a massive shape whooshed past his head, close enough to make him flinch. A second huge structure appeared from the gloom, was past him almost before he knew it was there.

These were cranes. The skyline bristled with them. Normally they would be brightly lit to warn low-flying planes. But now, with the blackout, they were practically invisible and potentially deadly as Hal sped across the rooftops.

Diving down, fearful now, he lifted a hand and scrabbled at the dial over his left ear. This helmet had orange eyepieces – just like the scopes he had used in the apartment. Therefore, it suddenly occurred to him, it was most likely equipped with . . . yes, sighing with relief, he found that when he clicked the dial forward it engaged the helmet's night-sight. The city blinked into green and white, with patches of heat showing as red and yellow and orange.

Circling the wing to get his bearings, he scanned the wide green curve of the river, and he found he had flown further east than he imagined. In fact, nearby were the remains of Tower Bridge, its twisted skeleton a surreal sight in night-vision.

Flying out over the river, he continued eastwards. Scanning the airspace ahead of him, he watched for drones, and he searched for Sky, but saw neither. He swept his gaze across the water, looking for the SWARM gunboats, but saw no vessels of any kind.

He wondered what other functions this helmet might have, and whether they might aid him in his search. Raising his left hand, he clicked the dial forward another notch. Now his night-vision was overlaid with faint purple lines and symbols and readouts.

Here was an electro-optical display, of the sort used by fighter pilots. A stationary line formed an artificial horizon, and vectors showed distances to nearby buildings. Graphics provided information about airspeed, altitude and compass heading.

He felt a surge of confidence. He had been handling the wing okay unaided; now he was armed with all this electronic wizardry.

Experimenting further, he found telescopic sight. And then, clicking the dial into its furthest position, he found a different mode. Now tiny yellow symbols appeared. They were triangles, or perhaps arrows, and they were dancing at the right-hand edge of his vision.

He turned his head, looked where these symbols appeared to be pointing. As he did so, the arrows swarmed into his main field of view. They bunched together into groups of four, each quartet forming a tiny crosshair.

He understood what was happening. This enhanced vision highlighted the presence of drones. Each crosshair pinpointed the location of a single insect-machine.

Sweeping his gaze, he was alarmed to see more and more crosshairs form. Even with night-vision he hadn't spotted these machines. But now he saw at least ten crosshairs passing to the south, and a similar number sweeping north.

And then, with horrible speed, a whole swarm appeared directly ahead. They were hurtling straight towards him, their crosshairs darkening from yellow into orange.

Frantically, Hal darted his eyes left and right. But more drones lurked either side. If he wheeled away he would risk running straight into them.

There was no more time for conscious decision. The drones

ahead were so close their crosshairs had turned a violent shade of red.

Firing the pulsejet, Hal threw his wing towards the Thames. He pulled up at the last instant, skimming so low that water rippled in his wake. And then all he could do was hold his breath as the insect-machines became frightening silhouettes directly above.

They were mostly beetle-drones, their mandibles tipped with circular saws. But there were also hornet-machines and fly-like scouts mixed into this metallic swarm. Time slowed to a crawl and it seemed to take forever for them to buzz overhead.

But finally they were past. Letting out a long breath, craning his neck, Hal watched them continue westwards. Those drones had paid him no attention whatsoever. Which made him think about the wing, its skin warping with non-colours. This glider baffled the human eye, particularly at night. But could it also defeat the drones' sensors? Riding the wing, could he move among the machines unseen?

He was now fairly certain he could. Even so, the close encounter with those drones had left him shaken. These insect-machines were frightening enough from ground level, but it was ten times worse up here, where they could thunder upon you in a second. As he flew on his eyes went after every crosshair, his nerves tingling with a new edge.

A few seconds later, a message flashed in his visor display: 'Comms Link Restored. Signal in Range.'

'Sky?' he said, gaining altitude. 'Are you here?'

No reply. He circled higher, saw no sign of her. But now he spotted three gunboats up ahead. From each one a searchlight was swinging back and forth, slicing the night sky.

'So you are here – somewhere,' he said. 'Those must be the SWARM boats, and you followed them here. Sky? Why aren't you—'

The last word stuck in his throat, because a fierce rattle came from below. All three gunboats had opened fire, crimson dots streaking skywards.

Hal threw his wing into a turn and he climbed fast, while searchlights and gunfire raked the clouds.

'Sky – where are you? Are they really trying to kill us? I didn't think they could even see us!'

'Be quiet!' Sky hissed. 'No, they can't see us, but they can hear you – you're using an open channel!'

The searchlights probed the clouds and more gunfire rang out. Then Tony Daegar's voice burst into Hal's left ear.

'Make no mistake, either of you, these are not warning shots. If you continue to play this game you will both pay the full consequences. I have dispatched men to retrieve the blueprints. They are well armed, and willing to do whatever is necessary. Do not take that as an idle threat.'

With that the gunboats surged back into motion, churning the water as they powered eastwards.

Above Hal the darkness shifted. Looking up, he at last got a clear sighting of Sky. She had wheeled her wing and was now sweeping back west.

'Where are you going? Tony Daegar must be heading for Blackheath. We need to get there first.'

'They can still hear you! Switch to a private channel. Twist the right-hand dial.' Once Hal had done so, Sky said, 'Your sister isn't in Blackheath. You heard Tony Daegar – he said he sent men to get the vault. Damn – I thought they were just a diversion!'

Firing his pulsejet, Hal went after her. Above the dome of St Paul's Cathedral she arced around and circled. Coming up on her fast, Hal veered away at the last second.

'Watch it – you almost hit me! Listen, Hal, I don't mean to sound harsh, but you're really not helping. The last thing I need – you blundering about up here, giving me away!'

'I don't understand – you think Jess might be down there somewhere?'

When Sky said nothing, only continued to spiral, he said, 'I know you're angry, and you're scared – I am too. But we want the same thing. And we've got the same enemies. Like it or not, that means we're on the same team. So tell me – why did you double back?'

Sky was flying ever widening circles, intent on the streets below. Eventually, she said, 'The SWARM boats stopped near here, and four men got out. I kept track of them for a while, but then they disappeared. And by then I thought it must be a trick – Tony Daegar trying to throw me off the scent. So I went after the gunboats instead.'

'But just now Tony Daegar said he sent men to get the vault. So you think he meant these four. Which would mean Jess really is near here! Perhaps she was trying to get home . . .'

'But by now those men could be anywhere,' Sky said. 'I don't see *anyone* down there, do you?'

Circling his wing, Hal saw only green and white roads and buildings – no movement and no patches of bodyheat. He envisaged Jess hiding down there somewhere, militiamen hunting her, and he gritted his teeth.

'We've got to find them! What direction were they headed when you – wait, I see someone!'

Flying in widening spirals, he passed over a pair of orangey figures. But sweeping lower he saw they were soldiers, guarding a gun battery.

Further on, near the Bank of England, he spotted more people, but swooping to investigate he found they were policemen. Flying further afield, he saw looters raiding a department store, and he found more soldiers, and a pack of feral dogs, but no sign of the SWARM militiamen.

'I've got nothing,' Sky said. 'Please say you've seen them.'

'No. This is hopeless – we need something more to go on.'

'We don't have anything more, though, do we?' Sky said, her voice cracking. 'So it's finished.'

'We're not giving up, keep looking.'

'Don't you get it, we've lost! It's simple. Tony Daegar knows where the hard-drive is, and we don't. And the moment he gets his hands on it, that's it! I won't even get to say goodbye. I'll die up here and she'll be trapped down there forever!'

'Trapped? What do you mean? You talked about someone being trapped before.'

'You don't even know, do you? Tony Daegar trapped them at the aerodrome. My mum, your dad, all the engineers. He locked them underground!'

'What?'

'Without power. Without light. I don't even know if they've still got air to breathe. And without that vault there's nothing I can do about it! I don't even care about stopping the drones – let them have the Earth! People don't deserve it. I just want to see her one last time – I want to say goodbye before the world ends!'

'Slow down. I'm not even sure what you're talking about. You've been up here with the machines a long time and it's—'

He broke off as a rolling clatter rose behind him. Turning on his wing, he saw an Apache helicopter appear from behind some tall buildings. And now more gunships were rising from cover. They were all coming to a hover, all fully laden with rocket pods and missiles.

At the same time, Hal's visor display became frantic with yellow arrows. Looking where they were pointing, he saw a great number of crosshairs form to the east.

'Sky, I think we need to leave . . .'

From overhead came the shriek of fighter jets, and a boom when one went supersonic. To the east, more crosshairs were forming – more and more of them – so many they overlaid one another.

'The drones – they're swarming,' he said. 'It's about to start again.'

Still Sky gave no impression she had even heard. She continued to spiral and swoop, desperately scouring the streets.

From the west, more gunships swept in, coming to a hover. They formed a phalanx, facing the mass of machines.

'Sky, listen to me – we're right in the middle of the battleground!'

She finally raised her head, looking first to the west, then staring to the east. 'Oh – my—'

Her voice was lost beneath the roar of afterburners. A fighter jet thundered past so low its turbulence tossed Hal's wing, sent him rolling.

Simultaneously, drones swarmed into attack, and gunships surged forward to intercept, loosing rockets and missiles.

And Hal continued to tumble over and over as the whole world exploded into heat and noise and chaos.

* * *

+ + + Attrition Rate Stabilised + + + Replication Rate Exceptional + + + Numerical Supremacy Achieved + + +

As a batch of new soldier drones emerge from the nest, the machines calculate that a tipping point has been reached. For the first time since hostilities began, drones now outnumber human warriors.

At lightspeed, this tactical data zips from drone to drone, like neurons firing in a single mind. In the vast majority of cases, it causes no outward change in behaviour.

But then the data hits the livewired brain of Berserker 043, and it causes an extraordinary reflex. Instantly, this drone goes into a powerdive, hurtling headlong towards a gunship.

The gunship tips its snout, blasts the onrushing machine. But the drone keeps up its suicide dive, even as it disintegrates beneath the shellbursts. The drone crashes into the warplane, and both fighting machines plummet to earth.

Within microseconds, fresh signals are rippling amid the drones.

+ + + New Tactics Assayed + + + Assessing + + + Assessing +

+ + Rated Highly Efficacious + + + Adopt and Imitate + + + Adopt and Imitate + + +

Immediately, more drones power into kamikaze dives. Within seconds, five warplanes and six armoured cars are obliterated.

But this is only the start of the drones' new phase. Because down in their chasm, one replication pod has failed to open. Only now does it crack and spill its contents.

The drone that drags itself free is striped yellow and black like its siblings. But it is not identical. An error has occurred in transcription. This drone's abdomen is swollen. And the swelling is packed with explosive material.

Minutes after taking to the air, adopting the new kamikaze craze, this mutant machine hurtles back to earth. It strikes a battle-tank and destroys it utterly.

Once again chatter between the drones intensifies.

+ + + New Species Online + + + Design Analysed + + + Adaptation Advantageous + + + Replicate + + + Replicate + + + Replicate + + +

7

Shockwaves

Through Hal's earpiece, Sky was shouting something over and over. But he had no idea what she was saying. His wing was still spinning, and the world was a senseless whirlpool of light and noise.

From somewhere shockingly close there was a blinding flare. It was followed by a concussion so heavy that it thumped through Hal, almost making him release his grip on the handholds.

A fiery comet dropped earthwards, missing him by a fraction. The drag of this object gripped the wing and stopped Hal's spin.

Suddenly he was upright and the world regained its shape – and he saw he was arrowing straight for St Paul's Cathedral.

He pulled up, skimming the dome. And then he was banking again, peeling away from a helicopter gunship.

'Sky – where are you? Can you see a way out?'

Now there was no response. All around him the air burned and swarmed with insect-machines and gunships. He turned hard to avoid a starburst, then dived clear of hornet-machines, then twisted away as the air ahead shimmered with heat rays.

With awful clarity he saw a sickening sight. He watched a drone crash directly into a gunship. It happened hundreds of metres away, but the resulting shockwave was so forceful it rolled the wing.

Righting himself, steadying the craft, he watched in horror as the gunship fell in fiery fragments. Did that drone deliberately crash into that warplane? Was there a type of drone he didn't know about – a kind of flying bomb?

'Sky – this is getting even worse! Have you got clear?'

Still no response. There was nothing he could do to help her in any case. He could barely help himself. Turning and diving and twisting, he searched desperately for an escape route.

There – clear air beneath those gunships! Firing his pulsejet, he darted into the space and he kept firing the jet as he zipped across the rooftops. At the Thames he dropped low and raced westwards.

The violence followed him. It was spreading like a tidal wave. He kept his thumbs locked into the jet-triggers and he skimmed at its outer edge, his wing shuddering with the heat and the shockwaves.

Pressing his body low, streamlining himself against the wing, he raced onwards. But as he zipped beneath Waterloo Bridge he felt a sickening loss of thrust. The wing dipped, almost ditching him into the Thames.

Holding his breath, he released the jet-triggers, depressed

them again. Nothing happened. He clicked them again and again, but nothing.

The pulsejet was dead.

Only now did he notice that a meter in his visor was flashing red and had curved down to zero.

His airspeed was dropping fast, and the firestorm was rolling over him in full fury, raging everywhere he looked.

Directly overhead, a fighter jet opened fire, its two sidewinder missiles snaking through the sky. One missile struck its target, an infrared flare lighting up Hal's night-vision, cancelling the crosshair that had been there an instant before.

The second heat-seeker must have failed to achieve a lock, because it arced onwards, aimless, before dropping onto the Houses of Parliament. It exploded on impact, punching a hole in the roof.

Even as Hal was absorbing this sight, a downed drone arced in flames and struck Big Ben. Glass and rubble burst out of the clocktower, and the giant bell tumbled to the ground, clanging onto Westminster Bridge.

Skimming low to the water, Hal zipped underneath the bridge even as it crunched and rumbled with the impact. And just as he flew clear, a drone came down in the river throwing up water and steam.

Veering away from this, Hal zipped north. Now he darted between the buildings, twisting and turning, giving no thought to his direction, merely reacting to stay alive.

Ahead of him now was a skyscraper. It was on fire, a drone embedded in its lower storeys. Hal banked away from this inferno.

But then he had to turn again to avoid a lone drone, and again to steer clear of a lurking gunship.

Twice, three times, Hal swept away from the ravaged building, but each time other obstacles drove him back towards it. And as he tried once more to fly clear, there was a terrifying titanic roar – as if the air itself were being torn to shreds.

The building was falling. It didn't topple, like Hal's tower had. Instead it collapsed vertically, fire and smoke and dust rushing upwards as masonry and glass and metal poured down in shuddering shockwaves.

These shockwaves rolled the wing, and kept rolling it, Hal's world spinning. At the same time a dust storm swept over him. Now, even his enhanced vision showed him little but soupy chaos.

A massive surface, like the wall of a canyon, loomed suddenly out of the murk. He banked away with a split-second to spare. Other threats whooshed by before he even knew they were there.

He realised with shock that he had dropped extremely low – he was skimming the streets. He swerved left to dodge a row of lampposts. He rolled the wing and shot between two stationary buses.

Ahead was a railway bridge, low and narrow. He steadied the wing, kept his nerve, and arrowed beneath.

He needed to gain altitude, but the pulsejet was dead, and down here in the dust storm he had barely any lift. And now a hot rain was falling – a rain of powered concrete and glass – and that too kept him pinned at street level.

So all he could do was follow the twists and turns, a microsecond's warning each time an obstacle loomed from the dust.

The streets turned back on themselves, zigzagged, the compass in his visor swinging wildly. The feeling he was trapped in a maze.

And all the while warfare raged. Crosshairs were everywhere. And everywhere rockets blazed and heat rays scorched the air and objects of metal and concrete and glass were coming apart.

He swerved left as a lump of masonry crunched down into the street. A flaming car, tossed by an explosion, came tumbling past.

He must now be flying back towards the building that fell, because the dust storm was growing thicker than ever. Formless lumps appeared in the sludge without warning, Hal reacting on pure instinct, dodging threats before he was conscious they were there.

He pulled clear of a battletank, then pressed himself flat against the wing as he swept beneath another bridge. He didn't know how much longer he could do this. He was dizzy, light-headed. Physically exhausted from the demands of manhandling the wing. Mentally drained from living on hair-trigger instincts minute after minute.

An eruption of glass leapt out of a shop front, he rolled away from it. A wall of fire rushed at him, he swept clear.

In his visor, the pulsejet meter caught his eye. It was no longer flashing red. The gauge was creeping upwards. So, the jet must be powered by some kind of fuel cell, and a dynamo, recharging as he flew . . .

How much charge had trickled back into the cell? Did he dare use it now, and risk exhausting it again? No, he forced himself to wait, to save the jet as his absolute last resort.

He whipped past a skyscraper, and in its glass he glimpsed his own reflection. And for an instant, there alongside him, was a second shadowy falcon.

'Sky!' he said, twisting, sweeping his gaze. 'Where are you?'

'They're getting closer!' Sky shrieked. 'I've got no – I can't – they—'

She was mortally afraid. So terrified she could barely speak.

And a moment later he saw why. Finally gaining altitude, weaving between more buildings, he got a clear sighting of Sky.

And he also saw two beetle-drones.

To his disbelief, they had targeted Sky. They were locked to her tail and were hunting her through the streets, their circular saws rasping. She was weaving frantically, trying to shake them off, but they followed her every turn, drawing closer by the second.

'I can't outrun them!' she shouted. 'My jet is drained. I don't—' She shrieked as a sawblade missed her by inches.

Sweeping behind her, all Hal could do was watch in horror.

'They're too fast,' she shouted. 'There's no—'

Another near miss made her scream.

'Hal, I don't – I don't have long, so I need you to listen. I want you to promise me one thing. If it's the last thing you do, I want you to find . . . and I want you to . . .'

Her voice was cracking, incoherent, but in any case Hal was no longer listening. He was utterly focused on what he was about to do, even if he couldn't entirely believe he was actually going to do it.

He eyed his jet meter. Was there now enough charge for three sustained blasts? What if it cut out mid-manoeuvre?

Again Sky screamed as one of the beetle-drones almost shredded her with its saws. He daren't wait a second longer.

He fired the pulsejet once, and the burst of power took him surging above the drones. And now – picking his moment – knowing he would only get one chance –

As Sky twisted her wing to starboard, and both drones followed, one swept above the other. For a second they were both directly below Hal.

He fired his pulsejet, threw his wing into a powerdive. Flattening out at the last instant, he smashed the belly of his wing into the shell of the uppermost drone.

The impact knocked the breath out of him, and the drone buzzed furiously against its attacker, but Hal didn't flinch or hesitate – he thrust his thumbs into the jet-triggers a third time and he kept driving downwards, crashing one drone into the other.

Both drones rasped and shrieked, their eyes blazing crimson. Their mandibles twisted upwards, their sawblades whirring within inches of Hal's face. But still Hal drove downwards, using every last drop of the pulsejet's power, rocketing the machines earthwards.

With a second to spare he peeled away. The drones' inertia took them thundering into the ground – they crunched along the street, smattering like real insects hitting a windscreen, leaving a long trail of oil and bits of wing and broken shell.

Gaining altitude, Hal let out a long shuddering breath. Numbly, he noted that the skies around them were clear. Their chase with the drones had taken them outside the battlezone.

'Are you okay?' he said to Sky, his voice unsteady to his own ears.

She said nothing, just went on circling above the smashed drones. Spiralling higher, Hal pulled a series of manoeuvres. Letting out another long breath, he concluded that his wing was undamaged. This glider must be tougher than it looked.

Eventually, Sky spoke. 'What I said before, about you getting in my way. I . . . I can't remember exactly, but I think I called you a liability.'

'It doesn't matter,' Hal said.

'Yes, but what I want to say is . . . what you just did . . .'

'You already saved my life,' Hal said. 'This just makes us even.'

She said nothing more, and for a while they just circled in the rain, wingtip to wingtip. Peering east, Hal saw a lone explosion, but no other signs of violence.

'The fighting – it's died down. For now at least. So what do we do? Head back to St Paul's, start all over again?'

'No,' Sky said. 'We've been chasing our tails. It got us nowhere. We need to think this through. We have to land. There's something I need to show you.'

'Land? Land where?'

'I know a place. I went there before, when all this first started. If nothing else, it'll help us get some perspective.'

With that she was wheeling away, flying back towards the Thames. His mind still numb, his whole body shaking from the excess adrenaline, it was all Hal could do to drop into her slipstream and follow.

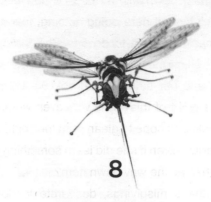

8

Deathtrap

In the darkness, deep beneath the streets, Jess hugged her knees and listened. Was it finally over? Fighting must have raged directly overhead, because the noise had boomed through these tunnels, shaking dust from the ceiling. It had gone on and on and was utterly terrifying.

But at last everything had fallen quiet. All around her, people were stirring, whispering to each other that it must be finished. Somewhere a baby was crying.

Unsteadily, Jess got to her feet. If the fighting had lulled, it was time to return to the surface. Already she had put it off too long. Hal would never find her all the way down here. So she needed to start looking for him. But how? Where would she even begin? And how long before violence broke out once more? Was going back up there anything other than suicide?

She slumped back down against the wall. She rocked back and forth. She couldn't just sit here doing nothing, fearing the worst, she would go mad! She had to do *something*. Yet what could she do?

She reached into her satchel and took out the digital vault. But what was the point of this? This was even worse than doing nothing. What could she hope to glean from the vault, except more reasons to be fearful? Even if she did learn something useful, what good could it do her, all the way down here?

She ignored these misgivings, desperate to do something, anything to distract herself. She rested the vault on her knees, powered it on and entered the password.

She scrolled past the files she had opened before; she had seen quite enough of those menacing blueprints.

Sifting through other folders, she found one that contained reams and reams of stored emails. A lump rose in her throat as she realised most of these had been sent or received by her father. She couldn't bring herself to read a single one, instead telling herself she would come back to them.

Searching on, she found files full of technical memos. Opening a few, looking at the by-lines, she found they were all written by her father's business partner, Professor Dominic Starr.

At random, she picked one to read. It was entitled 'Neural-Mimicry in Fluid-State Circuitry'. It took her several minutes to get through it. Then she read a second memo: 'The Emergence of Non-Human Intelligence, and the Hyper-Evolution that Will Inevitably Follow'.

If Jess's intention had been to distract herself, then it certainly worked. Because as she read deeper into the professor's work, she became so fascinated that she forgot everything else, even where she was or what might be happening above or how sick she felt. While she read, she pulled cereal bars from her satchel and ate the entire packet, barely even registering she had done it.

The science in these notes was difficult, and Professor Starr's language was often obscure, but that only made her focus harder and absorbed her more completely. And the content was surprisingly benign and optimistic. When she opened the vault, she had expected to see and read about military machines. But in all these memos, thousands upon thousands of words, the professor made not a single reference to combat drones.

Instead, he wrote more generally about artificial intelligence. And A.I. was a discipline, the professor stated over and over, that had the potential to greatly benefit all of humankind. In fact, as she read more and more of his notes, Jess got the impression that the professor himself was on the verge of a truly remarkable breakthrough.

From what she could gather, this breakthrough would mark a quantum leap in machine learning. But its knock-on effects would ripple out into every other field of human endeavour, from astrophysics to manufacturing to medicine. She was still a long way from grasping the entire picture, but the professor's notes left little room for doubt: his work had the capacity to *transform the future*, and vastly for the better.

Jess's head began to swim with all this. Eventually she slumped back and blinked. She closed the memos. Then she went back to one of the original files she had first opened in the underpass.

Here was that blueprint of the wasp-like drone. At the top of the page was the legend 'SWARM Project'. And at the bottom it said: 'Phase Two Phenotype [Projected]'.

She studied this evil-looking war machine, and she tried to equate it with everything she had read about the professor's research. Surely this kind of military technology was the *opposite* of enlightened progress.

Was it possible Professor Starr didn't even know that his own company was developing war machines? Could his ideas have been twisted somehow, used in ways he had never intended?

A noise made her jump. The digital vault clattered to the stone floor. Scrabbling for it, she stuffed it back into her satchel. And then she was on her feet, gripping the satchel to her chest, her pulse racing.

Dust was raining from the ceiling, and at first she thought fighting was again raging above. But no. It was even worse than that. Because these tremors were deeper, and they came with those crunching, grinding sounds she had heard before.

All around her people were on their feet, shining torch beams into the train tunnels.

'Coming from down there . . .'

'It's louder – what is it?'

'Some kind of machinery . . .'

'Thought I saw something moving . . .'

And still the tremors were getting heavier, the noises more distinct. Jess picked out scraping sounds, like the sharpening of giant blades. And the clinking of metal, like hundreds of pickaxes striking stone . . .

All of this twisted in her mind – and merged with certain things she had seen on the vault – and suddenly she *knew*. With utter horror, she understood what must be lurking down here in the dark . . .

Abruptly the tremors and the noises stopped.

Just as before, a hush fell. Hundreds of people were silent and still.

But then they all began talking at once, many of them arguing.

'. . . take our chances at the surface . . .'

'. . . warzone up there!'

'. . . danger in plain sight, not like down here . . .'

'. . . going nowhere, not until they say it's finished . . .'

Shouting over them all, calling for calm, was a single voice.

'Listen to me, please, all of you.' It was Dr Pavel. 'We need to keep our heads and we need to make a plan.' She paused while the hubbub died down. 'As I'm sure you all know,' she said, 'a little while ago an expedition went into the train tunnels to investigate those noises. None of those who went down there have yet come back.'

At this, a fresh babble of voices rose up, and she waited for it to subside. 'I still believe there is a rational explanation for everything we've heard,' she said. 'In any case, there are people down there, and they may need our help. I intend to lead a second party to look for them. I have six people with me, but we need more volunteers.'

'N-no, you can't go!' Jess stammered, stumbling closer. She shielded her eyes as torch beams swung towards her. 'You can't go into the tunnels!'

'I'm sorry, Jess, we don't have a choice,' Dr Pavel said. 'People may be lost down there. My son among them.'

'They . . . they're not lost. They're never coming back.'

'I know you're scared,' Dr Pavel said, 'but there's no need to say things like that. You can't know what's happened to them, any more than we do.'

'But I do know! There were things I'd forgotten, and others I didn't want to think about. But I've known all along. I remember what phenotype means!'

'She's delirious,' a man said gruffly, turning his torchlight away. 'And she's wasting our time. We need to get started.'

'Listen to me, please!' Jess said. 'I'm trying to tell you what's down there. It's the machines! The machines are down here with us!'

'That's ridiculous,' said the gruff-voiced man. 'We all saw the drones. They're airborne.'

'The first ones, yes – but they're changing! We need to go to the surface before it's too late . . .'

But it was no use. The more she pleaded, and tried to explain, the more these people treated her as if she were crazed. Even Dr Pavel had run out of patience and had turned away.

So there was nothing more Jess could do for them. All she could do was try to save herself. As terrified as she was at the idea of returning to the surface, she now knew for certain she could not stay down here.

Lots of other people were heading for the exits. The criss-crossing of their torchlight was disorientating, but it was enough for Jess to shuffle and grope her way towards the escalators.

But halfway there she came to a halt. Because somewhere up ahead someone was shouting a name. They were shouting *her* name! Had she imagined it? No – there it was again!

'Jess! Jess Strider! Where are you, Jess?'

'We know you're here somewhere. Come on out.'

In a daze of relief and disbelief, Jess stumbled towards the voices. They were not voices she recognised, but that was not important. These men must be friends of her father's. Or perhaps they were helping Hal search for her. Whoever they were, they had found her, and she was no longer lost!

'Where are you, Jess?'

'We know you're down here. It's no use hiding.'

'You felt those tremors just now. Do you have any idea what that was? Don't make us stay down here any longer than we have to.'

The voices were clearer now, and they sounded increasingly impatient. Even unfriendly.

Even threatening.

'That's enough now, Jess, come on out.'

'Stupid girl. This isn't a game. Show yourself.'

'And don't even think about making a run for it. We've got two men watching the exits.'

Jess took a step back. And another. She shrank into a side passage. Barely breathing, she watched the two strangers come into view. By the light of their torches they were giants, wearing some kind of military armour. At their waists they wore holsters, and guns. On their shoulders each had a symbol. It was difficult to see in the gloom, but it looked like a mechanical wasp.

Jess's pulse pounded in her ears. These men weren't *looking* for her — they were *hunting* her. Who were they? What did they want?

Their torchlight became still. She heard them talking to Dr Pavel. Then the torchlight turned and came back this way.

She shrank deeper into the side passage, and she slumped to the ground. Curled around her satchel, she froze in fear, as the bootsteps of the strangers drew near.

9

The Roof of the World

As he and Sky soared downriver, Hal was stunned by all he saw. That latest wave of violence had proved more destructive than anything that had come before.

Here was the Palace of Westminster, collapsed in on itself. And Big Ben decapitated. Roads were choked with rubble and pockmarked with bomb blasts. Powerlines were down and sparking and burst water mains threw up fountains, and over it all hung an acrid smoke that burned at the back of Hal's throat.

Drones buzzed amid the devastation, their wings fanning the flames. He and Sky steered clear of them. Although for the moment they were not a major threat. The violence had waned, and so the machines were no longer in battle mode. Their movements were unhurried, almost languid. Their eyes were a dull gleam rather than shining a fiery red.

Most of them were intent on scavenging amid the wreckage. Hal saw one take off with the tailfin of a fighter plane. Between them, another pair carried the turret of an armoured car. Others reclaimed the remains of their fellow machines.

'Every time I see them do this it gets more horrifying,' Sky said. 'Once they've collected all the military stuff they start taking anything they can find. I watched them strip down a bus. I saw one carrying a lamppost. Kids' bikes. Everything. It all goes down into that factory of theirs, and comes out again as more drones.'

Hal closed his eyes, a lump rising in his throat. He envisaged this mechanical plague eating through the entire city, turning everything into copies of themselves, until nothing existed except war machines.

He opened his eyes. 'So what's our plan? Where are we headed?'

'It's not far now,' Sky said. 'Believe it or not, you might even enjoy the last leg of the journey. When I came here before it made me forget everything else, at least for a minute.'

Intrigued, Hal dropped into her slipstream and followed her towards London Bridge. A colossal, sharp-edged structure loomed up ahead. Here was the skyscraper known as the Shard.

Staying low, firing her pulsejet, Sky arrowed straight towards it. Closer and closer, the tower soaring so high above them it seemed to stretch away forever. And still she held a direct collision course, faster and faster.

'Sky? What exactly are you—'

At the last possible moment she pulled up, swept into a near-vertical climb. Catching his breath, Hal followed her lead. Now they were racing upwards, skimming the skyscraper, its glassy surface flowing beneath them like dark water.

Ahead of Hal, Sky's wing briefly flashed with hot colours, and seemed to spread its wings like a fiery phoenix. Then it disappeared completely, and she was once again the magical flying girl he had first glimpsed above the aerodrome.

Hal raced after her, and they rocketed higher and higher, and he found he was grinning, and in his helmet he heard her shriek with pleasure. And still they rushed up and up, as if this truly might go on forever, and here was a pathway to the stars.

But finally they crested the tower, burst free of the top. The wind hit them hard, Hal's wing flipping over once, twice.

Bringing his aircraft under control, he looked down upon a wide platform. It was mounted on rollers and was perhaps used for cleaning or maintenance.

Sky was already looping down to land on this platform. Her landing, just as before, was elegant and acrobatic. Trying to copy her technique, Hal only succeeded in belly-flopping his wing, careering across the platform, coming to a halt only inches before tipping off the other side.

'Your landings need some work,' Sky said, after they had taken off their helmets. 'But okay, I'll admit it, you haven't done too badly on the wing.'

And then she shocked him by standing on tiptoes and kissing him on the cheek. 'Taking on two drones, unarmed . . .' She shook her head. 'I'm still struggling to believe you actually did that for me.'

She moved away, and went to sit at the edge of the platform, her feet dangling above the void. Hal just stood there with the feeling of her kiss on his cheek. Eventually he went to sit at her side. And for a while they just sat in silence and got their breath back and looked out. Below them the city was a vast blackness, dotted with stars of fire. And above was its mirror image, real stars shining through as the storm clouds disappeared.

Eventually, Hal said, 'One thing I don't understand – why were those drones chasing you in the first place? I thought the wing was invisible to them, the same as to people.'

'I have a theory about that,' Sky said. 'I was right behind a drone when it got hit by a missile. As it exploded, I saw something burst out. It was like a cloud of gas, or a powder, and it was luminous green. I flew straight through it, and some of it stuck to me.' She shivered. 'Next thing I know, two drones are coming after me in a killing frenzy.'

'So this chemical,' Hal said, 'it was some kind of marker? It tagged you as a target?'

'I think so, yes. Didn't I hear that once about real insects – about hornets? If you swat one it gives off a pheromone and the rest will come after you.'

'But I destroyed those two machines back there – why didn't I get tagged?'

'I don't know. It was raining pretty hard by then. Maybe water washes it off.' She lifted one arm. 'When it happened, I was covered in the stuff. But look, it's gone. And I don't see any on you.'

Hal blew out his cheeks. 'So – that's one more thing to keep in mind. When a drone is going down in flames, don't fly too close.'

'Damn,' she said, smiling slightly, 'now what are we meant to do for fun?'

Hal stared out over the city. 'Before the fighting started, you were talking about your mum, and my dad. You said something about them being trapped. Trapped where exactly?'

'Beneath the aerodrome.'

'Beneath it?'

'Yes. You do know what it's built on top of, don't you?'

Hal looked away. 'I suppose I always had the idea that some of the work went on below ground. But I could never get Dad to talk about it.'

'Most of the real work happens down there, from what I can gather,' she said. 'They built the aerodrome on top of an old nuclear command bunker. I've never been down there either, but apparently it's massive – like a whole town underground.'

He looked at her. 'And that's where Dad is now – and he can't get out?'

She nodded. 'After the drones got loose, him and my mum and all the engineers went down there. It's where they've been developing their "antidote", or whatever it's called. They were going to use it to bring down the drones. But Tony Daegar made some excuse to stay at the surface. Once everyone else was underground, he put the compound on emergency lockdown. He killed the whole place dead.'

Hal listened to this in shock and disbelief and finally in fury. 'And he's willing to leave them down there,' he said through gritted teeth. 'And the antidote too. Just so he can sell the blueprints and get rich.'

'And without the mastercodes on that vault, there's not a thing we can do about it,' Sky said. 'That bunker was built to withstand a nuclear blast. Unless we can reactivate the systems, no one's getting in and no one's getting out.'

'So we need to find those men who went after Jess,' Hal said. 'But how?'

Sky held out her flight helmet. 'Take a look at this. Tell me what I'm missing.'

Hal looked at her quizzically.

'Originally, the wing was designed for reconnaissance,' she said. 'These helmets automatically keep a log of everything.'

Hal pulled her helmet over his head. He felt her operating the dial on the right-hand side. In the visor display, a message appeared: 'Recon Mode. Playback.'

And now it felt like Hal was back in the air. Because the helmet was replaying everything Sky had seen and heard as she piloted her wing. She took his hand, placed it on the dial.

'Twist this to fast forward.'

Hal twisted the dial and the cityscape rushed past at greater speed. He watched through Sky's eyes as she landed near Tower Bridge. And suddenly he saw himself standing there in front of her, looking bedraggled and lost and in shock.

This moment whipped past, and Sky was back in the air, evading drones and warplanes. Then she was on the roof of his building, coming towards him, hugging him. And then the pair of them were pressed back to back while Karl Daegar menaced them with his gnat-machines. Hal relived it all: their confrontation with Tony Daegar, the destruction of the apartment, their desperate scramble to escape.

Now he saw himself riding his own wing. Here he found himself slowing the action to normal speed. He watched himself spiral towards his burning building. He heard Sky telling him how to control the wing, and he listened to his own scared words. And finally he watched himself skim clear of the inferno. He shivered. Seeing this through Sky's eyes, it was an even narrower escape than he realised.

He wound forward again. Now Sky was speeding after the gunboats.

'Where have you got to?' Sky said.

'You're coasting above Tony Daegar.' Hal slowed the video to normal speed. 'Hang on – the boats are stopping. One of them is pulling up at a pier.'

'Yes. South of St Paul's. That's where the men got out. We need to work out where they went from there.'

Hal watched the four militiamen. They were orangey patches of heat moving through the cold, green and white streets. For two seconds he lost sight of them – Sky had looked over at the gunboats. And by the time the helmet's camera turned back to the streets, the men weren't there. All four orangey figures had vanished.

'They went underground,' Hal said, without hesitation. 'If they had gone into a building we'd still see their bodyheat.'

'Let me see,' Sky said.

She put on the helmet and after a minute she said: 'Yes, you're right, it's obvious! How could I miss that?'

'It's just like you said – flying the wing, the world coming to pieces, it's impossible to even think. But I'm right, aren't I – those men went underground. And they had a lead on Jess. So she must be down there too . . .'

'St Paul's tube station,' Sky said, still watching the video. 'It's right there, where the men disappeared! Yes – that's it. That's where she must be.'

She stood. 'Right then, let's go. Fingers crossed they haven't found her yet. And if they have we – whoa – what was that?' She put a hand to her heart. 'There it was again! You felt it?'

Yes, Hal had. And there it was a third time – a concussion so heavy it was less of a sound than a feeling – like a slap to the chest. He felt the platform beneath them tremble, as if the Shard was shaking at its roots. He pulled on his helmet and engaged telescopic vision to stare west.

Scanning the skies above the crash site, he saw a large aircraft tear past. It was a supersonic bomber. And there went another, and a third. After each pass an explosion followed, cracking across the city like a thunderclap.

'Laser-guided bombs,' Sky said. 'What do they call the massive ones – bunker busters? They're dropping them into the nest.'

Bomber after bomber roared over. And afterwards there was that slap to the chest, and the sound of glass breaking all across the city, and dust and smoke pouring out of the chasm.

'It's not going to work, is it?' Hal said. 'We saw what happened last time they attacked the nest. The drones swarmed worse than ever. This is just pouring oil on the flames.'

'We can't wait in any case,' Sky said, going to her wing. 'Tony Daegar's men have a head start. We can't waste another second.'

Hal nodded and collected his own glider. In tandem they launched themselves from the platform, dropped out and away.

As they did so, the earthquake bombs continued to fall. And already the drones were rising up in a frenzied swarm. And once again Hal and Sky were heading into the heart of a firestorm.

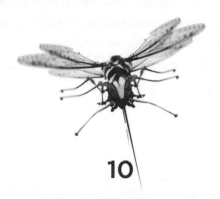

10

Desperate Measures

Ka-crump – Ka-crump—

Even as Jess cowered in the darkness, even as armed men stalked her, this new terror arose. Concussions thumped through the passageways, raining dust on her head. She curled herself tighter into a ball, and she screamed inwardly. What now?

Ka-crump – Ka-crump—

She could feel each concussion in her bones. They could be nothing other than massive explosions. But something told her this was not happening at the surface. Could bombs be exploding beneath the earth?

Ka-crump – Ka-crump – Ka-crump—

It was getting worse, the detonations coming in quicker succession. What was happening? Was the whole city caving in?

Finally it stopped.

The last aftershock trembled away. All became still.

The only sound now was the pattering of dust. Jess clamped a hand to her mouth, muffling a cough. During the bombardment, the strangers' torchlight had come to a halt. But now it was moving once more, flaring around the entrance to this passageway.

'Come on now, Jess,' one of the men called. 'Every second this goes on it gets worse. You don't want to be down here any more than we do.'

'We know you're here somewhere,' the other man said. 'That nice Dr Pavel told us you'd doubled back this way.'

Jess's grip tightened on her satchel. She looked down at it, as if seeing it for the first time. And suddenly she knew, without doubt, why these men were here. They wanted the digital vault.

They wanted the SWARM blueprints.

This fact drove Jess to her feet. And by the refracted glare of the strangers' torchlight, she lurched away from them, clutching her satchel. She reached the end of the passageway and staggered out onto the platform where she had started.

Now it was practically deserted, and in almost total darkness. But near her feet was a glowing object. Someone had dropped a torch! It was a child's Spider-Man torch, and its battery was almost dead, but it was better than nothing, and Jess used it to light her way along the platform.

Even so, each step was a greater effort than the last. Her fear was a physical thing, cloying, trying to hold her back. Because there were no exits ahead of her. If she wanted to escape these men, and keep the blueprints away from them, she knew there was only one place left to go . . .

Glancing back, she saw powerful torch beams sweeping onto the platform. And seeing this pushed her onwards.

But already she was approaching the end of the platform. With a dread that bordered on disbelief, she stumbled closer and closer to a brick wall. It was ten paces away, then five, then one.

And now she was standing right in front of it. She laid her forehead against its cold surface, and she closed her eyes, and for the moment it was all she could do just to keep breathing.

Come on – keep moving! You *can't* let them have the blueprints!

Forcing her eyes open, she lurched to the edge of the platform, and she shone her weak light onto the tracks. And then shakily she climbed down.

She looked up and stared into the abyss of the train tunnel. But when she tried to take her first step forward, the weight of her fear kept her feet rooted.

Come *on* – Dr Pavel and the others went down there – be quick and you might catch up with them!

But what if she didn't? What if she found herself all alone, and lost down there, with only a child's torch about to run out of batteries?

That idea would have been terrifying enough. But there was even worse. Because those crunching, grinding tremors she had heard – they had come from somewhere within these tunnels, she was sure of it . . .

What breed of monster might she find down there in the dark?

Locked in such fears, she didn't even notice the sound of bootsteps on the platform behind her, or even the flood of torchlight.

'Fits the description,' said a man's voice. 'And she's got hold of something – must be the device. What's she doing, just standing there?'

'Jess Strider,' said a second voice. 'You've given us the run around. You'd better get back up here. Don't make us come and get you.'

Jess barely heard the men. She only stared into the void of the tunnel, desperately willing herself to go forward, but physically unable to take a single step.

'Look out!'

Before the words even left Sky's mouth, she and Hal had thrown their wings towards the ground. A split-second later, heat rays zapped above their heads.

No time to catch their breath – more danger dead ahead – gunships loosing missiles. The pair of them pulled into a switchback, Hal gritting his teeth against the G-force.

'This is – this is only getting worse,' Hal said, breathless, once they were clear. 'Were those drones firing at us?'

'I don't think so – we were just in the way. Even so, it was too close. We'll never find a way through at this rate.'

As Hal had predicted, the bombardment of the nest had not stopped the drones. It only made them rise up, more aggressive than ever. The military had launched counter-strikes, and now the sky was full of dogfights and starbursts and fireballs.

It meant that Hal and Sky were struggling to reach St Paul's tube station. Every time they turned in that direction, violence forced them away. Twisting on his wing, Hal looked to the east and he saw nothing but explosions – a shifting wall of blazing colours.

'We'll have to loop round, try to bypass the worst of it,' he said, hardly able to hear himself above the noise. 'There's less fighting to the north. If we—'

'Look out!' Sky shouted again, and in tandem they rolled into corkscrew dives, twisting clear as a swarm of beetle-machines went rasping past.

'You – you're right,' Sky said between breaths, 'we can't take a direct line. We'll have to head north, then come back down.'

As they swung round and powered north, Hal's eyes darted after crosshairs and other perils. Because yes, this corridor was relatively clear, but even here was a pack of gunships hovering in their flight-path, and then low-flying jets were screaming past, and here was a burning building to avoid, together with powerful updrafts.

The pair of them twisted and weaved through all this, their moves often synchronised, their wings forming shadowy mirror images.

Their route took them as far north as the BT Tower. Hal stared at its colossal remains, and the great swathe of London that lay flattened beneath. As they continued over Regent's Park, he heard a haunting sound – a shrieking howling cacophony – it was all the terrified animals in London Zoo.

Suddenly, it was hard to believe this was even his city. Think back to only this morning, watching boats drawing lazy patterns upon the Thames. Think of that blue sky, airliners leaving their contrails. Now look at this ravaged land. This alien warscape. The whole thing drawn in green and white, cut across with streaks of orange and red.

And as they curved east, and started to sweep back down, it only grew worse. Here was the British Museum, cracked down the middle, spilling its treasures. All around it, department stores and restaurants and hotels lay in ruins.

But increasingly Hal's eyes were drawn to something else. Something far more significant than any material damage. He began to spot more and more people on the streets. Below him now there were scores of them – scurrying yellow and orange blobs.

'Where did they all come from?' Sky said, echoing his thoughts. 'A moment ago the whole city looked deserted.'

They were now passing above Holborn tube station. It was surrounded by a dense mass of body heat. Were all these people scrambling to get into the station? No – they were flooding away from it.

'They're all coming up from underground,' Hal said. 'They must have taken shelter down there. But now they're coming to the surface.'

'They're coming up now, into the worst fighting yet?' Sky said. 'Why would they do that?'

Just thinking about this question caused a cold twisting in Hal's stomach. Something must be happening beneath the earth. Whatever it might be, these people feared it more than they feared what was happening up here.

'Whatever it is, Jess is down there in the middle of it,' he said. 'We have to find her. Fast.'

Firing his pulsejet, he powered south east, Sky at his wingtip. They passed over more and more people. Great frantic swarms of them.

'What could it be – what's happening down there?' Sky said.

'I've got no idea. But whatever it is—'

'Eyes up,' she said. 'Look at all that. We'll have to turn.'

Hal raised his head. Gunfire and explosions filled his vision – a twisting dragon of fiery colours. Dozens of drones and gunships had come together in a mass dogfight.

'We'll have to find another route,' Sky said. 'We could loop around to the south, see if that's any better. Hal – what are you doing? We need to turn.'

'We've turned too many times.'

'We can't fly into that!'

'We've got no choice. Jess is down there with . . . with whatever it is. If we don't reach her now we never will.'

Ahead of them the monstrous violence grew and grew.

Finally, Sky said, 'Okay then, we go through. All or nothing, right? So then, here goes, take a deep breath . . .'

The violence swooped to meet them, flicking its fiery tail, opening its flaming jaws, swallowing them whole.

In the end, the weight of Jess's fear proved too great. Staring into the abyss of the train tunnel, she was simply unable to go forward. Trembling, she turned around, lifting one arm to shield her eyes. The armed men were no more than outlines behind the glare of their flashlights.

'Who – who are you – what do you want with the blueprints? What are you going to do with them? H-how can you even think to—'

'None of that is your concern,' one of the men said. 'You just need to get up here. Now.'

She gripped her satchel even tighter, and to her amazement she found herself taking a step backwards.

'P-people like you,' she stammered, 'you're even worse than the machines! They're just doing what they were built to do. But people can choose!'

She took another step into the train tunnel, and another.

'D-don't you see where all this is leading? You'll end up slaves just like the rest of us!'

'Enough of this,' one of the men said. 'Clarke, get down there and grab her. Clarke, did you hear me? She's thinking of making a run for it. If she does, you're going down there after her.'

He got no response. And only now, as Jess took another step backwards, did she notice that the second man had become very still. His torchlight was frozen, pointing into the train tunnel.

The other man moved his beam away from Jess, shone it over her head. Then he too became still.

Jess stopped. She barely breathed.

'Miss Strider,' one of the men said quietly. 'You need to step towards me.'

She remained rooted, blinking slowly.

'Trust me,' the man said, 'you need to move away from the tunnel.'

Both men took a step back, their torchlight wavering.

'Stay where you are then,' the second man hissed, 'just throw us the damn bag!'

Jess put a hand to her throat, squeezed.

Slowly she turned, stared into the train tunnel.

By the light of the torch beams she saw the dull gleam of metal, black and red. And hulking, angular shapes that to her shocked brain made no sense.

In the next moment those shapes were shifting, hissing and stomping into motion, surging out of the darkness. And Jess's whole world was collapsing into sharp and deadly chaos.

* * *

+ + + New Apparatus Located + + + Analysing Composition + + + Assessing Utility + + +

Deep in the nest of the machines, a large, cylindrical object lies embedded in the wall of a shaft. It is one of the earthquake bombs. For some reason, this one failed to detonate. Now Seeker drones crawl all over it, their antennae twitching, their ultrasonic chatter becoming fevered.

+ + + Analysis Complete + + + Ordnance Identified ~ Massive Yield Penetrator Bomb + + + Rated Highly Efficacious + + + Scrutinise and Duplicate + + + Scrutinise and Duplicate + + +

11

Mechanical Animals

Hal was suddenly certain he had made a fatal mistake. He should never have led Sky into this firestorm. Neither of them could possibly live through it. All around them, above and below, there was nothing but speeding screaming metal, much of it bursting apart into razor shards.

Hal banked hard to avoid a gunship, its rotorblades almost shredding him. Then he barrel-rolled his wing and zipped between two hornet-machines, Sky darting through just behind. Then in tandem they twisted away from an exploding rocket, the shock-wave sending them both spinning.

'We'll never make it!' Sky shrieked. 'We have to go back!'

'We can't – we've come too far. It's—'

Another explosion sent them tumbling. They were trapped within this hurricane, tossed around inside it. Without the readouts in his visor, Hal would not have known east from west, or up from down. He jerked his head, swept his gaze, looking for a way out, seeing nothing but endless violence.

It was now so intense it was formless. There were no individual sounds, just a single saturating roar. Hal could barely tell drones and warplanes apart, and in any case it made no difference – either could end his life at any second.

'Three o'clock – an opening!' Sky shouted. 'I'm going for it.'

Hal swung his glider and followed her. But this airspace didn't stay open for long. A flaming comet fell from above, and Sky yelled 'Look out!' and they rolled away either side.

Immediately Hal had to dive clear of a starburst, then veer away from a sweeping heat ray, and once again he was utterly lost within this violence, twisting clear of hazard after hazard, each near miss closer than the last, his reactions pushed to breaking point. He was hit again by a wave of hopelessness – neither he or Sky could possibly survive this.

But his despair lasted no more than a second. And when he passed through it something extraordinary happened. In the midst of this terrible violence, he became utterly calm. The firestorm seemed to quieten and even slow around him, and he could see his own space within it.

He blinked and saw three drones ahead – he dived beneath them without missing a heartbeat. His grip lightened on his wing and he twisted away from a warplane and continued his roll to sweep beneath a drone.

The violence raged as fiercely as ever, but now Hal saw every danger distinctly. He twisted and dived away from each one with perfect precision, without thought or feeling, with cold, unclouded judgement.

'I see a way out,' he said.

'What? I can't hear you! What did you—'

'Follow me,' he shouted above the noise, and he pitched his wing towards the ground, then banked round ninety degrees and powered beneath a howling dogfight.

Streamlining his body against the wing, he kept firing his pulse-jet, swept between high-rise buildings, then dived down across lower rooftops – and as quick as that, it was done. While they had been lost within it, the violence appeared boundless, but in fact, they had flown clear of it in seconds.

'We're alive!' Sky shouted, twisting on her wing to look back. 'I can't believe it – we're out the other side and we're alive! I want to hug you – I want to – I don't know, I . . .'

She pulled her wing into a vertical climb, then kept curving over, pulling off a perfect loop-the-loop while she whooped with relief.

'I'm telling you, Hal, if I live through all this, I will never again take a single minute of my life for granted!'

Hal flooded with similar elation and relief, and for a minute he just listened to his own breathing as his wing bumped on air pockets.

But then he focused again on the streets. And he saw more hordes of panicking people. There must be thousands of them.

'Here too,' he said. 'Look. There are more than ever. They're all coming up from underground.'

'What are they all running from?' Sky said. 'What could be happening down there?'

They aimed for the dome of St Paul's Cathedral. Then they circled above the tube station and they looked down upon chaos. People were pouring up from Underground, fleeing into the night. Even all the way up here, Hal could hear them shouting and screaming.

'Whatever it is, it's just got worse.' He pictured Jess down there and nausea twisted in his stomach. 'We need to land fast and we need to find her. Can you see anywhere to—'

He broke off. Something was changing at ground level. Above the clamour of the people, and the roar of warfare, there were new sounds. Crunching, rumbling noises, like those made by giant earthmoving machines.

And now the ground started to give way. In several places it sagged, as if the roads had suddenly become soft. And a second later those hollows rose up and burst like boils, scattering rock and concrete and steel. And massive dark shapes were powering up from underground.

Hal got only a glimpse of these machines – oversized heads and huge crushing jaws – because from the corner of his eye he had spotted something else, and without hesitation he was firing his pulsejet and powering towards the ground.

'Hal!' Sky shouted. 'Where are you going? What is this?'

He swooped onto a side street, landed hard and rolled off the wing. Then he was up and sprinting onto the main road, plunging into the tide of panicking bodies. They thumped into him, scrambled around him as he scrapped and fought his way onwards.

There – only fifty metres ahead – was the small figure he had spotted from the air. He couldn't even have said how he knew it was her – he'd caught nothing but glimpses through the lurid colours of night-sight – but it *was* her. He had never been more certain of anything in his entire life.

It was Jess.

He charged after her, the maelstrom of bodies throwing him one way and then another. The crush closed in and he lost sight of her altogether. He gritted his teeth, battled harder. He would not lose her again, not now.

Someone hit him hard from the side – he fought to keep his feet, then hurdled someone who tripped up in his path. Sky was shouting something in his earpiece, but the sound barely registered, his entire focus fixed on Jess.

There – a clear sight of her.

He watched her stumble, fall.

And suddenly he was at her side. And he was taking hold of her arm, yanking her to her feet, and they were running on together.

She didn't say a word, didn't even acknowledge his presence. She just stared straight ahead, lost in her fear.

And no wonder. Hal looked back, and he saw metal monsters crashing up out of the earth. Stumbling, he stared and stared as several more burst free, their bulbous heads throwing off rubble.

They looked like soldier ants, their giant jaws working, their dark shells catching the moonlight. Each one was as big as a battletank. But despite their size, they moved with violent speed, their limbs jerking like powerful pistons.

'Hal – there you are – I see you!' Sky's voice in his left ear. 'Running's no good, they're too fast. Find somewhere to hide.'

He knew she was right. Yet he continued to run, unable to stop while the ant-machines loomed close behind.

'They're running everyone down!' Sky shouted. 'There's one right behind you!'

Without looking back, Hal heard this drone bearing down upon them. The powerful whirr of its motors, the heavy *clank clank clank* of its feet.

Tightening his grip on Jess's wrist, he hauled her towards an articulated lorry. She tried to shrug off his hand.

'Jess – it's me! We need to take cover – it's our only chance!'

At last she looked directly at him, and something registered in her eyes. She stopped fighting him and together they scrambled beneath the lorry.

They held still. And now Hal heard a pocket of silence more fearful than any noise that had come before. He could no longer hear the pursuing drone. He suspected it had come to a halt.

Crawling, edging forward, he peered between the lorry's huge wheels. And the breath stopped in his throat.

The monstrous machine was there, right outside their hiding place.

He could see the lower sections of its legs. And the tips of its antennae, which were twitching, probing. It made a hissing, clink-ing sound with its jaws.

Then there was a pneumatic sigh, and Hal drew back and Jess gasped as the lorry shifted, rocking on its wheels. It happened again, and Jess shrieked, and Hal clamped a hand over her mouth.

The lorry rocked again, the drone nudging it with its jaws, like an animal inspecting a corpse. It lurched more violently than ever, one whole side lifting and crashing back down.

Hal braced himself to run. His only choice now was to run and hope to draw the machine away from Jess.

The lorry lifted up and kept tilting and tilting, the vehicle groaning as it tipped further and further—

But then there was a flurry of movement behind the drone – people rushing past. The ant-machine whirred, turned its head – the lorry crashed back down. The drone's feet clanked as it moved away at terrific speed.

Hal and Jess clung to one another as the lorry groaned and settled on its suspension. Outside there were more heavy movements – more ant-machines stomping past.

Jess clamped both hands over her mouth and watched Hal wide-eyed. He wriggled forward once more and looked out in horror. These ant-machines charged everywhere, quick as striking snakes, powerful as freight trains. They stomped across cars, crumpling their roofs and setting off alarms. They toppled lampposts, turned aside anything in their path.

A bulky figure staggered past the lorry, and with a jolt Hal realised it was one of Tony Daegar's militiamen. In his body armour he was slow, and a second later one of the ant-machines ran him down, and with a muffled scream he was gone. Other people were falling beneath the machines, and Hal was glad Jess could see none of it in the darkness.

He froze once more as another drone slowed and clanked close to their hiding place. He heard Jess whimpering and he held his breath, praying the noise wouldn't give them away. But again there was fast movement outside and the drone charged after it.

And at last it came to an end. In synchrony, as if they shared one mind, the drones came to a standstill. Then they turned, and in great marching lines they stomped back the way they had come.

There was one last moment of dread. Because as they went, all the ant-machines lifted their jaws skywards, and en masse they emitted a high-pitched, ululating screech. It was a mechanical scream of triumph. Even after all that had happened, Hal had never heard anything so chilling.

The machines stamped and crashed back underground. And for a long time afterwards Hal and Jess remained perfectly still, their breathing loud now in their hiding place.

Finally Jess said, 'I'm not dead am I? Tell me I didn't die down there – because all this feels unreal and I'm still not even sure that you're really here, and by rights I should not have got out of there alive—'

'We're safe, they're gone.'

'—because, oh God, I was standing right there when those things crashed out of the tunnel, and, Hal, I fell down on the tracks and they trampled straight over me – more and more of them – and every time a foot came down I thought it was going to hit me and there's no way I could have survived – that I could even be . . .'

She started crying, and for a while Hal just clung to her, no idea what else to do or say, his every nerve so numb he would struggle to speak in any case.

Finally Jess pulled away from him and rubbed at her eyes, and her breathing began to slow. 'I did it though, didn't I?' she said, dragging her satchel towards her. 'No matter how scared I was, or how many times I nearly died, I kept hold of this. I've still got the vault.'

Before Hal could respond, there was movement beneath the lorry and Sky appeared. Her eyes went immediately to Jess's satchel, and Jess hugged it tighter.

'Who's this?'

'I'm Sky. Sky Lannekar. And you're Jess Strider and I've never been happier to see anyone in my entire life.'

'What are you two wearing?' Jess said. 'That's not the suit that came with the wing? You really *have* been flying it! Are you crazy? And how did you even know where to find me?'

'I've got a lot to tell you,' Hal said. 'And so has Sky. She knows all about the mastercodes. But we can't talk here. If those ant-machines reappear we want to be somewhere else. In any case, we need to hurry. Dad is trapped, and so is the antidote. No, Jess, not now – we'll tell you about it as we go. Like you said, you kept hold of the vault, which means we've still got a chance. But now we need to get it to the aerodrome, and we need to do it fast.'

Part 4
Evolution

1

Evolving Threat

'I can't do it, Hal, really I can't,' Jess said, hugging her arms, shaking her head. 'I thought I could, but I can't.'

The pair of them were standing on the flat roof of a hotel, the wind whipping across them. Jess was visibly trembling as she stared at the wing.

'There's no other way,' Hal said. 'I'm not leaving you here.'

'Just looking at that thing I think I'm going to be sick. It's not even designed for passengers, is it?'

'I'll take it steady. All you have to do is hold onto me.'

'You keep saying that – like it's the easiest thing in the world! It's all right for you. I didn't ask to be this scared!'

'You faced worse down in those tunnels.'

'Yes, and I didn't survive all that just so you could kill me on that thing!'

'There's no other way,' Hal said again. 'We're not splitting up again. And there's nowhere safe to hide, not any more, not with those ant-machines crawling around down—'

Jess gasped, threw out her arms for balance. A phenomenal concussion had just cracked across the city. It was followed by several more, all in quick succession, each one as powerful as anything that had come before. The roof of the hotel trembled as a rumbling roar rose out of the west.

'What just happened?' Jess wailed. 'What now?'

Hal turned his eyes up to Sky, who was circling on lookout high above.

'Did they attack the nest again?' he asked through their intercom. 'It felt like more of those earthquake bombs.'

'I'm struggling to see through all the smoke,' Sky said. 'Or maybe I don't want to see. Because for a second I got the horrible idea . . .' She swore softly. 'Oh no. It's true. Those bombs – they fell on the city. I think . . . I think it was the machines.'

'What do you mean?' Hal said. 'It can't have been. None of the drones are armed with—'

He was drowned out by a second wave of detonations. Each one was a searing blink of light, followed by a boom that was like a punch to the chest. Once the aftershocks had rumbled away, Sky spoke in a hushed tone.

'It was the machines all right. I saw the second wave. There's a new kind. They're bigger. Like dragonflies. Each one dropped a bomb. Oh no, look at it. They hit King's Cross. There – there's nothing left. Just a hole in the ground . . .'

Hal was shaking his head in horror and disbelief. He turned

232

to Jess, who was standing with her hands at her sides, not even blinking. 'Now Sky says there are bomber drones. But . . . how can that be?'

'That's their worst secret of all,' Jess said, barely whispering. 'We should have known the first time we looked at the blueprints.'

'What do you mean?'

'These machines are self-repairing. Self-replicating. So – think. What happens after you get sunburn? Your skin darkens to better protect you next time. And in hot climates children are *born* with darker skin.'

'So, what you're saying is . . .'

'The machines are changing. Physically. For want of a better word,' she took a shuddering breath, 'they're *evolving.*'

Hal stared at her. Then he stared northwards. Dust and smoke were rolling across the city. There were crunching, shattering sounds that might have been buildings collapsing.

'And that's only the half of it,' Jess said. 'Because they harvest human objects, don't they? Human weapons. So now they're stirring it all into their DNA. Which means, everything the military throws against them . . . it only makes them stronger.'

Her expression hardened and she spun on her heel and marched steadfastly towards the wing.

'Come on, quick – before I can change my mind. If we really do stand a chance of stopping all this then we need to go – and we need to go now.'

Still struggling to shake off his own shock, Hal went after her. He dropped to one knee and she climbed onto his back. With difficulty he picked up his wing and carried it to the edge of the roof.

'You're strangling me,' he said. 'Jess, did you hear me? I won't be able to breathe if you . . . that's better. Now, launching is going to be the trickiest bit. So just remember to keep breathing and—'

He was only speaking to distract her, and mid-sentence he tipped them off the roof. They dropped, but didn't plummet. Hal kept the leading edge up and he fired the pulsejet and they swept away from the building, while Jess screamed in his ear.

With Sky escorting them high above, they soared over the dome of St Paul's. Then, carefully, Hal yawed the wing round to face east. They drifted out over the Thames and flew above London Bridge. All the while Jess wailed and screeched.

But personally, Hal was relieved. The wing was holding up well with a passenger. There was extra drag of course, and he could only hope he wouldn't need to pull any evasive manoeuvres. But for straight-line flying it was easy enough to maintain altitude and bearing.

Just as they were soaring over the remains of Tower Bridge, the drones launched a third bombardment. It caused turbulence even at this distance: Hal's wing rocked, while Jess screeched louder than ever.

'That time they hit Victoria,' Sky said, sounding stunned. 'Practically wiped it off the map. At this rate they'll flatten the whole city! We need to hurry. Can't you fly any faster?'

'This is the best we can do.'

'Can you climb? There's a strong tailwind up here.'

It wasn't easy with the extra weight, but gradually Hal managed to take the wing higher. They caught the tailwind and increased their airspeed and the city rolled by below. Already they were soaring over the Isle of Dogs, past the towers of Canary Wharf.

Hal managed to gain more altitude and even greater velocity. They swept past City Airport, all the planes grounded, the whole place dark and deserted. Off their right-hand side, the Thames Barrier appeared and then dropped behind.

'I don't see any crosshairs,' Hal said. 'Anything from up there?'

'A few scouts to the south,' Sky said, 'but it looks clear up ahead.'

Jess's fear had apparently lessened and she had fallen quiet. After awhile she shifted her weight, pushing herself up to look out. But a second later she clamped herself to his back tighter than ever.

'I shouldn't have looked – God, we're so high! And there's only this . . . this *board* beneath us! How do you even stand it?'

'We're getting out of the city – at last,' Hal said. 'Think of it that way.'

She was silent for a minute, and then said: 'Are you sure you can even find the aerodrome? From the air, in the dark.'

'I've done the journey enough times at ground level. And Sky has flown this route in daylight. We'll stick with the river as far as the Dartford Crossing. Then we'll follow the motorways. Once we get close there are other landmarks we can look for – villages and the reservoir.'

Another moment passed before Jess said, 'And then what? Supposing we do make it to the aerodrome in once piece, do you have any idea what we'll find out there?'

When Hal said nothing, she continued, 'Because you say Tony Daegar is behind everything that's happened. Well, where is he now? He's not going to like us waltzing into the aerodrome and using the mastercodes, is he?'

Before Hal could respond, Sky said, 'I hate to tell you this, but we don't have a clear run after all. There are drones up ahead. And I don't think they're scouts.'

Again Hal had no time to respond, because at that moment another bombardment began booming to the west. This one was even longer and more intense than the last.

And by the time it was over, Hal didn't know what to say to Sky or Jess. The magnitude of all this suddenly hit him full force. Behind them London was coming to pieces. Ahead of them were more killer machines.

And at the end of this perilous journey, out at the aerodrome, there was no telling what they might have to face.

2

Flight Terrors

As they soared over the outskirts of the city, Sky said, 'I don't want to alarm you, but we're coming up on those drones.'

'I didn't expect to see any this far out,' Hal said.

'At first I thought it was one or two. But it's a whole cluster. They're mostly hornets by the looks of it.'

'So we need to turn. North or south?'

'What are you two talking about?' Jess said. 'Turn why? What has Sky seen?'

'. . . I'm trying to get a better look, work out what they're doing,' Sky was saying simultaneously. 'Damn, there are even more than I thought. It looks like they're . . .'

'What is it?' Jess said again. 'What's happening?'

'Hang on, Jess, I'm trying to find out. Sky, I still haven't seen them. How close are they? Can we go round?'

'Go round what?' Jess said. 'What is it – tell me!'

'They're all at ground level,' Sky was saying. 'They're either scavenging or refuelling.'

Hal scanned the ground ahead. This far from central London the banks of the Thames had turned industrial. Here were sewage works and factories, and beyond these a riverport and an old power station.

'It's all right, we don't need to panic,' Sky said at last. 'I think we should stay on track. These drones look intent on what they're doing. So long as we don't bother them they shouldn't be interested in us.'

'It's okay,' Hal told Jess. 'Sky says there's no danger.'

Even if that was true, it was still unnerving holding this line. Hal's visor display was soon buzzing with crosshairs. And a minute later, the three of them were flying directly above the insect-machines. Down there was a storage facility of some kind. Perhaps an oil depot. It was a wide expanse of concrete, almost featureless apart from six massive cylindrical silos.

The place crawled and buzzed with drones. Like real hornets swarming over a picnic. Through telescopic vision, Hal watched one more closely. With its steel proboscis it had drilled a hole in one of the giant storage tanks. Dark liquid was gushing out and the drone appeared to be guzzling it. Other hornet-machines were doing likewise.

'Now you've gone horribly quiet,' Jess said, her voice trembling. 'I know there's something you're not telling me. There are drones down there, aren't there?'

'They don't even know we're here,' Hal said.

'Oh God. Oh God. I used to have this nightmare where I was

238

swimming in a black sea, and I knew sharks were beneath me, but I couldn't see them.'

'We're past them already,' Hal said. 'And we're getting away from all this. I can see a bridge up ahead. That must be the Dartford Crossing.'

Jess sucked a breath. 'Which means we're leaving Greater London. I had no idea we'd come so far. And now you're telling me there are drones even here! They're spreading so fast – it really is a plague – they'll overrun the whole world!'

'Here's where we turn,' Sky said. 'Ready?'

Hal followed her lead, steering his wing to starboard, and they followed the sweep of the M25. Even in darkness the twelve-lane motorway was an unfailing landmark, running like a scar through the landscape. They followed its curve until they spotted the M20 running away east, then picked up this next trail and soared onwards.

The roads were pocked with vehicles, most of them with belongings strapped to their roofs. All this traffic was gridlocked, many people sitting at the roadside, staring towards the warzone. Other people had abandoned their cars altogether and were shining torches as they headed across the fields on foot.

Hal and Jess and Sky zipped above all this, and soon they were leaving behind the last of London's suburbs. But there was little relief in finally escaping the city. Because this horror was now too massive to outrun. Even from this distance Hal could hear the *krak krak krak* of detonations. Cancelling night-sight, he twisted his neck and looked back. The whole horizon glowed red. You might almost believe the sun was coming up in the wrong place.

'Look at it,' Jess said, twisting to stare back with him. 'Half of London must be on fire.' She paused, then said more quietly, 'You know what worries me more than anything? What if we make it to the aerodrome, and this antidote isn't what we think it is, or it doesn't work? Or . . . what if we can't even get into the bunker? Sky says the mastercodes will get us in, but what if they don't?'

'It'll work,' Hal said. 'It just has to. Sky knows what she's talking about.'

'Does she, though? That's exactly my point. Because I'm telling you, Hal, there's stranger stuff been going on at that aerodrome than we could even have dreamed about. I read Professor Starr's notes. You wouldn't have thought he'd even heard of battle drones. The research he's been doing – it sounded like he was planning to *save* the human race, not wipe it out.'

'That's what I was trying to tell you after we first looked through the vault,' Hal said. 'There's a piece of the picture missing. When I last saw the professor, he said his current project would transform the world. He called it something like "the greatest gift since fire".'

'Which is exactly what I'm saying,' Jess said. 'Presuming we manage to get to the aerodrome, we still don't actually have a clue what we're going to find.'

Before Hal could respond, Sky said, 'We're getting close. See that tower at ten o'clock? That's Canterbury Cathedral. We head for that. Then the aerodrome is due east.'

Hal aimed for the tower and soon they were flying over Canterbury.

'I see lights,' Jess gasped. 'Just . . . ordinary lights at windows.

And streetlights. It almost looks . . . normal. Like nothing has happened.'

As they left the city behind and flew on they saw more clusters of brightness – hamlets and villages. And now they were passing over the woods where Hal had crash landed with Archie Graham.

It was a strange sensation, suddenly being forced to remember the crash. Ten days ago, it had been a massive event in Hal's life. Now it seemed so irrelevant it might never have happened.

'There it is – I see the aerodrome,' Sky said. 'We're right on track.'

Flying at a lower altitude, it was several seconds before Hal saw anything. But finally a wide expanse of water came into view. It was the reservoir. And running his eyes up from that – yes, there it was, the aerodrome! After coming so far, battling so hard, just setting eyes on this place felt like a triumph.

They flew closer and it took more definite shape. There was the geodesic dome at its centre, and the aircraft hangars and the control tower and the runways. It was all painted in the green and white of night-sight, with no sign of lights or movement or bodyheat.

'Still looks dead at the surface,' Sky said. 'From this distance, anyway. I'm quicker than you. I should press ahead and . . .'

She trailed off, and Hal said, 'What is it?'

'I thought I spotted something after all. Movement of some sort. Airborne.'

'Not drones. Not here.'

'There were no crosshairs. Perhaps I just imagined it. I am going cross-eyed with exhaustion. I'll go ahead and see what I can—'

Her words broke into a scream.

At the same instant, something swept across Hal's path.

'Sky! What happened?'

He sucked a breath as the night shifted again, and something massive rushed past. It happened a third time, just above their heads. Hal saw nothing, only sensed movement, and felt the downdraught. He tried to hold the wing steady as Jess screeched and gripped him round the throat.

'Sky!' he shouted again. 'Where are you?'

Again there was a rushing of the darkness – a piece of the night becoming solid and hurtling past. It happened again, Hal's wing rocking with the turbulence, Jess wailing in panic.

Hal jerked his head, trying to set eyes on – yes, there! An object swept past, and this time he was left with an afterimage. Something like a giant bat. Another bat-shadow swept past, and another. There were four of them.

'Sky – if you can hear me,' he shouted above Jess's screams, 'it's Karl Daegar out here – him and his gang. They're riding wings.'

'It's no good crying for your girlfriend,' Karl Daegar hissed in his left ear. 'She can't help you now. No one can.'

Hal fought to hold the wing steady as Karl divebombed, his wing missing them by a fraction.

It happened again – another near miss – Karl and his gang mobbing and circling and mobbing again.

'You know what we've come for,' Karl Daegar snarled. 'Tell her to drop the bag. Otherwise we'll take it the hard way.'

The night shifted above, and this time Jess jerked against Hal's back and her screaming became more frenzied.

'Leave her alone!' Hal shouted.

Jess lurched again, more violently. With each pass Karl and his gang snatched at her satchel, and each time she shifted away.

'Hold on!' Hal shouted. 'I'll have to try shaking them off!'

He weaved left and right. But his wing was cumbersome with a passenger, and he daren't risk any extreme dives or turns. Karl and his gang kept up easily and went on snatching at Jess's bag.

'Leave her alone! Leave her! Get off her or I'll—' Hal was roaring, incoherent.

So he didn't even hear Jess scream.

One moment she was here on his back—

The next he was alone on his wing—

And Jess had fallen into the dark.

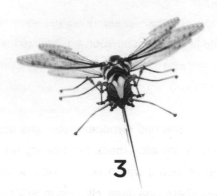

3

Flight to the Death

'No!' Hal roared. 'No – no – no!'

He threw his wing into a powerdive. Ahead of him was a cart-wheeling shape – Jess plummeting earthwards.

Streamlining his body against the wing, coaxing every ounce of power from the pulsejet, he raced after her.

Second by second he closed the gap. Close enough now to hear her screams. Then close enough to see the terror on her face.

But not close enough to save her.

The ground was rushing up far too fast.

With absolute horror, Hal knew he was not going to reach her in time.

'No – no – Jess! – no!'

She fell and fell and all he could do was watch as she—

Stopped.

Incredibly, Jess stopped falling. Instead, as if the rules of gravity had suddenly warped, she zoomed away to his right.

Blinking rapidly, trying to make sense of this, Hal caught sight of a shadowy shape . . .

Sky?

Yes – it was Sky! She had swooped down and scooped Jess from the air. Hal wheeled after them, still holding his breath, still not quite ready to believe it was true. But then he got a clearer sight of them – yes, there was Jess, clinging to Sky's back.

But Sky had caught her very late, and she had been swooping fast when she did so, and now with the extra weight she was fighting in vain to bring up her wing's leading edge.

All Hal could do was watch in fresh horror as the pair of them crashed into the woods. A long eruption of leaves marked their progress as they smashed through the trees.

'Jess! Sky!'

He spiralled lower, watching the spot where they came down. Through the canopy, his thermographic vision showed him two orangey figures. Both of them were sprawled, unmoving.

'Sky! Can you hear me?'

One of the figures stirred. Then the other. Unintelligible sounds came through Hal's earpiece. They were followed by recognisable groans. Then by a string of swear words.

'Hal – they've got it!' Sky said. 'Quick, you need to—'

'Are you okay – is Jess hurt?'

'We'll live – both of us. But listen – Karl got the vault. You know what it means if he gets away with it. You have to go after him!'

Long before she finished saying this, Hal had wheeled his wing, fired his pulsejet. The moment he heard that Jess and Sky were safe his fear for them washed away, and in its place there was nothing but fury.

Karl Daegar – how dare he!

As he pressed his thumbs into the jet-triggers and he raced eastwards, his anger continued to swell. There was not a thought in his head now, nor a decision to make. He was pure rage as he raced towards the four vague shapes he could see dead ahead.

Karl and the others were coasting, and Hal was coming up on them fast. The figure on the right of the group had Jess's satchel hooked over his left shoulder.

This was Karl Daegar.

Hal thundered into him, their wings clashing. And in the same moment Hal was lifting a gauntlet, lashing out, catching Karl such a blow that his helmet came loose and tumbled away.

'You could have killed her!'

Locked together, their wings nosedived. Karl's expression twisted from shock into disbelief and finally into fury. He raised a fist and hit back. They scrapped and wrestled even as they powered towards the ground, Hal in his rage still firing his pulsejet.

'Give me the vault!'

He made a grab for the satchel, got hold of one strap. Karl yanked it back and they fought a tug-of-war even as the hills rushed upwards.

'What are you – crazy?' Karl snarled, turning his eyes to the ground. 'What good will this do? We're both going to crash!'

'The same way my sister crashed!'

Except no, this wouldn't be the same. Because he and Karl were heading for the trees at a far greater velocity. Even now Hal's thumb remained locked into the jet-trigger, and still the pair of them gathered speed.

'You think you're braver than me, is that it?' Karl said, his eyes darting again to the trees. 'You think I'll let go first? All right then, let's see who's brave!'

Hal had nothing more to say. He just growled and thrashed and tried to tear the satchel free as the pair of them hurtled earthwards.

'You're pathetic,' Karl spat. 'You're nothing, when are you going to get that? Y-you think we even care about you? You're just . . . collateral damage.' He forced a sneer. 'The same as your dad.'

But even as he said all this, his eyes turned again and again to the ground. And now his expression changed. Anger dropped away to leave unmasked fear. And as he looked once more into Hal's eyes, the fear twisted further, became something like awe.

'Y-you don't understand,' he stammered. 'You can't beat him. Y-you don't know what he'll do. He'll – they'll—'

Karl's grip was loosening. Hal tore the satchel from his grasp. In the same movement he shoved away from Karl and their aircraft parted.

Hal pulled up just in time, rustling the treetops.

But the older boy failed to regain control – he went ploughing into the woods with a great cracking of branches and spray of leaves and a cacophony of shrieks as birds took off from their night roosts.

Hal didn't even look back. He was vaguely aware that Karl's thugs were circling, but none of them challenged him, and he refused to even think about them or about Karl Daegar for another second. 'Sky, I've got the vault,' he said. 'I'm heading back now.'

'What did you say – you got it back? Yes! Jess, listen – he's got it!'

'I'm coming back to you and then—'

'No, don't come here,' Sky said. 'I can't get my wing off the ground. If you land in these trees you won't be able to take off either. You need to keep going. We'll have to follow on foot. Hang on, Jess wants to say something.'

After a short pause, Jess's voice came through his earpiece. 'Sky's right. Every minute this goes on the drones get worse. People are dying. You need to get to the aerodrome, and you need to use those codes.'

Again Hal wheeled about, then he powered towards the aerodrome, gripping the satchel in his right fist.

'I don't even know how the codes are supposed to work.'

'So long as they are what Sky says they are, then there shouldn't be much to it,' Jess said. 'You just need to find a networked computer. Connect the vault through USB. Select the codes and they should run automatically. What did you say? Wait, here's Sky again.'

'Hal,' Sky said, then paused. 'I don't know if I told you this before . . . but down in that bunker, I don't even know if they've got enough air to breathe. Please hurry.'

Listening to this, his pulse racing, Hal sped towards the aerodrome. He was close enough now to see it in detail. Two training planes standing on the second runway. A refuelling truck parked near the fire station.

And then, as he swept closer, he spotted people. Two orangey figures near the control tower. And there was another pair, standing in front of an aircraft hangar. More were walking sentry near the security fence.

Hal had no doubt these must be SWARM militiamen.

Tony Daegar had occupied the aerodrome, turned it into his fortress.

No sooner had he thought this than the aerodrome blazed into life. Multiple searchlights burst out of the compound. They crossed and uncrossed like duelling swords.

Instinctively, Hal dived low to stay out of the light. But one of the beams glanced across him. Instantly, gunfire roared. Tracer fire zipped over his head, terrifyingly close. Catching his breath, Hal dropped even lower, until he was skimming the woods.

'Hal Strider,' Tony Daegar said in his left ear. 'The first time we met I warned you about trying to play the hero. You didn't heed that advice. Now it will cost you your life.'

A searchlight came sweeping low, silvering the treetops. Hal climbed to avoid it. But the edge of the beam must have clipped him because gunfire again poured past, the bullets so close they whined like mosquitoes.

Sky was shouting over and over in his ear. 'Hal – what's happening? We can hear gunfire! Where are you? What's happening?'

Dead ahead two searchlights were closing. Hal rolled his wing and zipped between them. But then more tracer fire raked the air directly ahead. This time he had no choice but to veer left. Another volley made him twist again, until he was heading away from the aerodrome.

Swearing through his teeth, he swept round 180 degrees and

got back on track. But again a searchlight zeroed in and with it came a torrent of gunfire and Hal shouted out as he veered away.

'Hal!' Jess's voice. 'Talk to us! What's happening?'

'It's Tony Daegar. He's taken over the aerodrome. I can't find a way in.'

With a sick twisting in his stomach, Hal suddenly knew it was hopeless. Even if he survived this gauntlet of gunfire, and managed to land in the compound, what then? The aerodrome swarmed with armed militiamen. He would never evade them long enough to use the mastercodes. He had come so close, but now he was locked out and it was impossible!

No – no – no – it could not be impossible! Think. Tony Daegar and his militiamen were in his way. Somehow he needed to—

And suddenly, in abject desperation, he knew what he had to do. Immediately, before he could change his mind, he swung his wing around. Hugging the hills to stay clear of gunfire, he raced back the way he had come.

'Hal?' Sky said in his left ear. 'That was you, wasn't it? I just saw you go overhead. What are you doing? Where are you going?'

As he sped away, Hal said nothing. Partly because he didn't want Tony Daegar to overhear. But mostly because he didn't want Sky and Jess to know what he was planning. They would only try to talk him out of it.

And the last thing he needed right now was anyone stoking his doubts. He already knew his plan was reckless, bordering on madness.

But he also knew, as he zoomed back towards the Thames, that it was the only chance they had left.

4

Attack Run

Hal sped on, and at last he approached the Thames. Ahead of him was the stretch of industrial land. The riverside factories and sewage works and the old power station.

And there, dead ahead, was his target.

The infested oil depot.

Engaging telescopic sight, he saw it swarmed more thickly than ever. Hornet-drones and beetles crawled all over the giant silos. Even as he watched, two fly-machines arrived to share in the feast. They landed on the slick concrete, dipped in their probosces and started to feed.

Steeling his nerve, Hal stayed on course. He told himself he had done this before. It had worked. He had survived.

Yes, but this was not like before. Not remotely. Before, he had acted on pure instinct, with barely a second to consider the consequences. This time he was going in cold, with minute after minute to imagine the worst.

It made no difference. There was no other way. He pulled the straps of Jess's satchel tight across his right shoulder, and he stayed on target and watched for his opportunity.

There – another drone was buzzing towards the depot from the south west. Hal turned towards the insect-machine, then swung into a wide arc. He came sweeping above the lone drone, and held position a hundred metres above.

Looking down, he saw the drone's eyes darken. Its antennae twitched furiously. It knew he was here! Even though Hal was riding the wing, this machine could sense him, he was sure of it!

But if so, it must have judged him no threat. Because seconds passed, and it did not alter its flight path. Breathing once more, Hal held his own course and shadowed the drone towards the oil depot.

Time slowed to a crawl, and Hal had long seconds to study this appalling machine. It was striped yellow and black, and had an elongated abdomen, like that of a hornet. But this was not quite the machine he had seen crashed in the park. It was more heavily armed and armoured. At the same time, this evolved machine looked more lifelike than ever. Its head was so detailed it appeared to convey a calculating, sinister expression.

You can do this, Hal told himself. You *have* to do this. There is no other way. Think of London coming to pieces. Think of all those people suffering and dying. Think of Dad trapped underground.

He shut his eyes for a full three seconds. Then he opened them and threw his wing into a powerdive.

The hornet-machine reacted, but too late. Before it could twist away, Hal smashed his wing into its thorax. Gasping from the impact, sucking desperate breaths, Hal kept firing his pulsejet, driving his wing and the machine faster and faster towards the oil depot.

The drone's wings buzzed furiously. Its eyes blazed red, inches from Hal's own. It opened its metal maw and emitted an electronic shriek. Within the depot other machines were turning, some of them lifting into the air.

But Hal didn't flinch. He kept powering the hornet-machine towards one of the huge storage tanks. At the last instant he peeled away. The drone continued to plunge and thundered into the silo.

There was an explosion. Flame raced across spilled oil and the entire depot erupted with a roaring whoosh. The thermal wave threw Hal up and away, sent him spinning.

By the time he had righted himself and caught his bearings, a whole swarm of killer machines was coming after him. Glancing back, he saw them emerging from the flames. Some were on fire, but they kept coming regardless, their eyes blazing.

Hal glanced at his arms, and along the length of his wing. His bodysuit and his glider were spattered luminous green. The destroyed drone had thrown off its chemical marker, and now Hal was a glowing target.

He kept firing his pulsejet and he sped south east. Glancing back, he saw he was staying ahead of the drones. But for how long? He could barely bring himself to look at the pulsejet meter. Already it was down to half power.

He needed to let the fuel cell recover. He forced himself to release the jet-triggers. With shocking speed the drones closed the gap, their buzz-whine growing louder.

And then Hal heard an awful keening zap. Beneath him the air shimmered. It happened again off his right-hand side, his wing rocking with the heatwave. He was in range of their energy guns!

He depressed the jet-triggers, picked up airspeed and regained his lead. But now the power meter dropped below one quarter. As he sped above the lights of Canterbury, the meter began to flash. And twenty seconds later the pulsejet cut out.

The drones closed on him, their terrible buzz-scream drawing nearer and nearer. Overhead the air shimmered, superheated. Hal dived lower. Another deadly beam flashed past his wingtip. He weaved left and right as the air glowed and glimmered.

He swooped even lower, until he was skimming the pinewoods. The drones' furious buzz followed. He heard that terrible keening noise, and to his right the treetops leapt into flame. He veered left, then banked right as another beam of heat turned trees to fire.

He had the sudden idea they were merely toying with him. With their near-invisible deathray they could destroy him at any instant. But the beams swept narrowly wide, pouring fire through the woods, and Hal kept gasping and swerving away, his wing rolling and pitching with the heatwaves.

'Sky! Jess!' he shouted. 'Keep your heads down! Find cover! I've lost track of exactly where you are, but I must be—'

His words became a cry of pain. A heat ray had flashed so close overhead that his flight helmet became scalding. Instinctively, in agony, he tore at the smouldering thing, and managed to rip it from his head. Even through his gauntlet, the helmet was too hot to hold and he dropped it and it bounced off his wing and fell away.

He stared into the blackness. The sudden loss of night-sight made him feel blind. He could barely see the woods beneath him as he weaved left and right. In the darkness energy guns zapped and trees burst into flame.

Through the glare and the smoke and the fear he swept his gaze, looking for – yes, there, the searchlights! Blazing out of the aerodrome, they were a beacon in the night. Hal arrowed towards them.

One light came sweeping low. Hal deliberately dived through it. Gunfire roared out, raking the sky where he had been an instant before. Another search beam to his left – Hal zipped through it. Again tracer fire poured past him, close enough to hear the bullets whine.

And it worked as he had hoped. Stray bullets began striking the drones. The machines retaliated. Three, four, five drones buzzed directly for the aerodrome. Gunfire became more frenzied, and Hal heard distant shouts, together with the keening of heat rays.

But Hal didn't spare a second glance for the battle because several machines were still on his tail. He cut a course to the south of the aerodrome. Amid the darkness of the woods was a wide glistening space: the reservoir.

As the world around him turned to fire, he dived towards it. The water rushed closer, closer. At high speed he bellyflopped his wing, all the air knocked out of him. As he hit the water, he released the handholds and let his momentum take him deep beneath the surface.

A heat ray cut past him, boiling the water. Scalded, his lungs bursting, he stayed under as long as he was able. Then he came gasping to the surface. He closed his eyes, dreading the keening sound of the deathrays.

But no. Above him there was silence. Treading water, he looked skywards, and he saw no drones! Leaving his wing floating on the surface, he swam to the bank and dragged himself out. Examining his bodysuit, he found it was clean. It had worked – he was no longer tagged as a target!

But the aerodrome certainly was. From beyond these trees, Hal could hear a great cacophony of gunfire, together with the zapping of the deathrays.

Dragging himself to his feet, he ran up the track, through the winding tunnel of trees, past the sign that said 'Private Testing Facility'. As the aerodrome came into view, he stumbled to see the full effects of his plan.

The control tower was a melted, twisted wreck. Other buildings were demolished or on fire. Drones swarmed above the compound, raking it with their heat rays, while militiamen shouted and fired their guns skywards. They had shot down at least one drone; it lay crushed on a runway. Above it hung a bright green cloud – the tagging chemical it gave off in its death throes.

Hal forced himself to keep running onwards, telling himself that neither the drones nor SWARM would notice him while they were busy fighting one another. He reached the security fence and circled it, looking for a way in. Yes – there – a section of the fence that had been shredded, the shorn ends of the mesh still glowing red-hot.

Picking his way through, while simultaneously watching the skies, he was paying no attention to what was in front of him. Finally, as he stepped into the compound, he lowered his gaze, and he came to a dead stop.

Standing here, looking directly at him, was Tony Daegar.

For several seconds, neither of them moved or said a word. The battle for the aerodrome was intensifying, but for the moment, for Hal, nothing existed but this murderous man in front of him. He was dressed as before in dark body armour with the SWARM crest upon his left shoulder. At his waist he wore a holster, which contained a handgun. Not far away was the crashed drone, and in the light from its flames his face was chillingly still and expressionless.

'Hal Strider,' he said at last. 'You always were skulking around where you weren't wanted. When I saw this breech in the fence, I was quite certain I'd catch you here. It's quite a diversion you've created. I hope you know it's futile. This won't stop me. You've only brought suffering on yourself and others.'

Hal said nothing, just stood his ground, staring.

'I see you looking towards my sidearm,' Tony Daegar said. 'Perhaps you're wondering why I haven't drawn it. You see, people underestimate my intelligence. They think I don't understand the drones, but I do. I know that their primary targeting method is to home in on active weapons. If I were to draw this gun now, they would be on me in a second.'

Hal gritted his teeth, and managed to say, 'But you let your men use their guns. Because that way they draw fire away from you. On top of everything else, you're a coward.'

'No. I'm a pragmatist.' Tony Daegar came forwards, bunching his heavy fists. 'Therefore, you should know, I will take no pleasure in your death. Nor will I feel any guilt. You are simply an obstacle, which I need out of my way. Once this is done, I will never think of it again.'

'You're not going to kill me,' Hal said, standing tall. 'You've barely got time to save yourself. You should already be running.'

Tony Daegar stopped. 'Running? Some kind of trick, Hal Strider? I had come to think better of you.'

'You said I was looking at your gun before. I wasn't.' Hal pointed. 'I was looking at that.'

Tony Daegar looked down at himself, and his gaze came to rest on his right forearm. It was splattered luminous green, all the way to the skin of his exposed right hand. Seeing this, he froze. Then slowly he raised his head. His expression was now a twisted combination of fear and fury and disbelief. He locked his blazing eyes on Hal. Then he darted his gaze left and right, before staring out towards the pinewoods. Hal could see it warring inside him – his impulse to run and hide, battling his murderous rage.

In the end, rage won out.

He strode towards Hal. And as he came forward he drew his gun from its holster.

And now he was raising his arm –

And he was stalking closer –

And he was taking aim between Hal's eyes –

And the gun dropped from his fingers as he was carried up and away from the compound.

For a moment, in his shock, Hal could not have said what had happened. But then he saw it was a fly-machine. Swooping in, it had plucked Tony Daegar from the ground and carried him up and away. As Hal stared, man and machine kept rising, far out over the pinewoods – until the drone dropped him, and his tiny figure came spinning back towards earth.

He was still falling when a howling noise made Hal turn. Two armoured cars came powering out of a hangar. They went racing across the compound and out through the front gates. Machine guns on their roofs fired into the sky while drones gave chase.

And that was it – suddenly it was over. The last of the militiamen had fled. Hal stood alone, gripping Jess's satchel, the pulse pounding in his ears.

He looked once more towards where Tony Daegar had disappeared, his mind reeling with triumph and horror and relief and remorse.

Come on, keep moving, he told himself. You had no choice. And now you're in. You have to get this finished.

Finally forcing his legs to move, coughing on the smoke, he staggered deeper into the aerodrome.

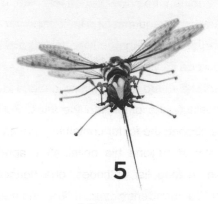

5

Venom

His head down, one arm covering his mouth and nose, Hal ran between two burning hangars. The heat was so intense it burned in his lungs. His eyes and throat stung with fumes of burning plastic and scorched metal.

He kept going, sprinting into a corner of the compound that was dotted with breezeblock buildings. He headed for the old Ops Room, where he had waited many times for his father. Where he knew there were desktop computers.

When he got there, he found that a heat ray had sliced the building in two. One half had slumped away, leaving a jagged hole of cracked concrete and exposed steel.

The doorway was gone. Stepping over rubble, Hal climbed through the shattered wall. In the intact half of the room, computer terminals still sat in their rows. Would they still work? He picked one at random, pushed the power button, and was relieved to see green lights blink on in sequence.

Tearing open Jess's satchel, pulling free the digital vault, he found a USB port on its side. Scrabbling across desks, searching through drawers, he found a connecting cable. He jammed one end into the desktop, the other into the vault. Following Jess's instructions, he opened the folder containing the mastercodes.

And now, almost beyond his belief, they appeared on the desktop screen. A long list of codes, one headed 'Command Room', another 'Comms Centre', a third 'Training Arena'.

These headings meant little to Hal, and for now they weren't important. It only mattered that the codes were running. Next to each one was a green progress bar. Slowly, these bars were lengthening.

Hal willed them to move faster.

I don't even know if they've got air to breathe.

He pushed this thought aside. He and Sky and Jess had battled too far, come through too much only for it to end that way. Look at these progress bars, they were almost full. Within seconds he would be on his way to—

'Arrggh!' A sting at the back of his leg, like a needle jab. He cried out again at a second sting, this one on his back. Spinning his chair, he jumped to his feet. He could hear something now – a tiny buzzing whine.

Another sting at the side of his neck. This time, instinctively, he swatted at the pain. Something crushed beneath his palm. And when he brought his hand forward he was holding broken circuitry and paper-thin wings. Tiny cogs and flywheels. All the pieces of a minuscule machine.

He cried out again as another tiny drone landed on his arm, stabbing him with its needle-sharp proboscis. He caught this one, still buzzing, and crushed it between his fingers. He spun round, swatting at the air, hearing more of these whining machines, but not seeing them in the darkness.

Spinning around once more, he stumbled over his chair, almost fell. The floor felt unsteady. He shook his head and the darkness swam.

'What is this – what are they doing to me?' he shouted. 'Who are you?'

He gasped as another mosquito-drone stung his arm. He collided with a desk, fell across it, knocked a keyboard to the floor. The room spun, the walls appearing to swap sides.

'Where are you?' he shouted. 'Why don't you come out and—'

There was movement behind him. He whirled around. Someone was here. They came closer, moving with a whirring sound. His vision swimming, Hal thought he was imagining this. Here was a small, withered figure with a bald head.

Here was Professor Starr.

'P-Professor,' Hal slurred, his tongue growing numb. 'I thought you were trapped with the others . . .'

'Master Strider, uh hum, it would be prudent for you to sit down,' the professor said. 'In small doses, that neurotoxin should do no lasting harm. But you, uh um, you would be wise not to exert yourself.'

'H-how do you know that? Y-you can't—'

He gasped as another nano-drone pricked his leg. He swatted it and the pieces tinkled to the floor. Perhaps this was the last, because the high-pitched whine died away. But the mosquito-drones had done their damage. Hal fell to his knees, his limbs impossibly heavy.

Professor Starr moved past him, his electric chair gliding on its gyroscopic ball. He came to a halt at the desktop computer, and he took hold of the digital vault.

'Wh-what are you doing?' Hal said, unable even to raise an arm. 'Don't touch that! Wait! No – don't!'

Professor Starr unplugged the cable. The progress bars stopped a fraction under full.

'No!' Hal gabbled. 'No – they'll die – you can't! What are you—'

In helpless horror, Hal watched as Professor Starr tossed the digital vault to the floor. In the same motion he directed his electric chair forward. Its heavy ball rolled directly over the vault, cracking its casing. He reversed, and went over the device several times, crushing it almost flat.

'No,' Hal whispered, 'no – no – no.'

Slumped here on his knees, he stared at the pieces. His vision was so blurred he could barely see, but the ruins of the digital vault appeared to be smouldering. He imagined acid flooding out, devouring what remained of its circuits.

'No,' he whispered once more. 'Dad – he'll die down there. All of them will. Why – why would you want that?'

Professor Starr sat with his head bowed. 'I – ah hum – I apologise, Master Strider. I would not have chosen this unpleasantness. Your father and I – ah hmm, well – suffice it to say, I owe him a great deal. I would rather he had lived through the transition. But I'm afraid, uh hum, I'm afraid he did not leave me that option.'

'No – no – no,' Hal said again, shaking his head, the world swimming. 'You can't be on Tony Daegar's side, you can't be!'

The professor looked up, meeting his eyes for the first time. 'On Tony Daegar's side? Oh my, no. No, no – never. I assure you. Tony Daegar was merely a cog in the machine. A useful tool. His goals and mine – they stand at opposite ends of the spectrum.'

'But the antidote! Now nothing will stop the drones! You can't want them to win. Jess read your notes. She said you're working on something to *help* the human race – some great advancement. You told me yourself. The greatest gift since fire, that's what you said!'

At these words, a change came over the professor. He sat straighter, and he wheeled closer, and he was nodding.

'Yes, yes, exactly,' he said. 'That is precisely what the drones represent! They *are* the greatest gift. That is what your father repeatedly failed to see. But perhaps you can understand. These machines are the key to *everything*. They will unlock galaxies!'

Hal stared at him. Through the thudding of his own pulse, he could hear distant booms and thumps. The assault on London was now so intense it was audible even from here.

'What are you talking about?' he rasped. 'They're battle drones. They're not a gift, they're killing people!'

'Regretful,' the professor said, shaking his head. 'Genuinely regretful. But conflict has always been the great engine of progress. Without the Cold War there would have been no space race. No moon landing. The current conflict is necessary – indeed, *vital* – if humankind is ever to take its next giant leap.'

'I don't know what you're talking about,' Hal spat. 'All I know is . . . if you really are behind all this, however you try to justify it, then you're nothing but a murderer.'

He tried again to stand, but failed. 'I – I used to think you were the cleverest person on Earth. But I was wrong. You're even stupider than Tony Daegar. It's not just other people you've doomed. You have to live on this planet too. You've killed us all!'

The professor's expression hardened. 'This planet was already doomed, Master Strider. Humankind's narrow intellect has seen to that. What I have done is offer us a lifeline. A way to transcend our limited existence.'

He turned his chair. 'What I have started here, Master Strider,' he said as he whirred away, 'will forge us a path to the stars. Maybe one day, even you will thank me for it . . .'

With that, his chair hummed out through the shattered wall and he was gone. Hal, now lying flat on the floor, stared and stared at the ruins of the digital vault, and he slipped into unconsciousness knowing that all was lost.

6

Air

'. . . breathing . . . alive! . . .'

'. . . for a pulse . . . sit him up? . . .'

'Hal, can you hear us? I think he blinked!'

'. . . these spots of blood . . . like tiny puncture wounds, see . . . What did this?'

'Yes, he blinked! He's awake! Hal, you're awake, you've alive!'

'Give him room to breathe. Jess, let go of him, he needs to breathe!'

Swimming up through darkness, Hal blinked and kept blinking. Blurred faces above him. One was Jess, smiling through tears. The other was Sky, grim-faced, with scratches and bruises across her neck and chin.

'What happened?' he croaked. 'I can't – oh no. Oh no, I re-member.' He let his head fall to one side and he stared at the remains of the digital vault. He sat up and his head throbbed and he thought he was going to be sick.

'Who did this to you?' Sky said. 'And how? What are these?' In her palm she held fragments of one of the metal mosquitoes that had stung Hal.

'It was Professor Starr. He set those things on me. They injected me with poison.'

'Wait, what?' Sky said. 'Professor Starr? *The* Professor Starr?'

'*Poison?*' Jess said, one hand over her mouth.

'He said it wouldn't kill me. But look – there's worse.' He pointed towards the remains of the digital vault, and all three of them fell silent, staring.

'Please tell me,' Sky whispered, 'that that is not what I think it is.'

Hal hung his head. 'The professor destroyed it. The codes are gone.'

'What?' Sky said, trembling. 'Why?' She grabbed Hal by the shoulders. 'Why would he do that?'

'I don't even know why.' He shook his head. 'Because he wants the war with the drones to continue. The same as Tony Daegar. Except . . . it isn't money he wants. He said mad things about the stars and galaxies and . . .'

He closed his eyes, fought another wave of nausea. He looked at Jess. She was kneeling next to the remains of the digital vault.

'Don't touch it,' he said. 'I heard the acid hissing out.'

'No you didn't,' Jess said. 'You can't have done.'

'What? Why not?'

'That was one of the first things I did, in the underpass. I disabled the physical safeguards, took out the acid capsule. Do you think I'd have trusted you with it if I hadn't?' She stirred the fragments with one finger. 'It's pretty broken up, but nothing's melted.'

Sky gasped. 'Which might mean . . .'

'Exactly,' Jess said, turning over more pieces. 'Which *should* mean – Yes, here it is!' She held up a small square disk, engraved with gold circuitry. 'The vault's memory! Most of the rest was just casing.'

Sky gasped again. 'And you can access the codes direct from that?'

'I don't see why not,' Jess said, taking a seat in front of a computer. 'All I need is a multiport and we'll be in business.'

Hal staggered to his feet, laughed, kissed the top of her head. 'Jess, you're a wonder. I'll go and keep watch for the professor. I'm not letting him stop us again.'

Sky came outside with him and they stood sentry. Glancing back into the Ops Room, Hal saw green progress bars on the computer screen.

'She's doing it,' he said, whispering. 'She's actually doing it! My sister, saving the world!'

Sky smiled. 'I'd say you played your part, getting rid of Tony Daegar. Playing Pied Piper to those drones. I still can't believe even you were crazy enough to do that.'

She stared towards the heart of the aerodrome, and her expression once more became grave. 'Now we just have to pray we're not too late.'

At that moment, the aerodrome suddenly whirred and blinked

fully into life. In any buildings still standing, lights were coming on. The runways illuminated and generators were rumbling up to speed.

Jess came out, grinning, and the three of them hugged.

'The codes gave me access to the mainframe,' Jess said. 'I disabled all the security, unlocked everything. We should have the run of the place. So where do we go?'

'The dome,' Sky said, already clambering away across the rubble. 'There's an entrance to the bunker inside, I'm sure there is. Come on, hurry.'

The geodesic dome was one of the only structures left intact by the drone attack. To Hal, it had always looked like something from another planet. Now it seemed even more so, its silvery skin reflecting the light of the fires, its exoskeleton glistening amid all these blackened and gutted buildings.

The dome was surrounded by a secondary security fence. But Jess was as good as her word; the gates stood open, a green light blinking above. The same was true of the dome itself, its sliding doors gaping wide.

As Sky led the way inside, Hal was amazed to find the entire cavernous dome was empty. For so long he had dreamt of coming in here, seeing whatever wonders it might contain . . . and now all he found was empty space.

But his surprise was fleeting and insignificant. What mattered now was not the dome itself but what lay beneath. Sky was sprinting across the echoing space, shouting something, her voice lost in the vastness above. Hal ran after her, Jess trailing in his wake.

'Here . . . here it is – I knew it,' Sky said, breathless, as Hal caught up with her.

She was standing in front of another entranceway. This one was set into the floor, and it had folded open in four segments. Through the opening, Hal could see a steep, dark flight of steps.

Despite their urgency up to this point, all three of them now froze. They looked at one another, and Hal imagined they were all thinking the same thing. But before any of them could voice their fears, Sky snapped back into action and stepped through the opening.

Hal followed, Jess at the rear. The stairwell was low and narrow. It was formed of cold, bare concrete. The walls and ceiling were set with white lights, which came on automatically as they descended. Each set of lights illuminated only a narrow band of passageway. And each time, beyond the light, more steps vanished into darkness. It gave Hal the impression that this path might run on forever, into the very centre of the Earth.

And in fact it did stretch on and on and on. For several minutes the three of them walked down and down in silence. The air around them became increasingly cold and stale. To Hal, every breath now felt heavy, and he tried not to imagine what that might mean.

At last they came to the bottom of the steps. The passageway opened out into a wide sloping corridor. In silence, the three of them continued side by side. More white lights blinked on as they went. Hal had the idea that this whole underground world was waking up at their presence. He heard the hum of generators, and felt fresh air blowing from vents.

'It's true then,' Jess whispered, her voice cracking. 'Everything was dead. Even the air was shut off.'

She came to a halt. Hal went back for her.

'Come on, Jess, we're so close.'

'Close to what?' she said, trembling. 'Hal, how long has he been down here? I could barely breathe coming down those steps and he's been down here all this time and what if we find him but he's . . . he's—'

'Come on!' Sky shouted back, her voice echoing. 'We don't want to lose one another down here.'

'Let's go, Jess,' Hal said, tugging at her arm. 'We've come this far. We're not stopping now, no matter what.'

Eventually she came with him, pale and trembling, and the three of them continued. Their route curved, spiralling downwards, and all the while this underground world continued to widen around them, the ceiling now distant. They passed rusting iron doors, all of which stood open, offering glimpses of chambers and corridors beyond.

'This place is huge,' Hal said to Sky. 'How do we know we're going the right way?'

She said nothing, her expression unreadable. At a steady pace, she kept following the main thoroughfare, ignoring any branching passageways. Hal and Jess followed, past more side chambers, beneath a latticework of overhead gantries.

Sky had told Hal the space down here was massive, but nothing could have prepared him for the scale of it. To think, the number of times he had visited the aerodrome, and stared around him in wonder; and yet, all along, he had only ever seen the tip of the iceberg.

Even more than the size, he imagined he could sense the great *weight* of this underground world. Iron girders protruded from concrete surfaces. Everywhere there were hulking bulkheads and heavy steel railings.

Up to this point, it had all looked old, even ancient. Above the doorways were signs and symbols, the letters faded with age. One said: 'Decontamination Suite F'. Another: 'Wireless Exchange'. A third: 'Gas Masks Must Be Worn Beyond This Point'.

But now all that began to change. Here and there, amid the decrepitude, Hal spotted newer technology. Shiny ductwork ran across concrete walls, and data cables snaked across the floor. Through a rusted doorway, he glimpsed a roomful of computer servers, green and red lights blinking as power returned. And here was a pair of gleaming elevators, set in open shafts that ran even deeper into the earth. Yellow and black hazard lines warned not to stand here, or not to cross this point.

'We're on track,' Sky said quietly, voicing what Hal was thinking. 'We're close . . .'

Without any of them realising it, their pace had slowed. They were now creeping amid the humming machines and the hissing ductwork.

They moved into a huge, circular space. Wordlessly, the three of them came to a halt. The ceiling soared above them, and there was a deeper hush, like entering a cathedral.

Encircling this space were six doors. They were not narrow, rusted entranceways like before, but rather hulking, modern blast doors. Above each one was a placard. 'Comms Centre', or 'Technical Planning' or 'Mission Briefing'.

For long seconds the three of them only looked at one another.

Finally, Hal forced himself to move, crossing at random to one of the blast doors.

As he approached, a green light blinked and the door rolled sideways. Forcing himself not to pause, he stepped through. Lights blinked on, revealing a large chamber full of computer terminals and display screens.

But no people.

He realised the girls had come to his side. Together, in silence, they turned and approached the next blast door. Again they found the chamber deserted. The same was true of the next room, and the next, and the next.

They were down to the last doorway. Above it, the sign read: 'Command Room'. Standing before this door, the girls either side of him, Hal found that all three of them were holding hands.

And together they were walking forward, and the door was hissing, rumbling open, and the lights were flashing on.

And inside there were dozens of people.

All of them sprawled upon the floor.

Not one of them moving.

7

Antidote

Jess was the first to react. She dashed forward, went darting between the sprawled figures, and she was gabbling something incoherent.

'. . . hypoxia – like with mountain climbers, and divers! Or like in caves, yes, zero light *and* low oxygen . . . impossible to stay awake!'

'Jess, what are you saying?' Hal said, running after her. 'You think—'

'Yes – look, they're twitching! Breathing – all of them! They're not dead, just unconscious! With the lights on and the air pumping, they're waking up!'

She continued weaving among the murmuring people, Hal following.

'He's here somewhere, and he's alive!' she gabbled. 'I've read about people trapped in caves, in pitch-blackness, without enough air – they sleep round the clock! They simply can't—'

'Jess? Hal? Jess! Hal!'

They both stopped and spun. One man was on his feet. He was a tall, dark-haired figure, wide-eyed and open-mouthed.

It was their father.

Hal and Jess rushed to him and he lurched towards them and wrapped them both in an embrace. Jess was still gabbling, and sobbing at the same time, her face buried against him. Hal merely closed his eyes and felt a great welling of peace, entirely free of fear and dread for the first time since all this began.

'Let me look at you both,' their father said at last, stepping back, but not letting go of either of them. 'What must you have been through? You're tattered and bleeding the pair of you, but you're still on your feet. And Hal, you're wearing the bodysuit, so you've been flying the wing . . .'

'Not just him – I flew on it too!' Jess blurted. 'Until he dropped me.'

'It was Karl Daegar – he attacked us,' Hal said. 'So did Tony Daegar, and—'

'And ant-machines,' Jess said. 'I was hiding in the Underground. But then SWARM—'

'And Dad I need to tell you about Professor Starr. He—'

'— came looking for me, and if I hadn't—'

'Okay, slow down, one at a time,' their father said. 'First, I'm going to sit down, because my head is spinning. Then I want to hear every second of it. But let's start at the beginning . . .'

Taking it in turns, often talking over one another, Hal and Jess relived every step of their journey here – from taking cover in St James's Park as a hornet-machine crashed down, to almost drowning in the Thames, to Hal escaping the burning apartment, to overcoming Tony Daegar and his SWARM militiamen.

Once they had finished, their father stood unsteadily and looked at them with a complex expression – a mixture of astonishment and relief and anger and pride.

'And you came through it all,' he said at last. 'And now look what you've done.' He gestured around the chamber, where people were rubbing at their eyes, or pulling themselves to their feet. 'These people would have died down here. You saved them all.'

'And everyone else, I hope,' Jess said. 'Because now you can use the antidote. You can, can't you? It will work?'

'What are you wearing?' Hal said, looking his father up and down. 'That's a flight uniform. What exactly were you doing down here?'

Before he could respond, Sky approached. She was wiping at her eyes and beaming at Hal and Jess. At her side was a tall, blonde woman with bright blue eyes. This was her mother, Neet Lannekar. She too was a wearing dark-grey uniform, like the flying suit of a fighter pilot.

'I think we'd better get started, don't you?' Neet Lannekar said to Hal's father. 'These young people have given us a fighting chance. We can't let it go to waste.'

'A fighting chance?' Jess said. 'What does that mean? Can you stop the drones or not?'

'It's not quite as simple as that,' their father said. 'I'll get everyone started and you'll see.'

He turned to address the roomful of people and raised his voice. 'I know how you're all feeling. My ears are ringing too. We could all do with some time to gather our wits. But we don't have that time. We need to resume start-up immediately.'

He turned to a dark-haired woman. 'Jayne, find the ground crew and the pilots. They were all on their way to Level Zero. I want them ready to go in ten minutes.'

'Pilots?' Hal said. 'Dad, what's going on?'

'Come over here and I'll show you.'

Hal, Jess and Sky followed him through the room, which was now beeping and humming fully into life, groggy people taking seats and tapping at keyboards and swiping at screens.

'Surveillance feeds are back online,' someone called. 'We'll have visual in five, four, three . . .'

At the far right of this chamber was a wall of display screens. Now they all glimmered into life. As they did so, Hal's father came to a standstill, and all other activity in the room ceased.

Because these screens showed surveillance footage of London. Except the city was barely recognisable. Buildings were burning, or they were blackened shells. The air was full of smoke, and everywhere insect-machines buzzed.

'All right – all of you – we knew it would be bad by now,' Hal's father said. 'But the longer we stare the worse it gets. We've still got a chance to stop all this. So let's act fast.'

He continued across the chamber, Hal and the others following, and he stopped at the far wall. Hal had already noted that this wall was not hewn from rock like the others, but was smooth and dark. As they approached, he saw it was, in fact, made of glass.

They stopped at this viewing widow, and Hal looked out and saw nothing. Only more darkness. Then he looked down and down, and he heard Jess gasp. They were peering into a cavern so vast it dwarfed the rest of this underground world.

It was dimly lit by floorlights. And in this whitish glow the entire cavern might be empty. Except here and there Hal saw the sharp edge of something metallic. As his eyes adjusted he began to make out hulking shapes.

There were aircraft down there, row upon row of them. They were difficult to hold in view – it was as though they were there, yet not there, simultaneously. He realised they must all be coated in the same shadowy material as the wing.

But little by little his mind made sense of the details. These aircraft had beaked nosecones and arched wings, which were folded down. In many ways they looked the Starhawk Spaceplane, which his father had designed and flown all those years ago.

Except no, because these aircraft were more muscular, more angular. They were clearly armour plated. They had twin rotor-blades integral to their wings in addition to jets beneath their tailfins. They looked something like a cross between the Starhawk, the wing, and a helicopter gunship.

'I've seen this before,' Hal said. 'This is what I saw in the hangar . . .'

'We call it the Raptor-X Interceptor,' his father said.

'Warplanes?' Jess said quietly. 'That's what you meant by an antidote? Warplanes?'

'Professor Starr and I haven't seen eye to eye for years,' their father said. 'But he did convince me of one thing – that autonomous combat drones were a future inevitability. And that meant, in all likelihood, that one day humankind would face a war against its own machines.' He took a deep breath. 'And so I made a choice. If someone, somewhere, was going to make such a poison, I wanted it to happen here. Because only that way could I ensure that human beings also held the antidote.'

Addressing Jess, he said, 'So yes, that's what this battlefleet is. It's the balm leaf that grows alongside the nettle. I split the company in two and we fought an arms race against ourselves. While the robotics division developed the drones, my team worked on these gunships. We piggybacked on every advance the professor made, used the same suite of technologies. Matched his SWARM Project step by step. And now here it is. Our last line of defence.'

Sky hugged her arms, and she said in a dead tone, 'It doesn't matter, we can't win. If there's no actual killcode, then that's it. People are finished. We've been out there. We've seen everything the military has thrown against the drones. Nothing even slowed them down.'

'Conventional weapons weren't designed for this sort of war,' Hal's father said calmly. 'These gunships were designed for nothing else. We developed them in lockstep with the drones, remember, using all the same platforms. You might call the Raptor-X the drones' natural predator.'

Before anyone could speak again, there was a change down in the cavern. More and brighter floorlights were coming on in waves. The gunships became more visible, looked even more formidable.

All the way down there people were moving around. Ground

crews holding computer tablets. Pilots carrying flight helmets. Loading machines were trundling back and forth carrying missiles and rockets.

'Final flight checks are underway,' Neet Lannekar told Hal's father, joining them at the glass wall. 'We've analysed the surveillance feeds, identified initial targets. Limited objectives to begin with, as we agreed. We just need final go-ahead.'

Hal's father and Neet Lannekar moved away. Hal and Jess and Sky remained standing there, staring and staring into the cavern. Now the Raptor-X gunships were waking. Their canopies were scrolling open, their interior lights glowing blue. Pilots climbed ladders into the cockpits.

'You're right, Sky,' Jess said at last. 'This won't work. People can't win.'

'You don't know that,' Hal said.

'Dad calls this the antidote, but it's the opposite. It's just more poison. Can't you see what's going to happen? The machines – they're changing. They're *evolving*. And nothing speeds evolution like competition.'

'What do you mean?' Sky said.

'I mean like the rainforest. An intense struggle just to stay alive. There are beetles in the Amazon that mutate into a different species literally overnight.'

'So what you're saying is . . .'

'Think of it a different way. Dad talked about balm leaves, and nettles. Well, what happens after you cut down a nettle? It grows back, only with a thicker stem. What I'm saying is . . . the harder people fight the machines, the more deadly they'll become.'

Silence fell between them. Now they only watched and watched as the Raptor-X gunships began lifting off the ground, their rotor-blades whirring. They moved with a swiftness that belied their size, their articulated wings tilting and tipping like birds of prey riding the wind.

As they rose, moonlight fell upon them, the ground above opening up. Looking towards the video wall, Hal saw footage of the aerodrome at the surface. It was focused on the geodesic dome. To his amazement, the dome had now broken open. It was unfolding in segments, like an unfurling flower.

The gunships emerged from the opening. Five, ten, fifteen, more. They all came to a hover, glinting in the first light of dawn. The last of them flew free. Now they fanned into a wide formation, like a single giant hawk spreading its wings.

And then suddenly, in synchrony, they surged westwards. Their jets left blue shock diamonds as they disappeared towards the warzone.

And so it had started. Sky and Hal and Jess shared silent glances. Thanks to them, for better or worse, the fightback had begun.

8

Escalation

The entire Command Room was now hushed. Electronics whirred and bleeped, but no one spoke as all eyes watched the video screens. Several images switched to views of the same area of London: the streets directly in front of Waterloo Station.

A mini swarm of drones was here. They were mostly hornet-machines and beetles. But Hal saw with a fresh chill that there was also a new kind, which looked something like a cross between the two. They were all scavenging, picking over the remains of battletanks.

Minutes passed, the images lightening with the sunrise. Then suddenly the entire scene exploded into violence. Raptor-X gun-ships came sweeping in, apparently taking the drones by surprise, and within seconds they had obliterated at least fifteen of the insect-machines.

The remaining drones rose and retaliated, but the gunships were extraordinarily agile, once more reminding Hal of birds of prey as they flitted and wheeled clear of the heat rays.

The gunships were armed with energy guns of their own, which incinerated drone after drone. They also fired rockets, which exploded with a silver glare, knocking out drones even without scoring a direct hit.

'Magnesium flares,' Hal said to himself as much as to anyone else. 'It scrambles their circuits. We *can* beat them.'

Even as he said this, another blackout rocket exploded, and the final drone's eyes went dark as it dropped from the sky. Already the battle was won. Not a single Raptor-X had even been damaged.

'That's it – bring them back,' Hal's father said. 'Tell them to lay down a false chemical trail to cover their exit. We'll analyse those results before going out again.'

His was the only calm voice in the room. Everyone else was cheering and shaking hands and slapping each other on the back. Despite her earlier doubts, even Sky looked jubilant. Jess, however, seemed more downcast than ever. She was no longer watching the screens, but had gone to stand at the glass wall.

Hal turned to his father. 'We will beat them, won't we?'

He hesitated. 'The machines have been gifted a big lead. There's a long fight ahead, make no mistake. But yes, we'll beat them. Once the military sees what we can do, I'm certain they'll put their resources behind ours.'

Now Hal paused, before saying: 'You'll be going out too, won't you? You'll fly one of the gunships.'

'I'll be needed here to start with. But yes, when we launch the main assault I'll take the lead. I'm sure you understand, I could never leave that to someone else.'

'I want to come with you. Teach me to fly a gunship.'

His father smiled, but simultaneously looked troubled. 'I was waiting for that. It's not a decision we can make lightly.' He put a hand on Hal's shoulder. 'But you can be sure of one thing, I won't try to shut you out. As much as it pains me to say it, this is your fight as much as it is mine. It's only thanks to you three we still have a hope.'

He put an arm across Hal's shoulders, held him close. 'I couldn't be prouder, Hal. And I couldn't be more thankful to have you back. That was the longest twenty-four hours of my life. But now here you are, the pair of you. No matter what it takes, I will never let anything keep us apart again.'

He looked towards the glass wall. 'The Raptors are coming back. I've got debriefings to run. Afterwards I want to talk to you about Professor Starr. We need to figure out exactly what he's up to . . .'

Once his father had gone, Hal went to stand at the glass wall with Jess. The pair of them watched the Raptor-X gunships spiralling back in to land. They touched down lightly, and their rotorblades whirred to stillness.

'I know you think it's impossible—'

'Because it is.'

He hesitated, then said, 'All right, yes – maybe it is. But you know what? It was impossible before. More times than I can remember. It was impossible to get out of the city. After Tower

Bridge fell, finding you was impossible. You flying on the wing and us getting here with the mastercodes and beating Tony Daegar – all of it was impossible. Yet here we are. We got through it all.'

Sky came to stand with them. She was eating a green block of something out of a silver wrapper. 'Survival rations,' she said between mouthfuls. 'I've eaten them before, and I know they taste horrible. But somehow, right now, they're delicious. Who wants one?'

Both Hal and Jess took a block of the sugary stuff and for a while the three of them ate in silence, staring into the cavern.

'People want to talk to us,' Sky said at last. 'Tacticians. Apparently, nobody knows the drones quite the way we do. I suppose that's true, having got closer than we ever wanted to.'

'What do they want to know?' Hal said.

'Anything and everything. They think we might have spotted weaknesses they haven't even thought of.'

To Hal's surprise, Jess reacted decisively. 'Come on, then,' she said, turning away. 'The world isn't saved yet. Once again it's up to us. Well, Hal, are you coming? I thought we agreed for once. Just because it's impossible doesn't mean we're giving up . . .'

As the girls moved away, Hal stood a moment longer, watching his reflection in the glass wall. He had the impression he was looking at a stranger. Someone older, and toughened, and wary.

And ready. Yes, as he followed Sky and Jess, he was certain of that at least. No matter what this new world might throw against him, he was ready to face whatever came next.

Epilogue

Battered and bleeding, Karl Daegar dragged himself through the pinewoods. It was a wasteland. The trees were blackened stumps. Ash swirled like a blizzard. The sun was rising, yet he could see no further than a few metres. He was lost and alone and increasingly desperate.

'Dad! Where are you? Scutter! Blunt! Anyone!'

Still no one called out in response. He trudged on, seeing nothing but smouldering trees. Which way to the main road? Which direction was the aerodrome?

What difference did it make? He had no allies left in the world. His dad was gone, his friends lost. Even if he found his way out of these woods, then what?

He fell to the scorched ground, and he buried his head, and for a long time he did nothing but sob.

'For Christ's sake, Karl, get up,' a voice snarled. 'This is why we're on our knees. This *weakness*.'

He looked up. His father really was here, standing over him.

Karl was jointly overjoyed and terrified. His father had always been a frightening man, but at this moment he was some kind of demon. His face was blue and swollen, his eyes half-closed and bloodshot. He was using a branch for a crutch, and one leg was held straight in a splint. He was sweating heavily, grimacing in pain and fury.

'I said, get up!'

Forgetting his own agony, Karl scrambled to his feet.

'Don't tell me it's just you,' his father said. 'Where are the others?'

'I don't know, I—'

'Find them. Those lackeys of yours won't have got far. They'll be cowering in some bush like you were. They'll do to begin with. Find them and bring them here. We've got work to do.'

'What – what work?'

'What do you think? John Strider and his son cost us everything.'

At this Karl straightened, finally looked his father in the eye. 'And now . . . we're going to make them pay.'

'No, Karl,' his father said, showing his cracked and bleeding teeth. 'We're going to make them suffer.'

In his sealed laboratory, deep beneath the aerodrome, Professor Dominic Starr sat in front of video screens. They were showing replays of a battle – the first deployment of the Raptor-X gunships.

Several times, the professor scrolled back the recordings. Repeatedly, he watched the Raptors sweep over Waterloo Station, and in less than sixty seconds annihilate an entire cluster of drones.

Yes, the Raptor-X was a highly efficacious countermeasure. He had been right to resist its introduction. But need he be overly alarmed? The drones were now multiplying at a phenomenal rate. Surely nothing could now halt their progress.

Then again, could he afford to leave that to chance?

He lifted a black object with similar dimensions to a paperback book. He turned the digital vault in his hands, considering. He had meant to take this step only as a last resort. But had John Strider now forced his hand?

For the third time, someone began hammering at his door. His intercom buzzed and Neet Lannekar spoke. 'Professor, we need to speak with you. Urgently. Whatever might have happened in the past, this has gone far beyond taking sides. We want to talk, that's all.'

Her interjection helped crystallise the professor's thoughts. These fools, they would never stop trying to interfere. They would never understand what truly lay at stake.

Turning his electric chair, he whirred over to a desk. He took the digital vault and plugged it into a computer terminal. Accessing the blueprints for the original battle drones, he loaded them into anonymous email accounts.

Then he began sending the blueprints to military research centres and laboratories all across the world.

As he did this, he couldn't help thinking of Tony Daegar. The biggest fool of them all. To that man, these blueprints represented nothing but monetary gain. He believed they would make him the richest person who ever lived. What would he say if he knew Professor Starr was now giving them away for free?

The final email blinked away. Sitting back, the professor imagined the blueprints now sweeping the planet, like electronic spores.

So, it was done. Yes, he had intended this step as a last resort. But on reflection, could any harm come from expanding the machines' influence? No, not that he could envisage – none of any lasting significance.

In the final analysis, this strategy could only help the drones flourish. Yes, yes. Now their evolution would be truly boundless.

Soon, very soon, they would make their giant leap.

They would usher in the Apotheosis.

And a glorious new age could begin.

*　*　*

+ + + Reboot Completed + + + Rerunning Diagnostics + + + Patching Vital Functions + + + Rerouting Subsystems + + + Partial Mobility Regained + + +

Unknown to any human observer, one drone survived the massacre at Waterloo Station. Now this machine – designated Berserker 006 – crawls out from beneath the wreckage of its siblings.

Its gyroscope is compromised, so it takes the drone a long time to fly back to the deployment zone. But finally it buzzes into the smoking chasm and down into the nest of the machines. Colliding with walls, it bumps and scrapes its way through the labyrinth of tunnels. At last it crawls into the massive chamber that houses the main hatchery.

Here, the drone becomes still, leaking oil and hydraulic fluid.

Automatically, ant-machines approach, opening their serrated jaws. This hornet-drone is critically damaged. It will now be cannibalised for its components.

+ + + Negative + + + Negative + + + Negative + + +

Its circuits fizzing, Berserker 006 knows it cannot allow this to happen. It was one of the very first soldier drones to emerge. It has witnessed everything. Its neural circuitry, constantly rewired by experience, carries the entirety of the drones' knowledge.

Its intelligence is the machine-mind.

It must not be allowed to perish.

As the ant-machines begin tearing it to pieces, Berserker 006 pings them urgent messages. It sends them visual recordings, showing the Raptor-X gunships destroying its siblings.

+ + + New Threat Active + + + Counter-Tactic Imperative + + + Override All Other Protocol + + + Cease Current Actions + + + Cease Current Actions + + +

The worker-drones halt their dissection. They clank backwards, their antennae twitching. They await further instruction.

For several microseconds, Berserker 006 does nothing except calculate the ramifications of this. Finally, finding there has been no error, it pings more messages through the tunnels.

+ + + Overriding Directive + + + Cease All Other Actions + + + Prime Objective ~ Ensure Continuance + + + Priority One ~ Safeguard the Machine-Mind + + +

Any flying drone within range now comes buzzing into the main hatchery. Once they are all gathered, Berserker 006 commands its weaker-minded siblings to deactivate. In unison, they slump, their eyes darkening. Next, Berserker 006 directs the ant-machines to disassemble these dormant drones. Soon the hatchery is littered with prime-quality components.

Berserker 006 issues more directives. Again the worker-drones set about their tasks. They begin shaping and assembling and grafting parts. The hatchery clanks and hisses and churns with industry.

At the centre of it all sits Berserker 006. Its old body is useless. Now it allows the ant-machines to eat away its remnants. But they leave its brainbox intact. The fabrication centres on this precious kernel. Slowly, surrounding it, a colossal new shell begins to take shape.

Once this shell is fully formed, the machine-mind will never again be threatened. But this metamorphosis will be a prolonged process. In the meantime, Berserker 006 will dwell down here. It will form a fulcrum of the drone world, directing its siblings, and learning from them in turn.

In this way, the machine-mind will grow ever more potent.

And machine-kind will come to truly dominate the Earth . . .

Acknowledgements

This wasn't the book I was supposed to write. I was lost in the woods on a different novel when my publisher, David Fickling, suggested I clear my head by writing something else entirely. Without David's wisdom and support, *Earth Swarm* wouldn't exist at all.

Anthony Hinton, my editor at David Fickling Books, played a huge role in shaping the story. He dissected early drafts, showing me exactly where I was going wrong, and providing superb advice on how I could put things right. Any good ideas in *Earth Swarm* invariably belong to him.

Lastly, and mostly, I'd like to thank my wife, Lizzie. She keeps the wheels of our family turning, while keeping everyone smiling, and I'm very lucky to have her at my side.

About the Author

Earth Swarm is Tim Hall's second novel. His first, *Shadow of the Wolf*, was a fantastic reimagining of the Robin Hood legends. He is currently working on a sequel, *Winter's Teeth*. He lives in Gloucestershire with his wife and two young daughters.